Pride Publishing books by Catherine Curzon and Eleanor Harkstead

Single Books
An Actor's Guide to Romance
A Late Summer Night's Dream

Captivating Captains
The Captain and The Cavalry Trooper
The Captain and The Cricketer
The Captain and the Theatrical
The Captain's Ghostly Gamble
The Captain's Cornish Christmas

Pride Publishing books by Catherine Curzon

Anthology
I Need a Hero: The Angel on the Northern Line

Pride Publishing books by Eleanor Harkstead

Single Books
The Low Road

I0658905

Captivating Captains

THE CAPTAIN AND THE THEATRICAL

CATHERINE CURZON &
ELEANOR HARKSTEAD

The Captain and the Theatrical
ISBN # 978-1-913186-24-1
©Copyright Catherine Curzon and Eleanor Harkstead 2019
Cover Art by Cherith Vaughan ©Copyright September 2019
Interior text design by Claire Siemaszkiewicz
Pride Publishing

THE CAPTAIN AND THE THEATRICAL

Dedication

CC — for the most fabulous of theatricals — they
know who they are!
EH — for Wai, Queen of the Eyeshadow.

Chapter One

As Captain Ambrose Pendleton strode through the gates of Vauxhall Gardens, he didn't see the crush of people or the lights in the trees, or hear the music. He was thinking only of seeing his friend Orsini once again.

But first there was the show, which Orsini had raved about in his letter. Cosima was from his stable of talent, and Orsini had been insistent that his friend watch the most remarkable, exquisite and well-formed young lady to grace the continental stage.

And her adorable performing parrot!

Ambrose entered the pavilion where Cosima was to perform. He took his seat and, as he waited for the show to begin, found himself enjoying the hubbub of ordinary people around him. How nice it was to be back among the throng of humanity, without the smell of gunpowder or the roar of cannon or the parade-ground shout. He glanced about the audience, wondering if his friend was there, but Orsini was nowhere to be seen.

The quartet struck a note, and applause rang through the pavilion as the velvet curtain was drawn back. The woman who emerged was tall and slender but, as Orsini had promised, well-formed. Here in a summer London, her diaphanous gown and tumbling curls transported Ambrose instantly back to his youth in Italy, to a world of classical myth and striking women, yet none that he could recall were as striking as the creature who now tripped across the stage, one slender arm outstretched for the bright blue parrot that perched upon her pale wrist, the yellow and red feathers beneath its wings and at its breast shimmering.

A woman in Roman dress and a parrot... It was very Orsini, if nothing else.

There was likely nothing else quite like it in London that night as the magnificent Cosima ran through her repertoire of silly stories—just the right side of bawdy—and Italian songs, sometimes accompanied for the sake of comedy by the bird and sometimes, for the sake of entertainment, by the quartet. Every man in the audience was enraptured by her, enchanted by each flick of her auburn curls, each sly aside, and every woman became a confidante, laughing behind ladylike hands at some wry comment from the performer on the stage.

Wherever had Orsini found her? Ambrose wondered, though he knew instinctively that some of this material must belong to his friend, for it had that same devilish mischief so beloved by Amadeo Orsini. They claimed that she was his sister but Ambrose knew better, for he had met Orsini's numerous siblings and none of them were La Cosima.

Yet she certainly could have been family.

The show ended with rapturous applause, Cosima curtseying to her admiring audience as the parrot took a small, proper bow. Reluctantly, Ambrose followed the crowd out of the pavilion and back into the balmy summer air. He would happily have watched Cosima and her parrot perform all evening, if not for his promised reunion with Orsini.

Off he went toward the Cascade, where they had arranged to meet. But he couldn't see Orsini anywhere. Where was the young man Ambrose remembered, always decked out in silks? He certainly would have noticed him among the crowd — unless, and Ambrose thought it most unlikely, the great impresario had adopted a somber guise.

But wouldn't he notice Orsini's dancing eyes, and his knowing smile, and his — what the devil?

"Now, madam, please stop that!" Ambrose laughed politely — as politely as a man could with a woman's hands over his eyes. He could smell her perfume and feel the lace of her gloves and hear her giggle. "You must have confused me for your husband, or your sweetheart!" *Or a paying customer*, but Ambrose thought it best not to voice that.

"Captain Pendleton," came the singsong-voiced reply from close to his ear. "The great Orsini begs your indulgence, but, alas, he is detained by matters feminine. He asks that I escort you to supper tonight!"

Ambrose clenched his jaw. Matters feminine? Was Orsini involved in some sort of intrigue with a lady?

And why did he recognize the woman's voice — but of course!

"Cosima!"

He turned quickly and took her hands as they fell from his face. There she was, standing before him, the leading lady of Orsini's show, a dazzlingly red shawl wrapped around her narrow shoulders. As much as he'd longed to see his friend, what an honor it was to be favored by such a performer—and the parrot too, who perched on her shoulder like a little admiral.

"How excited I am to make your acquaintance!" Ambrose bent to kiss her gloved hand. "I very much enjoyed your show this evening."

The parrot administered a sharp peck to Ambrose's hair and Cosima exclaimed, "Pagolo! Captain, forgive my little chaperone, he is so very protective of his Cosima and his applause!"

"I enjoyed your performance too, Pagolo, of course." Ambrose grinned as he gave the imperious parrot a bow. "How very remiss that I did not congratulate you, as well."

"His career has been long and celebrated." Cosima tapped her finger gently against the parrot's beak and he cocked his head to one side. "He might teach all of us how to improve our performances, he thinks! Now, sir, what delights might the gardens offer an innocent Italian girl and her escort?"

"We are stood before the marvel of the gardens, dear lady. The Cascade! Now watch carefully, for I think it is due a performance." Ambrose offered Cosima his arm as the crowd swelled around them.

He couldn't hold back his smile as the curtain lifted and Cosima's elegant fingers gripped his sleeve, her mouth falling open in an expression of perfect wonder. Before them the night lit up bright as fireworks illuminated the heavens and the gasps and appreciative murmurs of the audience greeted the scene of bucolic splendor. As the artificial metallic water cascaded down, a mill wheel gently turned, the intricately rendered bridge in the center crossed first by a coach and horses, then a whole troop of soldiers, strolling ladies and ambling gentleman. It was magnificent, Ambrose knew, but he took more pleasure in his companion's wonder than the mechanical marvel he had seen a dozen or more times.

"How is it done?" Cosima laughed, shaking her head in utter wonder. "What a thing engineering must be, it is all sorcery to me!"

Ambrose knew, but only because his father had told him, for he had an acquaintance who had known the fellow who had devised it. Even so, it still didn't make much sense to Ambrose, which gave him pause — how would he ever follow his father's wishes and turn industrialist now that he had left the Army?

"Cogs and wheels, I believe. Gears and pulleys." Ambrose wafted his hand, as if it was all thoroughly familiar to him and actually rather dull. "And such things of that nature. Now, may I offer you a refreshment? You must be in need of one after your performance."

"Cogs and wheels," Pagolo agreed, pecking at Ambrose's hair again. "Cogs! Wheels!"

"You should not pay him any heed." Cosima slipped her arm opportunely through Ambrose's own. "I confess, sir, I am of a mind to dance!"

A dance with such a lady as Cosima? Ambrose nodded, quite unable to form a coherent reply. His evening was not turning out quite as he had expected, but how lovely to lead Cosima toward the first dance floor that presented itself, and witness at close hand the glee leaping in her eyes.

"See? Is not Vauxhall Gardens the most splendid of places, Cosima? Have you ever known the like?" They stood, arms linked, on the edge of the dance floor and watched the couples in the set.

"Cogs," decided Pagolo somewhat archly, earning himself a sharp look from his mistress. She turned her gaze back to the dancers, tapping one silk-slippered foot lightly in time to the music as she twirled an auburn curl around her finger.

With Cosima absorbed by the dancers, Ambrose had a chance to see her unobserved. She was a dazzling lady, quite unlike the women Ambrose was used to, the daughters of ambitious parents keen to see their charge wed to a captain of industry's son. None of those girls had Cosima's grace, or her easy elegance, and certainly none of them could have put on a show such as Cosima had that evening.

The more Ambrose looked, the more he saw something oddly familiar about her. The large hazel eyes, for one, but perhaps that was not unusual among Italians. The rather prominent nose, but it wasn't shaped quite the same as Orsini's. Even so…

"Gosh, I hope you shan't think me an impertinent sort of fellow, but are you not—tell me now, if my dear friend Orsini had a sister, would she be you?"

"Alas, he does not have a sister, though the world thinks it is so." Cosima turned her head just a little, then dropped her voice to a whisper and asked, "Wasn't that a riotous night in Florence, Pen? You and that saucy old creature in the wimple, your eyes nearly popped out of your head!"

Ambrose Pendleton's eyes nearly burst from their sockets again as he realized his error. Unless Cosima was an exceptional mimic, but—

"Orsini! My dear friend!" He clapped the elegant lady on the back and pumped her arm up and down with eager enthusiasm. "As I live and breathe!"

They were now the object of some amusement, for what sort of a gentleman behaved like that to—as far as anyone else knew—a lady? Ambrose felt a blush rise to his face and the parrot glared at him from his perch on Cosima's shoulder.

"Unhand me, sir," Orsini—for it was he—teased in that delicate voice, the pretty young man of just a few years ago barely visible beneath the construct of Cosima. "Did you really not know your old friend? I take that as an exceptionally fine review of my work!"

"I own that I did not!" Ambrose offered Cosima—Orsini—it was confusing—his arm again. "I had thought there was something familiar about Cosima. Her humor on the stage, for one. And—" Ambrose cleared his throat. He tore his gaze from his friend and watched the dancers skip by instead. "And her eyes."

"Amadeo Orsini was simply one more pretty young actor in a sea of pretty young actors." Cosima pouted softly. "Cosima was merely intended as a party piece and yet her star soon eclipsed mine, and I could never hold back a beautiful young lady!"

"When you wrote and told me you'd given up the stage for the role of impresario, I had no idea that—" Entranced, Ambrose found himself gazing once more into the large hazel eyes of his friend. "My goodness, but you do make a very pretty lady."

"I have devoted myself instead to producing and managing the career of the dear, mysterious Cosima," he told Ambrose. "It allows me to see two rather different views of the world, I can assure you!"

"I'm not surprised!" Ambrose smiled to himself, rather pleased to have Cosima on his arm. "And I wager there must be quite a fight for your hand from king and emperor alike."

"All remain disappointed, for Cosima has yet to find the fellow who might claim her heart." He blinked, long eyelashes batting as he teased, "Perhaps that has changed tonight, kind sir!"

Heavens, what a thought!

"That depends—I have no title, but I do have a very wealthy father!" Ambrose patted Cosima's hand. A note of sadness came into his voice. "Alas, I believe that Father has found a wife for me—not that he has told me so, but what else can I assume when a young lady is so frequent a visitor to our house?"

"Oh!" Orsini sounded genuinely surprised by that revelation. "Tell, Pen. Who and what?"

"There is an industrialist, by the name of Mr. Tarbottom—"

Orsini opened his eyes very wide, then blinked as though he had something in his eye, the blinks growing more frequent until, with a hoot of noise, he broke into a fit of hilarity. He patted Ambrose's arm daintily and threw back his head, his laughter filling the air as Pagolo joined in for good measure.

"Yes, really—Mr. Tarbottom." Ambrose tried to narrow his lips in disapproval at his friend's reaction, but the gray cloud that had followed him in recent weeks began to dissolve in the face of such unbridled laughter. "Where was I? Yes—Mr. Tarbottom is an American industrialist, and he happens to have both an open position in his mines and a daughter of marriageable age. If I know my father, he will believe my fortune is set."

"A position?" Orsini nodded, his smile fading a little. "He must have mines in England then, yes? I am to remain here for a time, Pen, so I shall visit your mines and entertain the workers if you wish!"

"If only that were so." Ambrose's gaze passed slowly over the revelers and the pavilions, the garlanded trees and the musicians and dancers and tumblers. "I very much doubt I shall ever return, alas. The position Mr. Tarbottom would offer me is in America."

Orsini's chin dipped, his gaze falling away to the floor. He said nothing for a few moments, but gave Ambrose's arm a little squeeze. "You must be very excited, Pen."

Ambrose stared ahead, over the dancers, not really seeing anything, even though he knew that he was unlikely to visit Vauxhall again. He pursed his lips and shook his head.

"If Waterloo wasn't bad enough—I only want some peace and blasted quiet! Father is so desperate to impress the Tarbottoms, and he cornered me, saying 'Little Harriet has taken quite a shine to you, Amby! You could do with a wife, and think of all the money I've spent to raise you as a gentleman, and don't think I'll let you sit about here on the fruits of my labors. I don't care what you got up to at Waterloo, you're not a hero now!' Father's intentions are all too obvious, do you not think?"

"I am so very sorry, Pen, for I know how you dreamed of the theater, and I had never thought a fellow like you might be on the battlefield, let alone in industry." Orsini sighed and stroked his finger down

Pagolo's feathered back. "Can you not say no, thank you, Father, for the theater life is the one for me?"

"How can I not accept?" Ambrose gaped at his friend in surprise. No matter how odious the proposition was, the thought of rebelling against his father's will had to be dismissed. "Father decided my profession for me while I was yet in my cradle. I owe him my duty as his son—I cannot refuse his wishes."

"And what of the young lady in question? Is she as charming as Cosima?"

"Most certainly not." Forgetting himself, Ambrose touched a trembling fingertip to Cosima's cheek. But at a warning look from his friend, Ambrose shoved his hand into his pocket. "I barely know her. She is superficially pleasant, but..." Ambrose stared off into the middle distance again. He thought of Italy, of times long past and out of reach. "She doesn't make my heart dance."

"You cannot be stroking respectable Italian ladies in public, sir," Orsini informed him primly. Ambrose met his friend's gaze, glad to see a gentle humor reflected there. "Come, my friend, let us find an excellent wine and wander through the gardens? I think a little peace might go a long way."

They strolled to the nearest refreshment stand, and Ambrose bought them both drinks. He noticed the admiring glances they received and smiled to himself. They made a most handsome couple indeed.

"Let us be happy now, you and I, in the time that's left to us."

"Let us drink, Captain, and the fair Pagolo and Cosima shall turn our minds to the conundrum." She tapped a fingertip to the parrot's soft head. "You truly have no wish to be wed to the Miss Tarbottom in question?"

Ambrose sighed. "Not at all. But Father, as he never ceases to tell everyone, worked his way up from nothing, you see, so he wants me to work hard, too. No slacking, no living off his money. But I do not even like Mr. Tarbottom. He seems a most insincere sort of fellow — a very slick character. But I suppose successful types are."

"Slick cogs," decided Pagolo. "No slacking!"

"I cannot imagine you in America, Pen." Arm in arm they began to walk, strolling through the gentle pools of lantern light beneath the trees and deeper into the grounds. "And why must it be just as I reach English shores? I have long dreamed of recapturing the magic of our Italian summer, and here I arrive just in time to lose you!"

"What a wonderful summer it was!" Ambrose's voice was soft with nostalgia. "I truly believe that was the best and happiest time I ever knew. I often think of it, you know."

"I have never had such a time since, Pen. Tell me that you are still writing, at least? I have treasured my copy of *Of Fleet Fortune*." Orsini smiled and tossed his hair a little coquettishly. "For it gave Miss Cosima her name, of course."

"It did?" Ambrose chuckled as they ambled beneath the branches. "I have written many plays since, but none, you will not be surprised to know, have been performed. I write them more or less in secret, alas — for my own fun. I should not expect an audience to sit through a play of mine without dropping off to sleep!"

"Pen, please, you can hardly believe that. Why, you should be performed in the Haymarket every night of the week!"

Ambrose laughed. "You are kind to flatter your friend so. Although, I must say, you could play my Cosima very well — should anyone be mad enough to stage *Fleet Fortune*." How pleasant it was to speak of his playwrighting attempts without fear of mockery. "She's a sweet girl with a certain glint in her eye."

"But you would have to write a parrot in — although Pagolo tells me he is seeking retirement. He has earned his fortune and wishes now to enjoy it." She glanced at the parrot, then at Ambrose with a fond smile. "And if you were to show your father the play and tell him of your talent, would he not release you from your position in America at least?"

Ambrose shook his head. "You do not know my father! Industry, that's proper work in his eyes. I once had a poem printed in our local newspaper, and when I showed it to him, he said, 'Thank heavens they did not include your name'! That is my father's opinion of the arts. If I told him I was going to write plays and refuse his plans for America, I have no doubt that he would laugh in my face and — which does rather concern me somewhat — cut me off without a penny. Not that he has admitted in so many words, but he has made it clear that he will not put his hand in his purse for me a moment longer."

Orsini's immaculately shaped brows furrowed and he murmured, "And a soldier's pay is not a rich picking, is it? What a shame we have no real Cosima for you to show off to your father!"

He beamed then, puffing out his somewhat shapely chest and adopting a patrician tone. "Now look here, son of mine, what do you mean to tell me you had an Italian beauty hidden away all this time? And you have already made her a promise that cannot be undone?"

Ambrose laughed, the impression of his father only needing to be rendered in a Yorkshire accent to be spot on. "Well, Father, you would have me be a man of honor, and I could not breach my promise to the delightful Cosima."

"Well, now, this is a sorry pickle and a to-do to boot!" Orsini tapped his lightly powdered chin, still happily in character. "I seems to me that I have no choice but to pay off the Tarbottom girl and declare myself beat! Yet how could any man be angry when he is about to have the delightful, beautiful, witty and talented Cosima as his daughter?"

Halting at once, heedless of the crowd that buffeted around them, Ambrose clutched Cosima's arm. "That's it, is it not? Would he—oh, heavens, but I cannot go against the will of my father. What sort of a son would I be? And yet, the thought of going all the way to America, with a woman I do not—cannot—love... It's worth the attempt, surely?"

Yet Orsini was still laughing, clearly seeing only a fine jape in their conversation. He shook his head and asked, "Can you imagine, Pen, if only we could get away with it?"

If only, indeed.

It would be reckless, it might be silly, he could earn the eternal opprobrium of his own father, yet—

"How long are you to reside in England? Would a trip to Derbyshire present a pleasant diversion?"

"I end my engagement here tonight, though the papers and audiences are clamoring for more. A week is long enough to preserve Cosima's mystery and appeal," Orsini told him proudly. "I was planning merely to remain in London in my other guise and see my good friends—you are the best among them—and do little more than have fun. Yet a visit to your family pile sounds even more entertaining!"

"Would you dare, my friend? The greatest performance of your life—to be Cosima throughout your stay and save me from banishment!"

"Well, I have had a dozen proposals over the past six months"—Orsini informed him with a coquettish wink—"including a prince and a pair of emperors, so I believe I might be able to pass by a Derbyshire industrialist without arousing suspicion!"

"You had me fooled!" And that was quite something, because Ambrose knew very well that under the costume, Orsini was most definitely a man. A warm Italian afternoon, delectable wine over luncheon and a bracing sea was all it had taken for the two young men to run down into the water, casting their clothes aside as they went.

Orsini glanced over his shoulder before saying, "Then let us do it, Pen, if you are sure you want to. For once you engage Cosima, there shall be no going back to the arms of Miss Tarbottom!"

"Oh, please, saints preserve us from the likes of Miss Tarbottom! Now—let us sit and share a drink, and—Pagolo, what would you like?"

"Cogs!"

"A little water for Pagolo, for he shall not drink when preparing for a role, and preparing for a role he most definitely is!" They had paused in a serene clearing in which a scattering of quieter parties occupied tables, each liberally served by bottles. It seemed like a more secluded place in which they might discuss their scheme and these intimate groups were all too involved in their own chatter to be intrigued even by the celebrated Cosima.

"Would you be a love and find us some brandy?" Orsini addressed the request to an attendant who was hovering with such discretion that Ambrose hadn't even noticed his presence. Then the Italian settled neatly on a chair, adjusting the shawl around his pale shoulders, every inch a picture of pretty femininity. He brushed down the immaculate drapes of his Roman gown and murmured, "I believe I shall like England."

"Even if it is not so sunny as your homeland?" Ambrose toyed with the fringe on Cosima's shawl. "You are not cold, my dear friend? You do not fear our snowy winters?"

"Why, Captain, you always kept me warm on those heady Italian nights." Orsini was back in character, Ambrose realized, for it was Cosima who reached out and touched her fingertips to his cheek. "You shall not let me freeze in Derbyshire, I am sure."

"You can depend on your captain to keep you warm." Ambrose closed his hand over Cosima's against his cheek. Something — a word, a sentence — hung in the air between them. Just as Ambrose was about to speak, their brandy arrived.

He threw a glassful down his throat and wiped the back of his hand across his mouth. Adopting what he thought was a sonorous, thespian tone, Ambrose recited, "Drunk? and speak parrot? and squabble? swagger? Swear?"

Pagolo's head swivelled until his beady eyes fixed on Pendleton. As the parrot opened his beak to speak, Orsini said quickly, "Thank Thespis that you are a playwright and not an actor, Pen. Pagolo is quite distracted by your unusual delivery!"

"Thank heavens old Billy Shakespeare is long in his grave! Or was that bad enough to have roused him from his slumber? Perhaps his very ghost will chase me out of here!" Now that, Ambrose realized, wasn't too bad an idea for a play. The ghost of an offended playwright, haunting terrible theatricals. He could see it now. Maybe a lady playwright, and he could fashion the role for Orsini's Cosima.

Pagolo tipped his head to one side, a look so inquisitive in his eyes that Ambrose was convinced that the bird could read his thoughts. He would have to include a role for the parrot as well.

"That would be the most marvelous play," Orsini declared, his eyes sparkling with the thought of it. "Oh, Pen, I could play that dreadful actress, proclaiming woodenly from the lip of the stage to an audience who loathe me!"

Ambrose smiled and folded his arms. "Well, I had you down as the ghost of a lady playwright! But go on, audition for the terrible actress and try to convince me otherwise."

"A ghost? Oh now you have my interest, sir, tell me more!"

"What about, a lady playwright—with you in the role. A ghost. She's died—maybe, oh yes—maybe she's died because of bad actors murdering her work, so she haunts other bad actors from the grave!" Ambrose patted his pockets, hoping to find a lurking pencil stub. "Think of the novels of Walpole and Mrs. Radcliffe, then think—we can make this damned funny!"

"I adore her already!" Orsini pursed his lightly painted lips, clearly considering the possibilities of the piece. "And—oh—let us give her star-crossed lovers to unite, for what does an audience adore more than a love that conquers all?"

Ambrose held aloft a pencil stub, which he had found lodged into the corner of an inside pocket. "Paper, quickly—we must write this all down!"

"Where would I conceal paper in a gown such as this, sir?"

"Surely you must have a love letter from an *inamorata* down your—" Ambrose gestured vaguely toward the front of Cosima's gown, but was rendered awkward at once, as if Cosima really was a lady and he had caused her great offense. "Perhaps not."

"My manager, the great Orsini, does not allow me callers," Orsini told him innocently. "For he knows how my head might be turned by a strapping soldier."

"If only I hadn't resigned my commission!" Ambrose examined the pencil stub. What had—no, Orsini was only playing. He couldn't know.

"I am glad that you did, for every day that you were on the continent was a fresh torture to me, every report of another hundred men fallen in battle was—" He fell silent and shook his head, long-lashed eyes fluttering closed for a few moments. When they reopened the light had returned, and Ambrose recognized immediately that his friend had banished the memories of worry and was ready, as he so often was, for mischief. "I can keep the secret no more! I showed your *Of Fleet Fortune; or, The Duke's Disgrace*, to Viscount Hartington. We read it together and he adored every word. Will you permit him to make your play his next triumph, Pen? Say you will, then your father will have no choice but to celebrate your achievements!"

"Sorry—Hartington, you say?" Ambrose's thoughts had dwelled on Orsini's tender concern for him, but it took a few seconds for him to see the import of what he had just told him. "How you jest! Lord Hartington cannot possibly find that scrap of scribble in the least amusing. He might find a use for my manuscript by cutting it up to light candles with, perhaps, but not—" Ambrose lounged back in his chair, laughing. "You are a fine one for a jape, my dear friend!"

"There is no joke!" Orsini widened his hazel eyes. "He begged to meet the playwright, but I would not disclose your identity. I said simply that it was penned by a handsome traveler. Do you see? Penned, Pen!"

Ambrose barely heard Orsini's pun. Handsome traveler. Was that—did it mean that Orsini—? No, he was joking, that was all, because he was dressed as a lady, and anyone seeing them walk through Vauxhall Gardens arm-in-arm might conceivably think they were courting, and—except they weren't. And besides—Viscount Hartington?

"Hartington wanted to meet me?" Finally Ambrose was paying attention. "The producer? He wants to—my play?"

"He adored it. I believe he would stage it tomorrow, no, I know he would!"

Orsini wasn't joshing him, and Ambrose's face cracked wide with a grin. "I don't know what to say! It is so long since I read that play over—so long since I gave it to you as our parting gift when I left Italy for home. Do you truly believe that my youthful scrawlings have merit?"

"Tonight, sir, we shall retire to Pall Mall and read it again!"

"I should enjoy that—meeting Cosima, and Mr. and Mrs. Mallett and the Spanish *marquesa* again after all this time." Ambrose's world had been so gray without Orsini in it, and now he beamed at him with joy. "We will meet my long-lost friends!"

"Oh, don't look!" Orsini made a great show of turning away from a table a little to their left and in doing so, of course, simply drew his friend's attention to it and the lady who was sat there surrounded by clearly well-meaning friends, dabbing at her eyes. "A lady in distress, Pen, poor thing."

Ambrose looked because, as a playwright, he was unavoidably drawn to human drama.

"Oh good heavens, one speaks of Viscount Hartington and there is his mother, as if summoned by my very words. The dowager viscountess, poor petal," Orsini whispered, clutching his diamond necklace.

Even the ostrich plume rising from the dowager viscountess' coiffure had drooped, and her silk gloves had wrinkled. She was a picture of misery, so at odds with the frantic glee of almost every other guest at Vauxhall.

"The poor dear lady was the victim of a thief this past month," Orsini whispered, inclining his head in response to the bashful waves from the lady's attendants. "She had hosted a ball to celebrate the birth of her seventh legitimate grandchild and some terrible creature stole into her chambers and danced away with her treasured pearls! They were a betrothal gift from the late Viscount H. some five decades ago. This country is awash with villains and one of them is waltzing off with silver and jewels each time there is a ball!"

"Awash with villains? But what of your mountain paths garlanded with *banditti*?" Not that Ambrose had met with any on his Grand Tour, but even so. "Rascals are to be found amongst all peoples of the world, I fear—sadly for someone like the unhappy dowager."

"The poor lady, though." Orsini's full lips formed a perfect O of shock. "And the villain remains unapprehended, whoever he might be."

Orsini whispered something to the parrot, who took off at a fair flight, eventually settling neatly atop the table in front of the viscountess. Pagolo gave a little bow then without further ado, launched into a rather bawdy song of a sailor and his mate, entirely unsuitable for a noblewoman but eminently suitable for a lady who needed cheering up.

Ambrose couldn't help but laugh, and watched the parrot's performance and the viscountess' reaction. The venerable lady went from weeping to surprise then swiftly to amused before the end of the first verse. "Where did you find that parrot?"

"He found me, as I sat on the beach and looked at the sea and said a tiny prayer for a soldier in battle that I know," he said gently. "I had thought for a moment an angel had alighted on my shoulder, but it was just my Pagolo. I believe he has a lover somewhere for sometimes he will fly away for a day at a time, but he always finds me again."

"I hope he sang bawdy songs to distract you from gloomy thoughts about your soldier." Ambrose poured more brandy. "And of course, your soldier would have been singing bawdy songs too! Even while he thought of his friends far away."

"Did you, Pen?" Orsini blinked his long eyelashes and rested his elbow on the table, cradling his chin on his hand. "Did you think of your friend in Italy?"

"Yes—yes, of course I did." Ambrose couldn't bear to look at Orsini as he admitted this, and went back to enjoying Pagolo's performance. Too late, he realized that he had sounded rather short with his friend, but if Orsini had known what thoughts Ambrose had dwelled on, he might never speak to him again.

Orsini turned his head away to watch the parrot, suddenly silent. Ambrose felt as if he had scolded a child, as though that sharp tone had been meant unkindly and had sliced through his friend's cheer. Eventually Orsini murmured, "I did not mean to remind you of the battle, Pen."

"No—it is I who must apologize." Ambrose brought Orsini's hand gently to his lips just as if Cosima were real and not his friend's concoction. "I have many things on my mind, dear friend—which your warm company has almost made me forget."

"If we might free you from your marital servitude," Orsini mused, twining his fingers in her—his—own, "you would be allowed back to the theater! So we must decide, you met Cosima on your grand tour? And have we been lovers? Will I be a loud and difficult creature seeking the man who promised me his heart? What is our story, Pen?"

"If Cosima is an Italian actress, then I should be surprised if she were not loud and difficult!" Ambrose laughed. A memory of a theater in Florence and one actress in particular had sprung to his mind, a querulous lady who had demanded the two men accompany her about the city for an evening. And one evening had been more than enough. "But there must be sweetness in her too, or my father will not understand why his son fell in love. He thinks little enough of me now, but if he saw me bullied to the altar he would think even less! And yes — perhaps we were lovers."

Ambrose stared off at the lanterns as they trembled in a gentle breeze. "Just one snatched night, when we sloughed off our innocence in each other's arms."

Orsini nodded thoughtfully, tapping his finger against his chin. "I am, by nature, a calm and cheerful girl, but I do possess a temper when aroused and I shall demonstrate it if required. So, Pen, you will be glad to see me, yes? You have dreamed of one day embracing your Cosima once more?"

Ambrose sighed, assuming the role of a lover. If he acted his pretense, Orsini couldn't know what truth lay behind his words. "I have dreamt of nothing more these few years past but the moment when I might embrace my darling Cosima again. The memory of her beauty, of her sweet kisses and tender caresses, has been a torment to me. Every night I lie awake on my bed of thorns, unable to stop my thoughts wandering back to her — my darling, my sweetheart, my Cosima."

"And I, Pen, *amore mio*, I have never wanted another. When you left me, when our Italian summer ended, I wept until I had no tears left in me." He caressed Ambrose's face with his fingertips and dropped his voice to a whisper. "Let us hope some gossip reaches your *pappa*, of your liaison in the pleasure gardens?"

Ambrose moved his chair closer to Orsini's until they were side by side. He ventured to put his arm around Orsini's waist and rested his chin on his friend's shoulder. "There. Is that not fodder for scandal?"

"How scandalous dare we be in Derbyshire?" Orsini's mouth was very close to Ambrose's ear, his voice a low purr. "For your father's benefit, of course?"

"For Father's benefit, yes." And not for any other reason at all. No. None. Not one bit of it. "Perhaps a little kiss — upon the cheek, mind."

Orsini obliged, his pursed lips pressing softly to Ambrose's cheek. They lingered there, warm and tender, before he asked, "Like that?"

Ambrose couldn't reply at first. A sensation had shot through him that he was sure must be akin to a strike of lightning.

At length, he was able to croak his short reply. "Yes."

And he could say no more.

"Then I shall be sure that your father sees many such kisses," he replied softly. "And plenty of embraces besides."

His head resting on Orsini's shoulder, Ambrose whispered, "You are quite the actor, I must say! You do not mind, despite being a fellow, all — all this? Kissing…embraces…with me? Bearing in mind that I am a fellow too."

"It is a role, Pen, never fear. Unorthodox, I know, but if it might keep you here in England, Cosima is yours to command." Orsini was still whispering, maintaining the impression of some scandalous and unheard exchange. "And better with a performer who is known to you than a tavern actress, as long as you have no objections to a pretty Italian in a variety of beautiful gowns?"

"Who could possibly object to that?" Ambrose peered over Orsini's shoulder. A group of society people, whom Ambrose vaguely knew, had spotted him. From their eager gossip, Ambrose became aware that a novel subject for conversation would be on the lips of all. The Dowager Viscountess Hartington's unhappy theft would, with any luck, be unseated by the news that the second and youngest son of Mr. Barnaby Pendleton of Derbyshire was intriguing with a beautiful lady in Vauxhall Gardens. "And it's working!"

"Will we tell him that we have pined for one another?" Orsini smiled. "That it was on your Grand Tour that you fell in love with the toast of the Roman stage?"

Ambrose's heart bumped up against his ribs. He nodded, only now wondering if he could bear the subterfuge.

For in truth, he loved Orsini.

"Will you take me to Derbyshire with you? Or should my arrival be a surprise even to my lover?"

The thought of explaining themselves at every coaching inn between London and Derbyshire worried Ambrose. Besides, if his father was not expecting an Italian actress to turn up at his door, no matter what wisps of gossip might come his way, then all the better. "A surprise," Ambrose decided.

"When do you return?"

"Tomorrow." The word slid sadly from Ambrose's lips. "I am to visit my brother on the way back. Father wishes me to talk to him of mining matters. My brother runs several collieries — Father couldn't be more proud of him."

"One more question… They will suspect *issue*." He phrased it so delicately. "We are agreed that our night of passion did not lead to a surprise nine months later? For I expect the matter to be broached!"

"I am the putative father of no one," Ambrose assured him.

"And my figure thanks you!"

"I'll drink to that!" Ambrose went to pour more brandy, only for the bottle to present him with an insignificant splash. He mimed taking an almighty mouthful from his glass. "One must pretend, I am afraid."

"My Pall Mall sanctuary has plenty of brandy, if you are ready to depart?"

"Good brandy, too, I'd wager." Ambrose rose from his chair and offered his arm. "Unless you should like a dance first? But if we leave before closing, we give more fuel to the gossips than a spirited set of 'Hunt the Squirrel'."

"My Lord, Pen, you must have been hidden away! Nobody hunts the squirrel in Rome anymore!"

"It's all the rage in Derbyshire, I assure you."

Orsini raised his eyebrow and decided, "Pall Mall."

Chapter Two

It was long after midnight when the two men found themselves dancing merrily up Pall Mall and into the rooms that were Orsini's temporary home in London, Pagolo perched on Ambrose's shoulder and Orsini happily spiraling the gossamer shawl above his head. Knowing Orsini, Ambrose had hardly been expecting a run-of-the-mill lodging house, but the truth was even grander than he had allowed himself to imagine. During the months in which they had roamed the continent he had quickly realized that his friend didn't like to rough it, but these rooms would have seemed luxurious even to an emperor. It was a miniature Versailles, a palace's worth of splendor crammed into a suite of half a dozen chambers above a clockmaker's shop a few doors along from Ambrose's regular city haunt of Brook's.

Orsini shooed away the maid and valet who rushed to tend them, clearly under the impression that their charge was as female as the audience believed her to be. Finally alone he told Ambrose, "This belongs to

Hartington, you know. I rather think it's where he pops his mistress when she isn't bedding the king!"

It certainly looked the part, all marble and gold and ebony, vast swathes of red velvet and silk, mirrors and glass and ornate chandeliers as far as the eye could see. It suited Orsini too, whose own noble family favored a touch of the overdone.

"You shall find Pendleton Hall quite pedestrian, I'm afraid!" Ambrose was ushered onto an elaborate gold sofa, and he panicked as the pale silk upholstery came into contact with his outdoor clothes. But Orsini seemed entirely at home here, so Ambrose soon relaxed.

"Not at all!" Orsini threw his shawl down atop a gleaming walnut piano. "A touch of brandy? Oh, Pen, the scene in *Fleet Fortune* with Cosima and the brandy bottle — I thought Harty would die laughing!"

Ambrose gripped the arm of the sofa, awkward at such high praise. "That Hartington himself should find it amusing — well, it caps the globe! And yes, let's have more brandy and we shall raise a toast to Lord Hartington."

"Would I be right, Captain, in recognizing a fair few of our old Italian haunts within the more decadent scenes you have created? All those absurd dowagers and flighty Casanovas." He poured two generous glasses of brandy and waltzed them across the room to where Ambrose was sitting. Orsini's feet were sure and steady in their dainty slippers, dancing lightly over the deep Persian rugs despite the amount of alcohol they had enjoyed, his eyes half-closed as he hummed a gentle tune. "I am the luckiest fellow alive to have read it, and you are the greatest to have written it."

"But 'tis a trifle, my dear Orsini! You flatter me kindly, but I am not sure that it should ever be performed. What would my father say? A poem in the newspaper nearly sent him into apoplexy." Ambrose swirled the brandy in its glass and breathed the scent of an expensive make. He expected nothing less — Orsini had splendid taste in most things.

"No flattery, Pen, only an honest reading of an excellent debut." Orsini dropped down onto the sofa beside him in a cloud of lace and perfume. "I have read a thousand comic plays and appeared in the best and the worst and *Fleet Fortune* is the finest yet. It is a sorry thing indeed that the world will never see it!"

Ambrose did not believe that Orsini's sincerity was a performance. If his play really was as good as Orsini claimed, then Ambrose might dare to hope that there was something else in the world for him besides soldiering and industry. "It is an age since I last read it. Are you sure it does not sound like a mere youthful squeak?"

"I must tell you something else, Captain P. Promise you will not be terribly angry?" Orsini batted his long eyelashes. "It is a nice something, really."

"Really?" Ambrose settled against the cushions and grinned at his friend. "I promise not to be terribly angry, but depending on what it is — might I be allowed a tiny bit of anger? Which I shall dissipate by grinding my teeth for a few seconds? You shall barely notice, I swear it."

"You had asked me not to show your play to anyone in the whole world and I promised that I would not. And I broke my promise and showed it to Lord Hartington, as I have already confessed." He pouted, his full lips just turning upward into a smile. "And he showed it to Mr. Sheridan. And Mr. Sheridan showed it to the Prince Regent and he to Mr. Bannister and all of them adored it. They clamored for your name but I would not be drawn! Whenever — if ever — you escape the mine for the theater, you will have the most loud and well-connected champions."

Ambrose stared at his friend, dumbstruck by this revelation. He almost spilled his brandy.

"So — well, that certainly answers my question, then. Not a youthful squeak. Far from it. Goodness me!" Ambrose grasped Orsini's hand. "My silly play, with Mr. and Mrs. Mallett, and the beautiful Cosima, and the Spanish fellow and… My word. To think, I begged you not to show anyone, for fear they might think it foolish! Perhaps I am a little angry, but look — I have ground my teeth, and my anger is gone."

"Huzzah!" Orsini laughed, closing his fingers around Ambrose's hand in turn. "The Spanish fellow is adorable but it is Cosima they are falling over themselves for. I believe every gent would wed her if he could, that little minx you have created!"

"I must admit, she was the most fun to write of all the characters!" Ambrose held Orsini's hand a little tighter. "I had thought — daydreamed, in my idle moments — that you should make the perfect Fernando, but you are Cosima. You would have to play her!"

"And you can see that I am well used to appearing *en travesti*." He gestured to the gown. "It began as a little silliness for carnivale, and has become my fortune!"

Orsini's lips drew Ambrose's attention. They were so soft and plump, and red as cherries. A beautiful mouth for a beautiful woman. Gentlemen would swoon for them, searching out those lips for just one kiss, and fading away for want of the owner's affections.

"You will do my Cosima justice, I am sure of it." Ambrose raised their joined hands to his lips and kissed Orsini's. In jest. Of course.

"Sir, what if my father should see?" Orsini's voice had changed just slightly, the timbre raised a little into a softly feminine register. "We might not be so alone as we believe!"

Ambrose smiled, recalling the lines of the play that he had written in what seemed like another lifetime. Before Waterloo, before American industrialists and their awful daughters. He assumed what he thought might be a passable Spanish accent and spoke the lines of lovelorn Fernando. "*Señorita*, my heart's desire, no one passes by this bower. We shall love unseen and unknown!"

"One kiss," Cosima agreed with just the right combination of enthusiasm, desire and uncertainty. "And then fair Cosima must away, Your Grace."

Those lips. Goodness.

Ambrose grinned playfully as he leaned nearer to Orsini, as if he really was just about to —

Oh dear. Ambrose brushed his lips across Orsini's and felt once again that jolt, as if of lightning. He wanted to kiss Orsini, just as he had wanted to all those years ago when they had swum together in the sea.

He had never stopped wanting to.

Yet perhaps this happened all the time in theatrical circles, for Orsini simply fell back onto the sofa, laughing. He raised his brandy glass and told Ambrose, "We make the most marvelous Cosima and Fernando, hiding away in their little Italian paradise until the end of time, she innocent in her beauty, he handsome in her arms."

Ambrose unplaited his fingers from Orsini's and gripped the arm of the sofa again. A nice, solid sort of chair it was, a reliable, comfortable piece of furniture — and why did his heart beat so thickly now, pounding in his head as if his ears should burst?

"I do hope one day to see *Fleet Fortune* on stage." Ambrose took a long, brave swig of brandy. It burned its way down his gullet. "Perhaps you might tour it on the continent when things are more settled again?"

"*Of Fleet Fortune; or, The Duke's Disgrace*, by A Gentleman." Orsini took on a rather faraway look. "I simply will not allow you to be spirited off to America against your will. It is a fine sort of place, I hear, but surely a fellow should harbor some desire to move if he is to do so? One cannot force a playwright into a mining office and say to him, there, now make money and forget the stories you wish to tell!"

"I have no choice in the matter." Ambrose finished off his brandy and attempted a smile. "I have a vague notion, however, that Mama does not like the thought of me going beyond the seas. She complained of a nightmare the other morning — of a terrific storm and a shipwreck! I do hope that I shan't drown. It would be most inconvenient."

"You shall not be there at all, Pen, for Cosima is to descend on Derbyshire and demand the hand of her lover, just as he promised it to her all those years ago. Never fear, my friend, you shall be saved from your marital fate!"

Seemingly satisfied with that conclusion, Orsini snuggled closer to Ambrose. In the elaborate marble fireplace the fire was beginning to die, the room growing darker despite the overdone chandelier that hung high above them. It was the sort of room

Ambrose's father would no doubt approve of, for it screamed of wealth and opulence and the world that Barnaby Pendleton, born with barely a penny to his name, had managed to claw his way into. Barnaby, who had no education but possessed a fierce ambition and intelligence and the determination to make something of himself, and who had given his two sons every advantage that money could buy. The elder had already done his bit, an heir and spare, a wife, a hand in the family's industrial might, and now it was Ambrose's turn. Waterloo was two years ago — the time had come for him to join the firm too.

"I cannot bear the thought of leaving for my bed in the house on Cavendish Square. My dear friend, I am so contented here!"

"These are the rooms of a concubine, Captain." He raised one immaculately arched eyebrow, his slender face full of mischief. "Would you like to share my magnificent harlot's bed?"

"How jolly decent of you to offer, Orsini."

Ambrose watched the fire collapse in on itself. Having nearly kissed, was sharing Orsini's bed a wise idea? But Orsini had treated their near-miss as a joke — he clearly felt no awkwardness there. And surely he felt no desire for a pointless gentleman like Captain Pendleton, not when there would be all those pretty actresses at his command. Even if Ambrose desired him, even if having Orsini cuddled to him made his heart sing — Ambrose would not wish to embarrass his friend. If he kept to the edge of the bed, with Orsini on the other side, then all would be well.

"I've never slept in a harlot's bed before. It is really quite enormous?"

"Vast as an ocean, Pen, and a sight to behold."

"Lead on, sir!" Good. If it was as huge as Ambrose imagined, they could not awkwardly roll into each other. He'd had quite enough of that in rough-and-ready billets in the Army.

No one wants to wake up at five o'clock in the morning only to find a bristly old sergeant in one's arms.

"Come on, my harlot, shall we take the brandy?" Orsini stood and extended his arm to Ambrose, immediately assuming the plummy tones of a rather oily, rather seedy upper-class Englishman. "Come into my bedchamber, my dear innocent young creature, let me show you my ancient artifacts. I can assure you they will delight, amuse and leave you wide-eyed!"

Having never been called a harlot before, even in jest, Ambrose took a moment to recover from his surprise. "I'm...I'm sure I certainly shall be left wide-eyed!"

Was that a raise of the eyebrow from Orsini? Ambrose was struck by an image of writhing, naked flesh, which he very quickly dismissed from his mind. Only for it to be replaced by the memory of Orsini, naked as a babe newborn, dancing through the waves as they crashed along an Italian beach.

"Captain, would that you had seen my Little Pickle." Orsini imbued the character name with all sorts of other meaning. He seized Ambrose's hand and pulled him to his feet with such force that, for a moment, the two men collided. "We charmed the continent. Cosima must bless that rakish role every day, for it made her name! Orsini is the manager, the chap with the purse, but it is Cosima whom they cheer for!"

"Yes...yes, I'm sure you did charm the continent, and several other places too!" What a racy way to make one's name. Not with a Titania, no, nor even a Polly

Peachum. Ambrose glanced at Orsini's shining eyes and wondered anew if sharing a bed with him was a good idea. But it was all jokes and blather with Orsini – nothing untoward would go on.

Even if the devil in Ambrose wished otherwise.

"They offered Cosima Garrick's strange little bastardization of the piece for her London debut but in I said *no grazie*. Nice enough, but not when one has performed Wycherley!" Orsini laughed. "I am Orsini by day, Cosima by night, there is little I cannot tell you of life!"

Pausing only to snatch up the brandy decanter as they passed, juggling it rather nimbly with his glass, Orsini led Ambrose along the hallway, silent now but for their footsteps, and through a pair of double doors that already stood ajar. In the room beyond, a fire burned, illuminating a chamber of such ridiculous splendor that it took Ambrose a moment to fully appreciate it. If the apartment had been Versailles in miniature, then the bedroom was all of that and more, packed into one chamber. Across one wall was a dressing table already piled high with Orsini's cosmetics and jewels, a silk banyan abandoned rakishly over the chair.

And the bed... Well, he had not overstated it.

It was a canopied confection of dark wood, the pillars intricately carved with foliage and fruit, the canopy and textiles a deep, claret red on which patterns were picked out in gold and silver thread. The gold-tasselled edging fluttered in the breeze that blew softly from the grate and there in the pillow and on the covers was the slight shape of Orsini, who must have napped here before embarking on his evening.

"Hartington certainly knows how to have fun!" Ambrose couldn't quite believe that this was where he would be sleeping. Though his parents' houses were lavish and expensively decorated, they had nothing on this. The part of his brain that functioned as a chiffonier of random impressions, which he raided for his plays, busily absorbed every feature of the room. "Romping with his mistress, the naughty fellow!"

Ambrose shook off his already unbuttoned tailcoat and hung it over the back of a chaise longue. He bent to the mirror over the dressing table and fumbled with the elaborate knot of his cravat. Within moments Orsini was there with him, unknotting the cravat with an impressive turn of speed no doubt born of a lifetime in the theater. He pulled it clear with a flamboyant gesture and cracked the cravat like a whip.

"Picture this Orsini standing before his dearly missed father, the late Conte d'Orsini, who was full of horror when I told him I could not breathe if I could not act, but it was left to my mother to turn him to our scheme," Orsini told him. "After all, he was wed to an opera diva, how could he do any other!"

Ambrose dropped onto the edge of the chaise longue to pull off his Hessians. "Alas that my mother was never an opera diva, but merely a cordwainer's daughter!"

"But she was awfully well-behaved," Orsini furnished in a sing-song voice, as though it were the punchline to a bawdy joke. He disappeared behind a chinoiserie screen, undressing as any blushing young bride might, away from the eyes of her paramour.

"Not as such—my brother's birth came but a month after my parents' marriage!" Ambrose turned away as he unbuttoned his breeches. "But, as Mama is fond of saying, theirs was a love match. She fell for my father when he commissioned a pair of boots from my grandfather—how utterly romantic, don't you think? Anyway, you don't mind sharing a bed with an awfully well-behaved captain wearing naught but his shirt and his drawers, do you?"

"I sleep as God made me, but for you, Pen, I shall throw on a silky something," Orsini promised as he emerged. Cosima was gone, and in her place there was the young man from Italy once more, the auburn curls tied back in an elaborate queue finished with a red ribbon, and the dress replaced by...nothing. "I should not want you to feel inferior!"

The memory of the roar of the sea as it crashed along the golden strand filled Ambrose's ears. Orsini seemed entirely comfortable in his nudity, and his eyes danced with mischief. Ambrose dragged his glance away, but not before he had registered that the slim-hipped youth he remembered from Italy had become a slender, lightly toned man. And as for his little pickle—

No, a gentleman does not pass comment upon another gentleman's anatomy, and certainly does not allow his gaze to linger there.

"Let us see what we have," Orsini decided. He opened the linen press and rooted through, offering Ambrose a glimpse of the silks and velvets that made up his friend's flamboyant wardrobe. It was absurd, wonderfully so, and entirely unlike anything he had ever seen in Derbyshire. Finally Orsini withdrew a silk robe that was as red as his suit had been, and decorated with intricately embroidered golden flowers. He pulled it on with a swish of silk and tied the belt as he told Ambrose, "This was a gift for an attitude I performed for the Grand Duchess. I gave her a little Lady Hamilton, and she gave me this. I believe she may have thought me a young lady!"

She certainly wouldn't have thought so if she'd seen what Ambrose just had. But he chose not to mention it. "You do most certainly convince—very well, might I add."

"Let us just say that I have received more than a few proposals of marriage from the most surprising quarters." Orsini laughed, though he had the good grace to blush. "And one Russian gentleman in particular was most persistent, the poor soul. When I appeared to him in my suit and said, I am a fellow just like you, he merely cried, ah, here is my beautiful Cosima wearing the clothes of a gentleman, but I shall not be fooled! Happily, he has since wed a ballerina and forgotten all about his Cosima."

"I shall have to put that in one of my plays!" Ambrose laughed and pulled back the bedcovers. He paused, struck by a sudden, bitter barb.

"Well, I would do, if…" *If I wasn't being sent away.* But he and Orsini had a plan. "Anyway—I'm being very rude. Do you have a preference—which side of the bed is yours?"

He watched Orsini approach the bed on light feet, and Ambrose realized that he could see something feminine in Orsini that needed only costume and a small slicking-on of paint to transform him into a woman. And a rather beautiful one at that.

"I sleep on whichever side is empty," Orsini told him scandalously before drawing back the covers in climbing in. "Or here, alternatively."

Ambrose lay back on the bed and pillowed his head on his arm. He gazed up into the elaborate canopy, tracing the patterns in the gold and silver thread. "Is this bed usually quite full, then, Orsini?"

"Not so far," he admitted. "It is my first trip to London, I have too many exciting sights to see to spend hours in bed with whoever might be passing. So you are honored indeed, Pen!"

"I am!" Ambrose rolled over onto his side so that he could better see his friend. The Italian beamed back at him in the low firelight, his eyes alive with brandy and silliness. Really, Ambrose could not have asked for a better companion for those months of his Grand Tour.

"Just think, Orsini, this bed has seen Hartington in the altogether—the very idea of it!" Ambrose chuckled but soon found himself helpless with laughter at the thought. In a booming voice, he declared, "My darling Priscilla—that should be the name of his mistress— divest me of my breeches, for I wish to tup you!"

"Not until one has obtained one's rock from Garrards, my lord," was Orsini's coquettish reply. "Until fair Pris has her diamond, her gates must remain unbreached, no matter how you tempt!"

Ambrose winked. "Perhaps you will give your devoted Harty a little taste, my lady, before he heads to the jeweler's?"

"A little flash of my precious jewels?" Orsini drew the sheet up to his chin, batting his long eyelashes. "A lady might be ruined, Lord H., for it is not cheap to maintain one's modesty. A shoulder for a shilling, with the rest negotiable?"

"A shilling? Yes, a shilling it is!" Ambrose went on laughing, even though it seemed as if the viscount himself was there in the room, watching in horror at his mockery. Orsini howled with laughter and began to lower the sheet very slowly, stopping just before his pale shoulder became visible.

"All monies in advance, sir, for a girl cannot put too high a price on her modesty." He let out a hoot of hilarity. "Can you imagine, Pen, what sights this room has witnessed? Why, I'll wager it is no stranger to the royal favor, if you follow!"

Ambrose nodded conspiratorially. "Then this bed must be quite a feat of engineering not to have collapsed with old Georgie Porgie rolling about on it!"

"Let us hope he never sees the fair Cosima, or I may be the Princess Regent!"

"Don't worry, I shall defend your honor, my dear Orsini." Ambrose puffed out his chest. "I shall challenge him to a duel!"

"So long as it is not a duel to see who might stuff themselves with port and pie, you are sure to win." Orsini finally pushed the blanket lower, until it rested across his chest. "How civilized we are in our harlot bed."

Orsini's shoulder, now revealed, sent that jolt once more through Ambrose, enlivening his loins. He was relieved indeed that the bed was so large, otherwise the embarrassment of his erection might be rather obvious. Why must he desire Orsini? Why could he not desire the woman his father seemed so keen for him to take as his wife? Instead, here he was, in the bed of a mistress, lying beside an Italian actor, and all Ambrose could think of was how much he wanted to —

"I might have another splash of brandy before I sleep. What do you say, Orsini, to send us off to sweetest slumber?"

"Please do," he agreed. "It will give us pleasant dreams, I imagine!"

Ambrose slipped out of the bed, making sure he kept his back to Orsini. He poured two glasses from the bottle and took a large gulp. Returning to the bed, he hoped that the brandy would calm his embarrassment—and he hoped Orsini hadn't noticed.

"Brandy, my dear friend!" Ambrose climbed back into bed and passed a glass to Orsini. Did Ambrose catch a rather Puckish look on that all-too-innocent face? A slight quirk of his eyebrows and faintest hint of a smile?

No.

"You are blushing, Captain!"

Yes, then.

"Am I?" Words unspooled from Ambrose's mouth at speed. "I must say, I hadn't noticed. I can't think that I have reason to, I...I..." He put his glass down beside the bed and fussed with the blankets as he got comfortable again. "It's all this talk of goings-on, it had quite a strange effect on me."

"Then we shall talk of goings-on no more, but instead drink our brandy like respectable gentlemen in a harlot's bed."

"One feels very far from respectable indeed in this bed!" Ambrose retrieved his brandy and let the pillows swallow him as he reclined, sighing in contentment. Their plan to upset his father's nuptial arrangements would work—it had to. "Do you know, Orsini, I've not felt this happy in an absolute age."

Orsini beamed and shifted across until he could rest his head on Ambrose's shoulder, rather vexing Ambrose's schemes to keep himself at a respectable distance. The actor blinked up into the ornate canopy and murmured, "It feels just so, doesn't it?"

"It does." Ambrose draped his arm loosely around his bedfellow. It would have been rude not to. "I feel all warm inside, and I don't think it's only the brandy."

"Then it must be friendship," his friend decided softly. "For we have been apart too long."

"That must be it." Not desire. And certainly not love. Ambrose could never admit to that. "I've never met anyone half as fun as you."

Orsini laughed and told him, "And you will not again, especially not in America!"

"Indeed, unless I smuggle you out of the country with me." Ambrose tightened his arm a little around Orsini. He was comforted by the scent of him, even if his spicy, exotic perfume seemed designed to excite, not to calm.

"I shall snuggle into a trunk with my favorite suits," Orsini decided. "I wish you did not have to go."

"We shall not think of it. Not tonight, for I do not want anything to cloud our joy." Ambrose kissed Orsini's brow. Only once he had bestowed the kiss did something in his mind tell him that he should not have done so.

"Nor will it," came the soft reply. "Not tonight."

Ambrose yawned. He felt so warm and happy, and there was a look of such contentment on Orsini's face as they embraced. He would struggle to feel like this again.

"Sleep well, my dear friend," Ambrose whispered.

"And you, my captain," he whispered tenderly in reply. "My husband-to-be."

Chapter Three

Something brushed against Ambrose's cheek, waking him from confusing dreams of sharing a bed with Orsini. When he opened his eyes, he realized it was a length of Orsini's soft auburn hair that had come loose from its queue. This was no dream after all—he really had passed the night with his friend.

And Ambrose lay curled behind Orsini with his arm around him, as if they were lovers. As if they belonged together.

I must go.

Now that the London season was ended, he had to return to Pendleton Hall. And before the carriage left, he had an appointment with his tailor for a new suit of clothes, for it would not do to be a shabby gentleman.

Even if a shabby gentleman indeed flitted from a bedroom in the early morning without a goodbye.

Ambrose wanted to stay in bed with his arm around Orsini. He wanted to kiss him, even though he knew he mustn't want such a thing. Orsini was only playing. He could not possibly want the amorous attentions of a retired soldier and hopeless industrialist. And besides…a fellow could get into trouble.

Ambrose's head pounded from the effects of last night's brandy, and the weight of his impossible desires. He might have had the occasional interlude here and there with men before, but this was Orsini, his friend. He should not feel—he must not think of him that way.

It was best to go before Orsini awoke, before those long-lashed eyelids opened and Ambrose was caught in Orsini's gaze. He had been a fool to hope that their ridiculous plan would work. Orsini might convince as a woman in Vauxhall Gardens, but it was a stretch indeed to expect that Cosima could glitter in the drawing room at Pendleton Hall without something giving Orsini away.

Ambrose had to accept that there would be no playwriting for him. No theaters, and certainly no theatricals. It would be coal and industry all the way, just as his father had always planned. But what a terrible pang gnawed at Ambrose, banished from everyone and everything he knew, to start a different life in a faraway land. A life he didn't want, with a spouse he hadn't chosen.

Ambrose collected up his clothes and crept noiselessly out of the bedroom without looking back at the figure in the bed. He dressed quickly in the drawing room, hoping he would not wake Pagolo, who was asleep on his perch with his head tucked under his wing.

Despite the only pen he could find being made from a hugely elaborate peacock feather, Ambrose was able to write a note.

My dear fellow,

I have many and tedious appointments today which cannot wait. Would that I could have spent the day with you, but alas, this is not to be. Please do not think badly of me.

I must ask that you do not trouble yourself to travel to Pendleton Hall — our plan seemed so amusing last night under the aura of brandy and good cheer, but I cannot ask you to risk scandal or damage your career for me. I must accept my father's will with good grace, even if it is with a heavy heart that I do so.

Thank you so very much for your entertaining company. I wish we could have had many more evenings at Vauxhall Gardens.

Your loving friend,
Capt. Pendleton

* * * *

Each turn of the coach's wheels took Ambrose farther and farther from London. An oppressive load was upon him, as if he stood at the very bottom of one of his father's mines with an unconscionable weight of rocks and stones and earth above his head. Orsini's world of bright silks and parrot's wings was but an exotic dream in the world that Ambrose Pendleton inhabited. Their plan would never have worked, and Ambrose was cold with shame that he had even contemplated shrugging off his duty to his father.

Ambrose endured his melancholy reflections as he traveled alone along miles of English highway, rattled and shaken over potholes and sharp bends. Finally he arrived at his brother's residence, where he received a stiff, tight-lipped reception.

This would be Ambrose's lot. A valley of soot and grime, and a pinch-faced wife who spent her days wiping coal dust from her expensive ornaments.

That world of opulence and theatricality that he had experienced with Orsini was lost to Ambrose forever, like a man given a glimpse of heaven only to be thrown into purgatory. How soft that silk banyan had been against his hands when he had woken, how gentle his friend's sleeping breaths.

But Ambrose Pendleton was the base sort of fellow who kisses a gentleman's brow, embraces him all night and vanishes before breakfast.

What a dishonorable fellow I am.

The coach turned in at the gates of Pendleton Hall and rattled along the ruler-straight drive. Ambrose flipped open the window and leaned out to see the house up ahead, a vast Palladian effort which had tried to bring a dash of Italy to Derbyshire.

But not the dash of Italy that Ambrose longed to see again.

There, standing atop the steps beneath a monumental portico, framed by pillars that would not have been out of place in Ancient Greece, was his father.

Barnaby Pendleton would certainly have been out of place in Ancient Greece, no matter how many temples to Diana he commissioned to stud the grounds of his home. As small and round as his son was tall and athletic, he stood with his hands on his hips, master of all he surveyed, master of Pendleton Hall, the self-made king inspecting his realm. Coal had built this house. Coal and hard graft and knowing how to cut a deal before you could even read, let alone sign your own name.

'There'll never be another me,' he never tired of telling his family, his plump cheeks red with satisfaction and port. *'You'll not see my like again.'*

"Here's a welcome sight at last!" Mr. Pendleton descended the steps on his small feet, as undersized as everything else about him was oversize, a little toad balancing on dainty toes. "The lad come home to roost!"

As Ambrose climbed down from the carriage, the family crest on the carriage door glittered in the sunlight. The gold shield crossed with a pickax had cost Mr. Pendleton a pretty penny from the College of Arms, but he was a man with plenty of money to spare.

Mr. Pendleton seized his son's finger in his bear's paw of a hand and slapped his palm down against Ambrose's shoulder. "Was it a worthwhile trip?"

Ambrose winced as his father energetically pumped his arm up and down. "Met an old friend, saw my tailor, called in on my brother, slept uncomfortably in a coaching inn." What more could be said? *Slept in a harlot's bed curled around a beautiful Italian theatrical, who I will never see again?* "How goes life at the Hall?"

"The family Tarbottom are in residence and Miss Harriet has spoken of nothing but when you might return. She'll make a bonny bride, fortune favor you, young Captain Pendleton!" He squeezed Ambrose's shoulder and grinned. "You and I have the business of men to discuss."

Ambrose clenched his jaw. Couldn't he come home and collapse onto his bed and not be expected to see a solitary living soul for at least ten minutes? His teeth were still jangling in his head from being jolted about in the carriage. The business of men, indeed — the business of Mammon, more like.

"Best get on, then." Ambrose bit off the words, not even trying to sound enthusiastic. He strode up the steps to the front door, his father hopping up each one in Ambrose's wake.

"Mr. Tarbottom has much to tell you of his mining interests in America, and it seems his daughter carries with her quite the dowry if her betrothed is a man of wisdom and business sense," he said. "The lucky fellow will have the management of five establishments and a good many thousands of men. Coal and cash, Captain, coal and cash!"

Ambrose paused on the step. A small seed of hope stirred inside him, even without Orsini's plan. "Five, eh? Brave man fixing on me, when I have nary the vaguest idea of how one mine works, let alone five of the dashed things!"

"Ah, but the husband-to-be will be guided by Mr. Tarbottom in all things, learning his business, but he hopes for a young man with mining in his blood. Cut us Pendletons in half and we bleed coal dust," Mr. Pendleton told his son with a hint of smugness. "This time next year, Captain Ambrose Pendleton, hero of Waterloo, might be a byword for mining endeavor in America. What say you to that, son?"

An image of Orsini fluttered before Ambrose, a will-o'-the-wisp that shivered in a heat haze then was gone.

"I say I'd be bally well surprised, Father!"

Ambrose grimaced under the heat of his father's answering glare. Perhaps he shouldn't behave like a petulant child.

"You won't need more than ten minutes to refresh yourself, then along to the east drawing room." Mr. Pendleton said the words proudly, for the east wing of the house had been years in the creation and was now complete, transforming Pendleton Hall from a *mere* mansion to a magnificent mansion. "You'll find the Tarbottoms there taking tea with your mother. Young Harriet awaits the company of her gentleman. She's a fine sort of filly!"

Ambrose swallowed every sour remark that was rising up his throat. He couldn't avoid his duty. But by

Jove, it pained him beyond all reckoning. He nodded to his father and trudged off into the house.

* * * *

Ambrose paused just outside the drawing room's doorway. His parents were holding court from armchairs elaborate enough to be thrones. Sitting opposite them, ranged along the width of an overstuffed, silk-upholstered sofa, were the three Tarbottoms.

Mr. Tarbottom was a tall, broad-shouldered man with a scattering of gray in his dark hair and a piercing stare that reminded Ambrose of a hawk. Mrs. Tarbottom was a poised, confident woman, well aware of her abundant personal charms, whose full lips were frequently home to a lazy smile. And Miss Tarbottom sat between them, smiling sweetly at Ambrose's mother with the wide blue eyes of a china doll.

Most men, Ambrose supposed, would look upon Miss Tarbottom and think her pretty. They would look upon Mrs. Tarbottom and be glad that in twenty years' time, if the daughter followed suit, they would still have an attractive wife on their arm.

But Ambrose did not have the taste of most men, and Harriet Tarbottom could never please him because she failed on one vital point.

She was not a man.

"And fine tea it is too," came Tarbottom's answering drawl. How Ambrose had come to resent that drawl and the tall, saturnine figure to whom it belonged. He resented his mirthless smile and his wealthy mines and his daughter, whom Mr. Pendleton intended to call family before the year was out. "Thank you, Mrs.

54

Pendleton, for your hospitality. You have made our little family happy indeed."

"Don't mention it, we're glad to— Oh, my word, it's my boy!" Mrs. Pendleton shot out of her chair to embrace her son. "Amby, my darling, back home safe and well. I tell you, last night, I had the most terrible dream—anyway, pour yourself some tea and—"

She grabbed his lapel and told him, in the least subtle whisper she could manage, "Say hello to the Tarbottoms!"

Ambrose bowed neatly to them. "Good afternoon, all."

Harriet giggled prettily and Ambrose pretended he hadn't noticed. He turned his attention to the tea table. "I see we have seed-cake, Mama—how splendid."

Tarbottom left his stead and moved to stand beside the ornate fireplace as though this was his house, and he was not about to allow Ambrose to ignore him. He advanced on the younger man in a few long strides and extended his arm, seizing Ambrose's hand whether he wished it or not and pumping it a little too forcefully.

"Good day, Captain Pendleton. We have just been discussing you!"

With effort, Ambrose quirked one eyebrow in response. "Have you indeed?" How very tedious.

"We have been talking of life in Pennsylvania. Of business and entertainments." He met his wife's gaze and inclined his head respectfully. "Of worship and good works too. Mrs. Tarbottom devotes her days to her philanthropic works and when Miss Tarbottom is married, good works and raising a fine family will be her vocation too."

Mrs. Pendleton nodded with good humor and gestured to the guests as if encouraging her son to offer an impressed response.

How dreary.

With one eye on the cake, Ambrose asked, "And what does one do for fun in Pennsylvania?"

"Fun?" Mrs. Tarbottom gasped.

"We gentlemen have our clubs just as you do here, and there's plenty besides," was Mr. Tarbottom's reply. "Our city is vibrant, Captain, and would offer any entertainment that you—forgive me—would give the suitable candidate for Miss Tarbottom's hand more than enough with which to fill his days. Most of all, though, it will give him business!"

"Business!" Mr. Pendleton echoed.

Ambrose quipped, "And we all know how fond my father is of that!"

Mrs. Pendleton laughed, but stopped suddenly as if she wasn't supposed to find her son's remark so amusing. Mr. Pendleton nodded keenly though, then instructed, "Tell our guests a Waterloo story, son. Something heroic with our cake."

Ambrose picked up the cake knife but as the light glinted from the blade, he heard the thunderous roar of cannon once more. His hand trembling, he returned the knife to the table. Though the battle had been two years before, sometimes it was all too present to him.

"Gave the French what for! Rode like the wind over that battlefield—chased them halfway back to Paris!" Ambrose nodded toward their guests. That's what they wanted to hear, wasn't it, not the story about the soldier who had kicked an advancing cannon ball and had his foot torn off, or the weeping camp follower who had bandaged her injured husband in the churned earth.

"Is it true you took tea with Wellington on the eve of battle?" Mr. Tarbottom asked. "The captain is destined for great things, Harriet, great things indeed."

Ambrose glanced at Mr. Tarbottom in surprise, but turned his head at a discreet cough from his mother. She gave him an encouraging smile.

"Yes, it's quite true, we did indeed take tea," Ambrose replied. It wasn't true at all, but he was loath to catch his mother out in a lie.

"How fabulous, to meet a man like him," Mrs. Tarbottom purred. She patted her daughter's arm. "My Harriet dotes on heroes—she followed the exploits of your Wellington in the newspapers. Of course, we always got the news some months late, but you were agog, my dear—were you not?"

"Oh, yes, Mama, indeed. And to know you took tea with him!" Harriet clasped her hands in a girlish fashion and fixed a beaming grin on Ambrose. He responded with a nod and picked up the cake knife again.

"How handsome your son is in his portrait," Mr. Tarbottom observed with all the sincerity of a shark. "A hero above all, and soon to be an industrial titan in the footsteps of his father and elder brother!"

The portrait, in pride of place above the mantelpiece, had been commissioned when Ambrose had entered the Army. His parents proudly showed it to everyone who came into the house, a straight-backed vision of bravery decked out in a red tunic with gold buttons.

"A Wellington indeed!" Tarbottom declared, earning an obsequious laugh from Mr. Pendleton.

"A true hero needs a true beauty on his arm, does he not?" Mr. Pendleton asked, clearly seizing the opportunity to be matchmaker. In reply both of the Tarbottoms nodded their enthusiastic response as Harriet continued to grin. "And a true profession, for one cannot be a retired captain forever, when one is so young as Ambrose here!"

"Why did you leave your commission?" Mr. Tarbottom inquired. "Though I can hardly say that I blame you. A good many men I know would clamor to do business with a genuine hero, it makes good sense!"

"I…" Ambrose plunged the knife into the cake. He pressed his lips together, stopping himself from saying, *I just want to write plays*. "I knew Father wished my brother and I to follow in his footsteps. The time had come for me to put soldiering aside—the Army was no longer for me."

"He still has his uniform, though." Mrs. Pendleton's voice was warm with pride. "He looks so handsome in it, my little Amby a great, brave man!"

Mrs. Tarbottom and her daughter chuckled gaily at this, while the hero from Waterloo tried to maneuver his slice of cake onto a plate without spilling crumbs everywhere.

"Anyone else for cake?" Ambrose asked. The slice that had seemed so inviting. The flavor of home and the fond memories it evoked, looked dry now, as if it would choke him the moment he put it on his tongue.

"Why, we love a hero back home," Tarbottom told the room in general with a bright grin, ignoring Ambrose's question. "And how many men can say they saw off Bonaparte? Now, I know there's a thorny briar between our two lands on the matter of the French, sir, but you'll hear no talk of revolution from me. I'm just a simple man who had a simple dream and the hard work to make it come true."

"As am I, Mr. Tarbottom," Mr. Pendleton told him approvingly, shifting into his oft-told fairy tale. "A pick and a meadow and a nose for coal can carry a man from one room and an empty belly to the house you stand in now!"

"Let me tell you about my newest acquisition — " Mr. Tarbottom was silenced by the opening of the door to admit the porter, usually so unflappable yet apparently a little flustered today. He carried a visiting card upon a small tray but, as he passed it to the beaming industrialist, murmured something that left Mr. Pendleton's grin looking somewhat less sure than it had.

"Pardon me," Mr. Pendleton told the assembled group. "I am required elsewhere for a moment or so."

Mrs. Pendleton stared after him. Perhaps worried that their guests might find her husband's sudden disappearance somewhat rude, she clutched her hands together and smiled at the Americans.

"Amby — would you tell us what you got up to in London? What one can get up to there out of season!" Mrs. Pendleton chuckled. "You've been to London, Mr. Tarbottom, Mrs. Tarbottom, have you not?"

"Only when personally invited by the prime minister." Tarbottom laughed as he settled into a chair, his long legs crossed at the knee like an insect's. It was clearly intended to be self-deprecating even as it set out this man's stall clearly. Influence, money, power, all the things that Barnaby Pendleton held dear, and all the things that Theodore Tarbottom could provide. "Why, as I said to Mrs. Tarbottom, first the president and now the prime minister, perhaps this is the good Lord's way of suggesting that my little business isn't so little at all!"

Ambrose wandered off to the window and stared outside, his back to the room as he nudged the unappetizing slice of cake about the plate. He knew exactly what his father would say if he told him he had no wish to go to America. 'Don't you care about your family? Have you no thought for the sacrifices I made, nor the sweat of my brow?'

"So you've met some important people, Mr. Tarbottom! I cannot say that I have, apart from…" Mrs. Pendleton fell silent. The sound of approaching feet and the swish of silks signaled the arrival of more visitors. "I wonder who this could be? We're not expecting anyone."

"We do have other guests at the present moment." Mr. Pendleton could be heard, his cheer getting more forced the closer it came to the drawing room. Whoever had arrived, Ambrose could already hear that they had thrown Pendleton senior into a confusion. "Not that you are not welcome, of course! Your note did not reach us, I'm afraid—"

Ambrose put aside his plate and readied himself to bow. He glanced at the Tarbottoms, wondering what they would make of the arrival of more guests, wondering himself who on earth they could be.

Blushing, Mrs. Pendleton rose from the sofa and caught her son's glance. Her surprise was palpable. The Tarbottoms rose too, exchanging a rather quick and unreadable look in the moment that their own gazes met.

"Madame, please—" Mr. Pendleton gave a shriek and ducked to avoid the bright blue parrot that passed over his head in full flight. Pagolo was no longer slumbering on his perch in London, it seemed, but here in Derbyshire, large as life.

He swept over Mr. Pendleton's head and made a lap of the room before settling on the mantelpiece and squawking, "*Ciao!*"

"That was…unexpected." Mrs. Pendleton smiled awkwardly at the Tarbottoms.

Ambrose stared at Pagolo, who stared back at him as he bobbed his head up and down like a boxer preparing for a bout.

"Madame!" Cosima exclaimed from the hallway then there she was, making straight for Mrs. Pendleton. That beautiful creature whom Ambrose had seen onstage at the Pleasure Gardens, who had transformed into the exquisite Orsini in the blink of an eye. The young woman, artful, innocent, beautiful, who had sprung out of Ambrose's imagination during that marvelous Italian summer.

Tall, beautiful, intensely and perfectly feminine, Amadeo Orsini's always rather pretty face was transformed once again by the magic of powder and rouge into a creature of gentle, unaffected beauty. He — she — looked like a woman, there was no denying it. There were even bosoms beneath the demure pale blue gown she wore, a delicately embroidered shawl draped just so over Orsini's shoulders. The glossy hair that had brushed Ambrose's face as he slumbered was hidden beneath an intricate turban, just a few auburn ringlets peeping from beneath, while a vast ostrich feather towered over her head, bobbing with each step she took toward the parrot.

"Signora Pendleton." Cosima — no, Orsini — passed the bird and extended one gloved hand as he did, allowing it to hop onto his fingers. Only then did he glance around the room, his gaze meeting Ambrose's for a moment before it moved on. Orsini fell to his knees before Mrs. Pendleton and took her hand, kissing it. "Mamma."

Everyone in the room had been stunned into stillness by the arrival of Cosima and her parrot. Ambrose stammered helplessly.

This wasn't meant to happen.

Orsini must not have seen the note. The plan was still going ahead, it seemed. It was madness, utter madness — Ambrose's father would put his foot to his rump and send him flying out of the front door, without a farthing.

"My dear Cosima, how very kind that you would condescend to visit Pendleton Hall." Ambrose bowed and folded his hands behind his back as he took in the gaping surprise of his parents and the Tarbottoms. "May I introduce the Contessa Cosima d'Orsini, an acquaintance of mine from my days in Italy? I hope you will enjoy our English hospitality, Cosima—pray, will you take tea with us?"

"Signora, forgive me?" Orsini raised his—no, Ambrose decided, her head and blinked her large, dark eyes. "To arrive here without sending word, for my Pagolo to invade as though he were a feathered Napoleon—this is not the introduction I would have wished for!"

Mrs. Pendleton closed her hand over Orsini's and smiled. "My dear girl, it's a lovely surprise! Any acquaintance of my son is welcome at Pendleton Hall. And their parrots, too!"

Ambrose suspected that his mother had not been charmed by the Tarbottoms, so the surprise arrival of a young Italian lady presented an agreeable distraction for her. And, as her gaze moved from the surprise visitor to their parrot, Ambrose noticed his mother's smile grow larger.

An ally, Ambrose realized. Perhaps all was not lost after all.

"You will have some tea, won't you?" Mrs. Pendleton gestured toward the pot.

"I have traveled since dawn, I am beside myself." Orsini rose delicately to his feet and nodded toward the Americans, who stared at him in mute disbelief. "Tea would be very welcome. I fear I will swoon!"

"Swoon," Pagolo repeated, nodding in his businesslike fashion. Then he turned his beady gaze on the Tarbottoms but said nothing. He simply stared.

"Tea for all!" Mrs. Pendleton enthusiastically poured the tea, wielding spoon and strainer like weapons. "So unexpected to have a houseful! Aren't we lucky, Mr. Pendleton — hmm?"

Ambrose caught an edge to his mother's voice, which usually signaled the beginnings of conjugal discord.

"Blessed," her husband replied in a clipped voice. "Surely you are not traveling alone, miss?"

Orsini settled elegantly on the sofa beside Harriet, offering the girl a cherubic smile that Harriet returned, though her eyes narrowed just a little as she took in this new arrival and possible pretender to her crown.

"I have been with my brother in London. He is both father and business manager to me." Orsini's gaze shifted to Ambrose. "When Amadeo told me that he had seen the *capitano*, I admit that I lost my head. As soon as the sun rose, I left my brother's rooms and hastened to your home in pursuit of the man who still has my heart. I have braved the road alone these past days. My brother thinks I am intriguing in London and will be seeking me there — I am not proud of the falsehood!"

Ambrose had to remind himself that Orsini was playing a role. The lovelorn, abandoned contessina. Ambrose passed Orsini his tea, the cup rattling discreetly against the saucer in his trembling hand. "Contessina, your tea."

"*Grazie, Capitano*," Orsini said sweetly, taking the cup, yet the look he gave him was meaningful, imbued with longing and not at all subtle. "I had hoped you might call on me in London, for you have not always been so shy."

Before Ambrose could summon a response, Mrs. Tarbottom emitted a scandalized gasp and clutched at her throat. "Harriet, you should not be listening to this."

Mrs. Pendleton intervened. "Oh, nonsense, Mrs. Tarbottom—I'm sure the young lady merely means that when Amby was younger, he bounced with vitality. He's a more sober fellow altogether now that he's a gentleman. Is that not what you mean, Contessina?"

"He was not at all sober as I remember him," Orsini purred. "And my brother tells me that Captain Pendleton was raising hell in your capital. Women, brandy, carousing in the squares! Amadeo is a man of respectable birth—noble birth—he was in an outrage at your behavior, sir. Yet still I adore you. You have bewitched me time and again!"

As Orsini buried his face in her handkerchief, Mr. Tarbottom told his wife and daughter, "This is not appropriate for ladies such as you. You are excused, Mrs. Tarbottom, Harriet."

A look passed across Harriet's face and was mirrored in her mother's. Only a flash, but it was there long enough for Ambrose to notice their shared look of calculation.

"I'm sure your brother exaggerates, Contessina." Ambrose sighed. "I should explain—I traveled Italy with Amadeo Orsini. He and I were excellent friends. He is the son of a count, of an ancient line. And while in Italy—" Ambrose could feel the bristling interest of his father from the other side of the room, so he plunged on regardless. "—while in Italy, this young lady and I became—ah...rather well acquainted, you might say."

"Ladies," Tarbottom said firmly, dismissing his wife and daughter with a stern nod that this time, they obeyed. Mr. Pendleton watched them depart then coughed and gave a nod of his own.

"Mrs. Pendleton, you too are excused."

"But—" Mrs. Pendleton looked from her husband to Cosima and finally to Ambrose. Her lace cap had begun to slip. "Shouldn't I stay? The young lady surely requires a chaperone."

"Amadeo shall be furious already. I cannot say what he will do should I be alone without a chaperone," Orsini agreed. "*Capitano*, speak up, is my brother not a man of violent passions and masculine fury?"

Ambrose was sure his face had betrayed him, for he struggled to picture Orsini, who at this moment was convincing so well as a lady, in a masculine rage. But he nodded vigorously nonetheless. "Oh—oh—! Indubitably. No one should want to get on the wrong side of that warm Mediterranean temperament."

"And this brother is in London?" Tarbottom nodded in reply to his own question. He cracked his knuckles and, with that gesture, told Ambrose that he wasn't beaten yet. "What of your parents?"

"My father is in heaven. My mother even now travels for England hoping to see me. What she will say, I cannot guess!"

Mrs. Pendleton patted Orsini's shoulder and flashed her husband and Mr. Tarbottom a defiant look. "You must not fret, my sweet, for you're a guest in my house and you are not friendless."

Orsini lowered his handkerchief and blinked his large, dark eyes at Mrs. Pendleton. His creation really was quite stunning, Ambrose thought, because she was quintessentially Orsini. The most eligible women in the land had been presented at Pendleton Hall over the years and no matter how pleasant, how winning, Ambrose had remained impervious to their feminine charms. In Orsini though, in the fair Cosima, he saw all that was beautiful, inside and out.

"Contessina, is it?" Mr. Pendleton asked, his voice betraying a note of interest. A title versus industrial might, Ambrose could almost hear the inner struggle. Which is better when bragging at the club?

"*Si*," Orsini whispered, his gaze flitting across to Ambrose again. "I am the youngest daughter of the late Conte and marvelous Contessa d'Orsini. I am in the care of my brother, Amadeo, and—"

"A brother who brings you to London?" Mr. Pendleton blinked in surprise. "Alone?"

Once again that dark gaze settled on Ambrose and he felt a stab of guilt, as though he truly had seduced and abandoned this young, innocent creature.

"Before her marriage, the contessa was famed for her soprano and I have inherited her theatrical muse," Orsini explained, his voice trembling as Mr. Tarbottom's lips grew thin with distaste at the very thought of it. "I had always wished to be on stage and *mamma e papà*—"

The thought remained unfinished and he dissolved into tears behind his handkerchief again.

Mrs. Pendleton slipped her arm around Orsini and threw a glare—this time at her son. "Now, now, let's not have your pretty face stained with tears."

"Pray do not weep, Cosima." Ambrose nodded stiffly. "Whatever is there to cry over?"

"You stole my youthful heart as the waves crashed against the Italian shore," Orsini told him tearfully. "And since that day, my heart has been yours alone."

Embarrassment flared in Ambrose's cheeks. He looked at Orsini again and was caught in his gaze.

"I…I—goodness me. I'm so—gosh, my dear Cosima, I'm so sorry."

I'm so sorry, Orsini, for running out on you before you had even woken up.

"I had thought you might carry me away to the altar." He shook his head and dropped his chin, evading Orsini's gaze. Then she murmured, "Yet I adore you still."

A guilty shiver went through Ambrose.

Would that it were true.

"You," Orsini hissed toward Ambrose, casting a wide-eyed glance at Mr. Tarbottom, who was taking all this in without a word. "Sir, you broke my heart, but it is aflame for you!"

"By heck!" Mrs. Pendleton gasped, her lace cap slipping further sideways on her head. "Amby, you—you profligate—oh, my word, I had no idea, that our boy—oh, Barna—Mr. Pendleton, oh—oh!" She gripped her husband's hand, her knuckles white.

Ambrose dropped to his knees in front of Orsini, his head bowed. How strange that so much guilt could wash through him for something he hadn't actually done. "Gosh. Sorry."

"You might tear my beating heart from my breast, and I would forgive you, *amore mio.*" Orsini ran his fingers through Ambrose's hair then, quite unexpectedly, caught him tightly by that same, now rather ruffled hair and jerked his head up. "Would you tear my heart out, *Capitano*?"

"No one's tearing anything out of anybody," Mr. Pendleton told them. "Come on now. This is not the continent!"

"Seed cake?" Mrs. Pendleton held out a slice on a gilt-edged plate. "It's very good."

Memories of the night in the harlot's bed flooded Ambrose's mind as Orsini grasped him by his hair. Those near-kisses, his embarrassment making itself known, and Orsini's body, curled around him through the long, dark hours of the night. And after sharing his bed, he had run from Orsini like a base cur.

Ambrose's hand trembled again as he took Orsini's. A sigh forced its way out of him. "Oh, my darling Cosima, forgive me!"

"Did you use me, sir?" Orsini eyes were wide and dark, as gentle as those of a fawn, and his lips settled in a sad pout. "Or were your words of love from the heart?"

"I meant every word I said," Ambrose told Orsini. "I love you, my darling Cosima."

The slice of seed cake skidded off Mrs. Pendleton's plate onto the floor. "My word," she breathed.

"And your question to me, the question that you asked me as we strolled in the surf..." He blinked again, holding his gaze, as beautiful as the brightest star. "You still wish me to take me for a wife?"

Ambrose had thought back so many times to that swim, as the surf crashed over them, when they had been young and free and happy. Yes, so very happy. If only — "A hundred, a thousand times — yes! My sweet, darling Cosima, be mine, oh, won't you please? Marry me, darling lady!"

"Now, just wait—" Mr. Pendleton began, but even he was silenced by Cosima's exclamation in reply.

"I shall, my love, I shall! Oh, how I have longed for you, ached for you, dreamed of your loving embraces that I once knew." Orsini put his lips to Ambrose's cheek and kissed him, before finally releasing her supposed lover's hair and lifting his head to address the Pendletons. "Your son is a man in every sense of the word now, yes?"

The plate followed the slice of cake to the floor as Mrs. Pendleton gasped again. "My word..."

Ambrose returned to his feet and included everyone in his neat bow. "Mother, Father—a man has many duties. To his parents, yes, but also to—to those he loves. And who love him." He reached for Orsini's hand. "Do I have your blessing, my dear parents?"

Mrs. Pendleton's lace cap slipped even further sideways and she smiled at the hopeful couple. Ambrose followed her glance until it alighted on his father, and her smile withered away.

"No, no you do not have my blessing," Mr. Pendleton told him sternly, gesturing toward the white-faced American. "I will not be humiliated, sir. If you think for one moment that—"

"Come now," Mr. Tarbottom soothed. "The lad is young and carried along by love. Let us not be too quick to condemn. Why, Captain Pendleton, did you not speak of this young lady before today?"

Ambrose mastered himself. He had faced down the French on the battlefield at Waterloo—he could face down an American in his father's drawing room.

"I did not, because..." Ambrose clutched Orsini's hand. "Because I thought it was hopeless. I thought that because I had dashed off and left her that she could not possibly still love me, even though I have never stopped loving her."

"And I you, my love, from the first moment we saw one another, you have held my heart." Placid once more, he settled his dark gaze lovingly on Ambrose. "*Amore mio*, how I have missed your embraces."

"And I...I have missed yours. So much."

"Mr. Tarbottom—" Mr. Pendleton began, his face white with fury, but the American cut him off with a smooth, smiling reply.

"I'm a man of the world, sir, and a man of business. There's nothing here that I'm sure we two cannot negotiate on." He nodded toward Orsini politely, Ambrose clearly not to be included in discussions of his own destiny. "All this talk of love is for novels and poets."

"Novels and poets!" Pagolo repeated. "Novels and poets and Tarbottoms!"

Mrs. Pendleton shifted in her chair, her silk dress puffing up around her as she nodded to her husband. "And young men without a shilling to their name, who moon after cordwainer's daughters—is that not right, Mr. Pendleton?"

"Aye, well, maybe..." He shook his head but Ambrose saw a softening in the industrialist at the reminder of his own youth, his own meeting with the woman who became his wife. "It's a different world we're in nowadays, Mrs. Pendleton."

"It most certainly is." Mrs. Pendleton flared her nostrils. Talking to Pagolo more than anyone else, she said, "How money changes a man!"

"For shame!" Pagolo squawked. "For shame, Mr. Pendleton!"

Mrs. Pendleton nodded firmly, and this time her lace cap did not move. "That's right, Pagolo, that's it—for shame!"

Orsini, however, had turned his attention to Ambrose once more, gazing softly at him even as he murmured, "When shall we be wed?"

"Wait one moment!" Mr. Pendleton's voice boomed across the opulent drawing room, enough to silence them all. "This liaison, and the young lady doesn't seem sure there was one, was during a tour a half dozen years ago or more. Now, I see no child, I see no one calling of ruin other than the lady here. There'll be no weddings on the strength of five minutes spent being bellowed at by an Italian!"

"I'll arrange the marriage license." Ambrose stood in front of Mr. Barnaby Pendleton with all the firmness of a captain in His Majesty's Army. "I shall marry the woman I love—I must do my duty by her. You have always told me, a gentleman must honor his debts—and I shall honor that owed to my sweet Cosima. I have only to call on the reverend, and all shall be arranged. You need not involve yourself in the matter, Father."

"We shall discuss this later," Mr. Pendleton told his youngest son firmly, his eyes filled with anger. "I'll not be made a show of."

"Come along now, Mr. Pendleton!" His wife was at his sleeve, smiling at him playfully. "No need for grumps! We shall all be best of friends as soon as we sit down to dinner, eh?"

Ambrose returned to Orsini and sank to his knees again, taking Orsini's hand.

"The boy shall not speak to me so in my own home," Mr. Pendleton said firmly. "I'll not have us shown up, Mrs. Pendleton, not by our own lad."

Mrs. Pendleton turned rather pale and returned to her armchair, her lace cap farther askew. Ambrose knew there was no point in forcing the issue any further at the moment—his father was as receptive as a piece of slate once he was stoked with ire. Ambrose nodded to Orsini and withdrew to the window seat with a cup of tea.

"Madame." Orsini addressed Mrs. Pendleton gently, the parrot silent now. "We have come into your home and behaved disgracefully. I am so very sorry, it has been a long and tiring journey from our homeland."

Mrs. Pendleton glanced at her glowering husband. Surely his own father wouldn't hurl her out on her ear? But Mrs. Pendleton smiled gently to Orsini. "It's quite all right, dear, I get fractious myself after being thrown about in a carriage for hours on end!" When Orsini smiled back after this remark, Mrs. Pendleton grinned broadly in return.

Ambrose managed to restrain a sigh of relief but, all the same, he wondered how his mother would react once she realized that her new acquaintance was only an invention and that Cosima was only present for a deception.

"I can't pretend I'm happy at all I have heard." Mr. Pendleton looked pointedly at Ambrose. "But let us speak of it no more today. The fault is not yours, young lady, but Captain Pendleton's."

It made a change for Ambrose to incur his father's displeasure for something he hadn't done. And to be glad of it, too. Ambrose smiled at Orsini, impressed by his friend's acting skills, because the character of Cosima gazed at him as if she actually loved him. As the notion crossed Ambrose's mind Orsini smiled, a radiant, beaming smile.

But a terrible notion struck Ambrose. While his alleged profligate behavior could save him from banishment to America, might his father not consider such ungentlemanly behavior worthy of punishment? Ambrose might be rewarded with a trip beyond the seas after all.

"We'll get all this sorted out, I am sure," Mr. Pendleton told him. Yet Ambrose knew they must play this unexpected scenario with infinite care. There would be questions, of that he was sure.

How had he not mentioned her since his grand tour? Was this not just a seduction, a fancy? And, of course, there could be no wedding, for there was no real Cosima, there was only Orsini, an actor playing a role.

"Mrs. Pendleton, perhaps you would take the young lady to a nice quiet chamber where she might gather herself. Mr. Tarbottom, you and I shall retire to my study and discuss business. Ambrose, go about your own business, if you would, sir."

Ambrose bowed to his father then made his way to the door. "Very well, Father. I shall be in the library if anyone needs me."

"I shall see you in my study in two hours," his father said, rising to his feet as Orsini and Mrs. Pendleton stood. "Good day, ladies."

Chapter Four

The library had been Ambrose's favorite place in the house, where he had spent many a happy hour poring over plays and poetry alike. But the two hours he spent there awaiting his father's pleasure were not unlike waiting for the enemy to attack. He could not settle and he moved from chair to chair, no words making an impression on him from anything he tried to read as all he could see were the faces of the Tarbottoms looming before him.

Ambrose stood at the window, gloomy as he stared out at the shimmering summer's day, wondering what on earth Orsini — Cosima — was saying to his mother. If even she believed Cosima to be a woman, maybe the plan could just work.

The clock on the mantelpiece struck the hour.

Ambrose went through the house at a march and knocked sharply at the door to his father's study.

"Enter!" Mr. Pendleton called and Ambrose obeyed, stepping into the room and closing the door behind himself. His father was sitting behind his vast desk, its waxed surface reflecting a shaft of bright summer sunlight that spilled through the window. Atop the desk sat a glass of brandy and Mr. Tarbottom, standing at the window, held another.

At the sight of Ambrose, Tarbottom lifted his tall figure onto the tips of his toes momentarily, his long limbs those of an insect preparing to strike, then lowered down again with the sound of his creaking leather shoes as an accompaniment.

"Now then, this is a business, eh?" Mr. Pendleton asked, knitting his fingers atop his blotter. "What have you to say?"

"I love her." Ambrose shrugged. "What more is there to say besides that, Father?"

"Mr. Tarbottom and I have negotiated a betrothal between you and young Harriet and a business partnership between we two gentlemen." Mr. Pendleton said it as though the marriage was likewise a business deal, and perhaps, to him, it was. "Theatrical sorts are given to emotion and she has no doubt drawn you in with her tears. We shall summon her brother and convey her safely into his custody with a little token of our consideration. It is a fancy, no more."

"Cosima is deserving of more than a little gift, Father." Ambrose placed his hand over his ribs, under which he was fairly sure his heart resided. "You will break her heart—and mine—by insisting on my marriage to Miss Tarbottom. If you cannot see that the contessina and I are in love—if you force me into wedlock with a woman I barely know—it is with a heavy heart that I do my duty to you."

"Son, what evidence have I that her parents approve this match?" Mr. Pendleton asked, his tone surprisingly kindly. "Am I to break Miss Tarbottom's heart and cause the good Mr. Tarbottom professional embarrassment only to find that Miss Cosima's family will not agree to your wishes? Is Miss Tarbottom not accomplished and pretty and charming, is—"

"Am I not offering you the opportunity to enter the American mining world?" Mr. Tarbottom asked Ambrose shrewdly. "Are you not about to conquer an untapped landscape that is crying out for men like you? Wise, self-made? Men who place head above heart? We have all had fancies in our youth, sir, but we leave them where they belong. In the past."

"Only, when I saw her all the love I have for her returned to me once more—threefold." Ambrose clasped his hands behind his back and took a plunge into a lie. "I happened to see her during the season—she has been in London with her brother all this time. When you thought I was at my club, I was in fact—do not think badly of her. We talked so often of our marriage that in our hearts we are as good as engaged."

"You came back from your tour, full of some theatrical fellow or other, no mention of a girl!" Mr. Pendleton's expression hard grown harder, like the rock he had hewn his fortune from. "Off to the Army, off to war, and suddenly you're madly in love? Come now, lad, why have I never heard of a Cosima before today?"

"Oh, surely you have heard of her?" Tarbottom gave an indulgent chuckle. "She glides across the comedic stages of the continent. They say kings have long pursued her. Your son has regal tastes!"

"I chose not to mention Cosima out of deference to her reputation. Ever since I first met her in Italy, she and I have corresponded all this time via her brother's letters." That at least, Ambrose decided, wasn't a lie. "Indeed, all this time she has accepted no proposal, neither from lords nor princes, but as you say, Father—"

Ambrose turned back to the window, concerned that some twitch of his features might betray him. "As you say, the coal mines of America beckon."

"And what would you have me say? Gallivant off and live a theatrical life?" His father frowned and pinched the bridge of his nose. "You are no longer a soldier, sir, and Mr. Tarbottom offers you and I a considerable opportunity."

"I must say, young sir, I take your rejection of my daughter with no small amount of insult." Tarbottom sighed. "There is only one thing to do, Mr. Pendleton. The brother must be summoned!"

Ambrose turned away from the window to face the two men.

"Quite so!" Mr. Pendleton nodded. "And if the mother is bound for London, she too must come to Derbyshire and retrieve her daughter!"

"I cannot ask for a fairer hearing than this. Thank you both. I shall summon Orsini at once." Ambrose bowed. Surely Orsini had brought at least one outfit suitable for a gentleman? "And please be assured, Mr. Tarbottom, that no insult was meant to either yourself or your family—when I made my promise to the contessina, I had no inkling that my father had been matchmaking on my behalf."

How this would play out Ambrose could hardly guess, but surely even Orsini could not be two people at one time? And how was he to secure a private conversation with his friend when all eyes were surely on them? One thing was certain, he could achieve nothing while stuck in this stifling room with these men of business.

"Let the gentleman know that he cannot delay a moment," Mr. Tarbottom instructed. "For the happiness of two young maidens —"

The American paused and gave a low laugh, then corrected himself.

"The happiness of one maiden and one" — he raised his eyebrows and glanced toward Mr. Pendleton — "theatrical depends on this matter being swiftly resolved."

The ungentlemanly cur.

"I shall write to Orsini at once. Good day, sir. Good day, Father." Ambrose bowed again and left the two industrial patriarchs to their business.

Chapter Five

With enough ink on his fingers to make it seem as if he really had toiled away at a letter to summon his friend, Ambrose returned downstairs to find everyone in the drawing room once more. An uncanny sense of calm filled the room, the sort that came before the weather changed.

"Good afternoon, everyone." Ambrose drew a chair up to the group and sat down. Sandwiched between her mother and her rival on the sofa, Harriet was doing a marvelous job of pretending that Orsini was invisible. Instead she was sharing a story of some dance or other with some duke or other, her laughter tinkling and Mr. and Mrs. Tarbottom looking on in obvious adoration. Only when her story drew to an end did Ambrose find his greeting properly returned, and Harriet was the keenest of all, demurely batting her eyelashes.

Orsini, however, appeared to have recovered his own good humor and was watching Pagolo with a gentle smile as the parrot sat happily on the back of Mrs. Pendleton's chair. Orsini nodded toward him and asked, "I believe Pagolo adores you already, signora! Would you like him to sing you a little song of thanks?"

"She would not," Mr. Pendleton replied on his wife's behalf, though he had the good grace to ask, "Would you, Mrs. Pendleton?"

"I—well, I don't know."

"Mama should like him to, Father." Ambrose would stand up for his mother, even if he could do no more to stand up for himself. Besides, if Pagolo started to sing to her, there was the chance that he might choose the same song from his repertoire as he had for the dowager viscountess. And as much as he did not wish to rile his father too much, the thought of the parrot singing a salty song in the drawing room was dashed funny. "She was saying only the other day that she should like to have a bird in the drawing room. Weren't you, Mama?"

Mrs. Pendleton looked across at the bird, dampened longing in her eyes. "He's certainly a handsome creature, is he not? Such a lovely shade of blue. I tried to get curtains in that color for the ballroom, but I couldn't find such a hue for love nor money."

"I might help in that," Orsini told her, earning a noisy huff from Mrs. Tarbottom and a cool look from Harriet for his troubles. "For I know a lady in Italy who used Pagolo as inspiration for her textiles. She certainly does have his blue in her collection."

She rose from her seat and glided across the room. On reaching Mrs. Pendleton, Orsini sank to kneel on the rug at her feet and held out his gloved finger as though conducting a miniature orchestra. Then he said, "Pagolo, *pronto*."

"*Ciao!*" Pagolo nodded and turned a pirouette on Mrs. Pendleton's outstretched hand. "*Ciao!*"

"He adores you already. You go well together." Orsini beamed then tutted, "But he has knocked your cap, how careless he is!"

Orsini stood and gently corrected the cap that was so askew, sliding the pins securely into place. Ambrose couldn't help but smile at his friend's kindness, for he knew that the parrot has been nowhere near his mother's badly behaved headpiece.

"Aren't you a love, Cosima, dear!" Mrs. Pendleton patted her cap. She peered at Pagolo, who began to chatter at her. "Hello, Mr. Parrot! What's this he's saying, dear? Is it your Italian?"

"He says you are very pretty," Orsini told her warmly. "And that you smell like roses!"

"Fancy!" Mrs. Pendleton blushed at the compliment and shaped her lips into a kiss. "And you're a very pretty parrot!" She glanced at her husband. "How I should love to have a parrot of my own, Mr. Pendleton."

"I believe Pagolo should love to have a Signora Pendleton of his own too!" Orsini laughed, his merriment utterly outdoing Mr. Pendleton's look of stern disapproval even as Harriet's smile grew more frozen and shark-like. The parrot chattered on in Italian, its head bobbing this way and that, beady eyes fixed on Ambrose's mother. "Heavens, he has taken a shine to your mamma, Captain Pendleton!"

"A parrot of excellent taste!" Ambrose smiled. "Do you not agree, Father?"

His mother whistled and chirped at Pagolo, as if she was learning to speak the language of the birds.

"On that point I cannot disagree," he was forced to admit.

"Now, again. *Pronto*!"

This time, Pagolo began to sing, treating the assembled gathering to something that sounded rather like an avian version of the Queen of the Night's aria, his head bobbing merrily as he trilled. Mrs. Pendleton was entirely conquered. She gently hummed along, utterly charmed by the parrot.

"What a handsome little man he is!" She beamed. "Look at him, just look—he's like a little fellow who's got lots of business to attend to, look!" She bobbed her head with Pagolo. "Have you got lots to do, Mr. Parrot? Have you? You'll sing me a song and you'll eat some of this lovely cake—can parrots eat cake? Well, if you can't stomach the cake, we'll send for something parrot-y from the kitchens for you, won't we, dear heart."

Ambrose chuckled. His mother evidently had a penchant for small, busy men.

"I must warn you, madame, that my Pagolo is seeking a happy home in which he might retire from public life." Orsini stroked his finger down the bird's wing. "He may decide to make it here with you!"

"Might he?" Mrs. Pendleton grinned. "Signor Pagolo, eh, would you like to live here in Derbyshire with me, in Pendleton Hall?"

"Mamma!" Pagolo cooed, turning in another pirouette. "*Ciao!*"

"Oh, he thinks I'm his mother—bless his little heart, what a dear!"

Ambrose watched the feathery actor with amusement. "Mother, shall we leave you to become further acquainted with your new son?" *Who sings raucous ballads at Vauxhall Gardens.* "Cosima, my dear—a turn outside in the gardens, perhaps? It is a beautiful day now the clouds have shifted."

Harriet looked urgently toward her mother as Mr. Pendleton turned his attention to his wife again, very briefly shaking his head.

Defiance shone in Mrs. Pendleton once more. "A little stroll? Whyever not."

"Signora Pendleton, would you care to hold Pagolo if I am permitted to walk?" Orsini asked. "We will stay before the windows. You need not fear."

"I'd be delighted to, my dear." Mrs. Pendleton beamed as Pagolo hopped merrily from one foot to the other and rewarded her with a polite nod. "I can trust you both to behave decorously, but for propriety's sake, yes—stay where we can see you."

Ambrose smiled. "Thank you, Mama."

"Stay before the window," Mr. Pendleton reminded them as Orsini curtsied and took Ambrose's arm. "If it is the continental way, so be it."

Then, with her hand gently holding Ambrose's arm, Orsini allowed the soldier to escort him from the room and out into the gentle summer breeze. For a moment they paused and, as one, drew in deep, relieved breaths. Then they began to walk, demure and proper and utterly respectable.

Chapter Six

As soon as they were out of earshot of their respective parties and the Americans, Orsini asked, "Am I doing justice to your creation, Pen? I must say, she is rather good fun to play!"

"You are perfect as Cosima—more perfect than I could even write her." Ambrose chuckled as he recalled his mother and Pagolo. "And how marvelous that your parrot has taken a shine to Mama. May I hope he will sing us a jaunty yet piquant sea shanty over tea, or a tragic execution ballad at dinner?"

Orsini laughed, but his face grew more serious when he asked, "How went the meeting with your father and Mr. Tarbottom? Are you safely released from your not-quite-engagement?"

Ambrose shook his head. He cast a glance back at the house and lowered his voice, though no one could possibly have overheard him. "My father wishes to seek your family's permission—having heard that Cosima's brother—I mean, you—that is, Orsini, is in London, and he wishes to see him. As well as your mother. Now, she is real enough, of course, but surely you cannot split yourself down the middle and appear in this place as two people at once! What on earth shall we do?"

"My mother is safe in Scotland with a frightfully dull earl of some sort," Orsini assured him. Then he narrowed his eyes, his brow furrowing. "Hartington asked for my hand in marriage not two hours after he had dined with Orsini. Even he did not see we are one and the same. Of course, theatricals often ask for one's hand. They do not intend for one to say yes. If we need Orsini, then Orsini we shall have!"

"You brought a suit of his clothes, of course?" Ambrose tweaked his neckcloth. "Oh, and I told a little lie—I am sorry, but it was to assure my father we had met recently. So"—Ambrose took a deep breath—"you and I enjoyed covert meetings of a particularly intimate nature during the London season. I do apologize for compromising you—I so hope that Cosima's reputation shan't be sullied by all these intrigues."

"My heart beats only for you." Orsini chuckled. "And not saucy old Harty nor any of those other stage door callers who swoon for Cosima's fair favors!"

Ambrose turned slightly to smile at Orsini. "Mine also, sweet Cosima. No young miss sent to tea at Pendleton Hall could ever take your place."

"I received your note when I awoke in London," he told him. "And ignored it."

"As I had suspected!" Part of Ambrose wanted to laugh, but the boy who still dwelled inside him feared his father's roar and bristled at the fact that Orsini had brushed his concerns aside. "But why come all this way and risk scandal?"

"Because I have never been a hero." He smiled. "And I thought it was your turn to be saved."

Ambrose let Orsini's simple words wash through him. "I am humbled beyond measure, truly I am. That you should go to such lengths for a friend—but we must be careful and not overplay our hand. Ah, if only Cosima were real!"

Orsini frowned and opened his mouth to speak. Yet he said nothing and instead glided serenely between the flowers, ethereal and untouchable. Cosima was an illusion, Ambrose reminded himself, born out of his love affair with Italy, forged in the heady heat of a continental Grand Tour when anything seemed possible. Back in the days when he thought he might be a playwright, before battles and brides and business came calling to steal his happiness.

"I do apologize, dear lady." Ambrose ran his hand through his hair. "You are real."

"I feel very real." Orsini glanced back at him, his eyes a little less lively. "And we have not thought out the ending of our performance. How will you go about not marrying Cosima once Miss Tarbottom is vanquished? I confess, I had quite wrapped myself up in the role. I fancied myself a bride-to-be!"

If Ambrose had believed that his love for Orsini was returned, then he would have suggested they make the attempt at matrimony anyway. But this was all an act, and it was fortunate that Ambrose seemed so good at his role, despite not being a theatrical himself. How easy to pretend he was in love with Cosima, when he loved the man beneath the gown.

"Erm…" Ambrose stroked his chin. How would he have resolved this in a play? Of course, it would depend much on whether it was comedy or tragedy. "One of us could die?"

As soon as Ambrose said it, he heard how ridiculous his idea was, and he laughed. "Maybe not."

The look on Orsini's face was one of pure horror and he shook his head keenly. "Orsini is one pretty actor in an ocean of pretty actors. Cosima is celebrated, adored, a muse, Pen. She cannot die!"

"No one dies. So we'll not have a tragedy — a sad tale's not best for us." Ambrose stroked his chin again. "A comedy, then — but they always end in a wedding. Perhaps we shall find Orsini a bride."

"Orsini is quite content to remain as he is — how would he ever explain Cosima to his intended?" He laughed softly at the very thought of it. "No, but perhaps Cosima shall decide that her pledge belongs to Thespis? She cannot love a mortal man, Pen, she must dedicate all that she is to the theater. And filthy songs."

She pantomimed a swoon, placing the back of her gloved hand to her forehead. "Can you forgive her, darling? Will you still let her lead your *Fleet Fortune*, even though you must adore her chastely from afar, beside those kings and princes who have begged for La Cosima's favors?"

Ambrose placed his hand over Orsini's. "I should love nothing more than to see you on stage in *Fleet Fortune*! And I shall — no America and certainly no Tarbottoms for me."

"Your father shall deny permission for the wedding anyway, so our finale has already been written." She patted his hand. "That is our aim, remember, to put a stop to your nuptials and save you from the mines of America!"

"Yes! And I must make efforts to swerve away from future threats of nuptials." Visions of dreaded afternoon teas and insipid dances crowded in on Ambrose's mind. "Once we have brought an end to the Tarbottoms' plans for marriage, the ambitious aunts and matchmaking mamas will return. Do you intend to stay in London, my friend? For I might move there and give my plays a bash—that would keep the mamas at bay, would it not? And just think of the times we shall have at Vauxhall!"

"I have found London to be most impressed by my talents, and I intend to remain and make it known that you and Cosima have an understanding!" Orsini said merrily. "And that, though you love her from afar, you will not entertain the prospect of another. For, tragedy of tragedies, you cling to the hope that one day she will forsake Thespis for as strapping, handsome soldier."

Now Orsini paused and gave a mischievous grin that was pure Orsini, the same grin he had worn as they'd cavorted in the Italian surf. "And all the time, as Cosima supposedly retires to her chambers to rest, Orsini and Pen shall be out on the town! I declare, old friend, there is much to be said for playing two roles!"

Ambrose immediately warmed to the idea, but it sparked off another in his mind. "Perhaps I could don the garb of a lady too, and Cosima and I might...might do whatever it is that ladies do?"

"Some men, and I am one of them, are rather more of the feminine appearance." And it was true, for Orsini was slender, his features delicate and soft. Even his feet and hands were dainty, his limbs lithe. "Others—you, for instance—are so perfectly, beautifully male. I cannot see you in a female guise!"

Ambrose ran his finger down inside his collar, as if it was suddenly too tight. "I suppose the disguise might be rather difficult, for I am rather—" He held up his large, square hand. "Broad. But I am told that I take after my mother—indeed, I am not so short as my father. Speaking of whom, do my parents not seem familiar to you?"

"Well, one might see a little of Pagolo in your father, I think?" Orsini tapped his finger to his chin. "Yes, a busy, stout, noisy little fellow who struts and puffs but means no harm!"

"The similarity had not passed me by!" Ambrose laughed. "But truly, my parents served as the models for Mr. and Mrs. Mallett in *Fleet Fortune*. And perhaps…" Ambrose tipped his head to one side, watching for Orsini's reaction, "There is even a little bit of my friend, the wonderful Orsini, in Cosima."

"Oh, Pen, truly?" He blushed beneath his powder. "I feel that I know her intimately!"

Ambrose whispered, though no one was near, "You inspired me, Orsini! Cosima, the charming Italian girl—well, not that you're a girl, but even so."

"If only I were, Pen, for then you might marry me and escape all of those mammas in one fell swoop!" Orsini laughed, the nudge he gave to Ambrose more rogue than ladylike. "Cosima Pendleton, wife of a captain who is not broad but, let us say, beautifully proportioned."

I would wed you in a heartbeat.

But Ambrose couldn't say it—his friend would flee if he knew what desires lurked in the shadows of his heart.

"Cosima Pendleton indeed!" Ambrose snorted with pretend amusement and came very close to slapping

Orsini on the back in matey fashion. He stopped just in time, as he remembered they were being watched, hawk-like, from the drawing room.

"As long as you would not flee and leave your Cosima sleeping?"

Ambrose's blood turned to ice. His hand was trembling again. "I'm so sorry — for running off as I did, without saying goodbye. You must have thought me so rude. To wake up on your own, after — after —"

After one of the most marvelous evenings of my life.

"I sleep late, Pen, we theatricals always do...especially after a wonderful night and a nice dream." Orsini gazed up at Ambrose, long eyelashes fluttering. "Wasn't it a splendid evening?"

"It was," Ambrose said softly. "I wish there might be many more. And — what was your nice dream? Was it about Vauxhall?"

His companion didn't answer immediately, but instead lifted one gloved hand to his lips and gave a gentle laugh. Then he looked around the garden, bright in the autumn sunlight, and declared, "It was wonderful. You have a most beautiful home, Pen — it puts the old Orsini palazzo rather in the shade!"

"But Pendleton Hall is so new. And your palazzo is so charming! It has so much history." The house's many windows glittered in the sunlight like jewels along a necklace. Ambrose squinted against their brightness. "Even so, I should miss the place if I had to go beyond the seas."

"Which you shall not. I have promised to save you, and save you I shall!" How overwhelming, how Ambrose's heart beat faster at the thought — of not being sent to America, of not being married to Harriet dratted Tarbottom! "And we shall laugh about this as we walk in the Italian sunlight again!"

Overwhelmed with impulsive glee, Ambrose forgot himself and grasped Orsini in a tight embrace. "We shall, my dear friend — oh, we shall!"

From the house came the sound of a fist furiously knocking at the glass and Ambrose knew without looking that it was his father, keen to save them any scandal — or any further scandal, given the Italian revelations that day. Reluctantly, Ambrose released Orsini from his embrace. He turned to the house as he took Orsini's arm again in an unobjectionably chaste manner, so that his father would see he was heeding his rules.

They had reached the edge of an ornamental lake. A bridge crossed over it to an island in the middle with a pagoda and a willow tree. Ambrose could see that his companion was enchanted, but he could feel the heat of his father's eyes on him. They could go no farther.

"There is much to show you of these grounds, my dear friend — there's grottos and bridges and statues and temples — but I fear we must remain within sight of the windows."

Orsini laughed again, then swatted one gloved hand against Ambrose's arm. The actor let it linger, not so long that Mr. Pendleton would have cause to complain, but long enough to leave him in no doubt as to the feelings of the young lovers. What an actor the Great Orsini was, it was remarkable.

Without thinking, Ambrose touched the edge of his finger to Orsini's cheek, smiling gently at him. He had to remind himself that Orsini was only acting — Cosima was not real and no matter how convincing it might feel, Orsini was not actually in love with him.

Ambrose dropped his hand away and was suddenly awkward as they walked back toward the house. His companion, happily, did not tease him over his silence but instead was the picture of stately femininity, gazing around at the grounds as they strolled. She hummed very gently, Cosima as demure as Orsini was garrulous, and every bit as enchanting.

"So, Pen, what fun awaits? Your father, Pagolo Pendleton, was chattering about a ball when he tried to stop me from invading the drawing room, something about my not being on the guest list. Is there to be a party?"

Pagolo Pendleton. All Ambrose could see before him was his father, rushing along the marbled corridors, his arms replaced with wings. Those beady eyes that observed all and missed nothing would have been more suited to a bird than to a man.

"Party? Oh, a ball, yes, to celebrate the completion of the ballroom. A chance for Father to strut about on his perch before the great and good and wave his cuttlefish about. And — so he thinks — to celebrate the impending nuptials of one Captain Pendleton to the daughter of American industrialist Theodore Tarbottom!"

"A chance for Cosima to shine!" He released Ambrose's arm and turned in a neat circle on the spot. "And to dance with her *capitano!*"

"Mother is insisting I wear my uniform. She was most disappointed when I told her I couldn't possibly dance with my sword or I would trip over it!" Ambrose babbled, trying to push aside the thought of two men, dancing together at a ball, and only they would know.

Orsini nodded and told him, "I must send to London for a few extra little baubles. Is our Hartington invited? He might carry them north for me!"

"Hartington? Here?" Ambrose gawped about at the many-windowed frontage of the house again. "Would he wish to? Gosh—perhaps. Yes, let's invite him—he might work on my father to convince him that playwrighting is not a fruitless endeavor!"

"Pagolo Pendleton does not need to like me, only to realize that I am a force to be reckoned with." He winked one hazel eye cheekily. "You mother, on the other hand, is quite the most adorable lady I have ever seen!"

"My mother *is* adorable—but I thought you would find her terribly provincial, after all those grand people you've known."

"I am very good at being very loud and knowing exactly what to say and to whom, whether I am Orsini or Cosima," he admitted. "But if I am allowed to choose between a braying city sort and a kind lady with a misbehaving lace cap, I shall choose the latter every time. How fortunate I was that Cosima and her captain met and fell in love on the warm Italian shore."

Orsini paused, clearly waiting for Ambrose to confirm the fiction.

"Fell in love…in Italy…" Nostalgia washed through Ambrose. He had, yes, he had fallen in love in Italy. He was no actor, but this was a role he could play.

Yet Orsini frowned, his pretty face clouded by pantomimed confusion. "Pen—you do realize that I'm not really a girl who might steal your heart? I am an actor, a man. Am I so believable?"

"Worry not…" Ambrose lowered his voice and turned his head so that his lips brushed Orsini's ear. "I know that you are very much a man."

"And very much more popular on stage as a woman!" She winked. "Let us return to the parents before they imagine all manner of wrongdoings and a carriage for Gretna Green!"

Chapter Seven

A silver bowl containing a selection of nuts was balanced on the arm of Mrs. Pendleton's chair. She took first one, then another, the parrot nodding and opening his beak, or shaking his head if it wasn't to his liking.

"I see Pagolo's moved in," Ambrose remarked as he and Orsini returned to the drawing room. "If he's not careful, Mother will feed him up and he'll be too fat to fly!"

The atmosphere was frozen, Mrs. Tarbottom and her daughter still on the sofa, their smiles as pious as they were false, while Mr. Tarbottom and Mr. Pendleton poured over a portfolio of his father's mines as though it was the finest continental art.

"Mamma!" Pagolo announced, happily peering at his new best friend. Then he began to whistle a sea shanty, nodding his head in time to the tune and his gaze remaining merrily fixed on Mrs. Pendleton.

She wrenched her attention from the parrot to address Ambrose and his Italian lady. "Now, Cosima, what did you think of our gardens?"

"I think you are very lucky," Orsini told them, demurely taking a seat beside the hearth. "You have a beautiful home, so peaceful. Or peaceful it was until Pagolo arrived!"

"He's been keeping us entertained!" Mrs. Pendleton stroked the parrot's head. "Hasn't he, dear husband?"

All eyes turned to Barnaby Pendleton.

"Well, he's a cheeky enough fellow, I shall certainly give him that." Mr. Pendleton sounded just a touch grudging. "Reminds me of someone, but I'm at a loss as to who that might be!"

He took a sip from his teacup and blinked, in time with the parrot's blinks. Ambrose hid his smile behind his hand and pointedly avoided Orsini's glance in case it made him laugh. He, however, remained as placid as ever, and addressed Mr. Pendleton politely.

"I shouldn't like to do business with him." Tarbottom laughed, though the joke seemed forced even as his wife and daughter laughed demurely behind their fingertips. "I believe he already thinks that this house is his, Mr. Pendleton. Will he also be a partner in our joint mining endeavor?"

"He looks like he might!" Barnaby Pendleton nodded and laughed as Pagolo nodded in response. Ambrose noted this with interest, wondering if his father might be won over by a parrot. "And we shall celebrate that endeavor and hopefully more happy news at our ball next week, shall we not?"

Ambrose made an attempt to head off his father. "Perhaps we should enjoy ourselves and dance, and not think about—"

Ambrose was silenced when Orsini, who had been at his side, suddenly held his hand to his forehead and stumbled, falling back against him slightly. Orsini gave a murmur of discomfort and blinked, as though dazed, before laughing with embarrassment.

"Forgive me, I—"

"A swoon," squawked Pagolo as Orsini stumbled again, catching her fingers in Ambrose's to keep himself standing. He caught Orsini about the waist, aware again of his friend's talents but more than that, of simply Orsini. He swooned so beautifully, so convincingly, and Ambrose knew that this was a ploy, even if he didn't know to what end.

"Oh, my word!" Mrs. Pendleton rose with effort from her armchair but was thwarted by Harriet, who was at Orsini's side in a moment.

"Contessina—you must lie down. Here, let me help you upstairs." Harriet took Orsini's elbow, but Ambrose still had his arm around Orsini's waist. Ambrose saw Mrs. Tarbottom give a soft nod of approval though she remained otherwise still, as though the sight of a young lady in such obvious distress left her entirely unmoved.

What a cold sort of woman.

"Miss Tarbottom, thank you." Orsini inclined his head very slightly, the feather atop his turban bobbing softly. "I believe a rest will do me no harm."

He gave Ambrose's hand a surreptitious squeeze then released it, acquiescing to Harriet's attentions. Whatever this new scheme was, Ambrose decided, he would follow the theatrical's lead.

Ambrose released Orsini's waist. "But you will send notice if you require the attentions of a physician?"

"I'm sure it's nothing that a noseful of smelling salts can't remedy," Mrs. Tarbottom remarked with a grin. "We women are martyrs to swoons—are we not, Mrs. Pendleton?"

Mrs. Pendleton was still hovering above her armchair, as if she couldn't quite believe that Harriet had usurped her. A puff of air escaped her as she finally dropped back into her seat. "Oh, indeed, Mrs. Tarbottom. Indeed. In this weather, too…"

"Indeed," said Pagolo, and hopped across onto her shoulder. "Quite so."

Chapter Eight

As he found himself being escorted from the drawing room by Harriet Tarbottom, Orsini reflected that he hadn't quite anticipated this new wrinkle in the plan. His intention had been a simple one, to retire to his rooms and prepare for the arrival of Amadeo, the man who even now was hidden beneath dress, padding and makeup. He had foreseen time in which to pull out the male clothes he had brought with him, which were few but flamboyant, and contrive a way to exit unseen and arrive unexpectedly, for he had a feeling that brother Orsini shouldn't wait to receive Ambrose's summons but should appear with every gun blazing, furious and filled with righteous indignation on behalf of his sister's lost virtue. Yet fury and indignation were not emotions that Orsini was particularly au fait with, let alone fears for his fictional sibling's virginity.

What fun the role will be. Amadeo but not Amadeo, a man of action rather than rouge and powder.

Yet what if Harriet, his so-called rival for the hand of Ambrose Pendleton, was not so concerned with money and status as he suspected? What if her heart was a kind one and she would appoint herself nurse and companion, at Cosima's service as she was taken unwell? What if Orsini's intended request to be left alone to rest until the morning was ignored and he found himself laid in bed with Harriet sitting at his side, reading from the Psalms and administering tonics?

No, that would never do.

"Mrs. Pendleton" — Orsini turned at the doorway to address his hostess — "I wonder if you might permit me to remain in my bed undisturbed until tomorrow. The day is a fine one and I am sorry to miss dinner but I think it will be to my constitution's benefit if I am able to rest?"

"It's the springs in the coaches, that's what it is." Mrs. Pendleton nodded to her assembly with the sagacity of an expert. "It really does shake one's constitution, especially over a long journey. Yes, my dear Cosima, you shall rest as much as you need."

Harriet fluttered her lashes over her doll eyes. Her grip was getting tighter. "Do let me escort you to your chamber, Contessina."

"This is what happens when young ladies travel alone," Tarbottom decided. "Why, Contessina, my wife and daughter have a handful of attendants each and we will lay them at your disposal during you brief stay here!"

"Oh, there is no call for that," Orsini told him, the thought one that hadn't occurred until now. Attendants? Why hadn't he thought to bring a dresser or an actress at the very least, someone trustworthy to play the part of maid? "I left London with such haste that my ladies were all still sleeping. I am afraid I am too shy to be tended by a lady that I do not know. It is my Italian blood, you see."

Even Orsini was forced to admit that everyone in the room showed their acting talent then. She was a theatrical, after all, a fallen woman who had lain with Ambrose Pendleton, and here she was too shy to take a maid?

The thought of lying with Ambrose Pendleton was a distracting one, though, and he remembered that night in the courtesan's chambers, the strength of Ambrose's body pressed to his through the night, recalling memories of the Italian ocean and long, drowsy afternoons.

If only Cosima were real.

Orsini blinked away the thought as Tarbottom told him, "My wife's and daughter's attendants have been with them for many years, they are as sober and Godfearing as Mrs. Tarbottom herself. You need not be shy."

"*Grazie.*" Orsini nodded gently, then looked to Harriet. "I should go to my bed, I think."

Harriet smiled kindly on her, as if they had been particular friends since girlhood. "Come along, Contessina."

"You are very kind," Orsini told her as they made their way along the hallway. Perhaps Harriet was as much a pawn of her own father as Ambrose was of his, for all her glittering jewels and rustling silks. Maybe she too was being pressed into a marriage for which she had no enthusiasm. Many was the girl who knew about that. "I am glad that we can be friends."

"Oh, yes, excellent friends." But there was something brittle in Harriet's tone, and her grip had grown so tight as to be almost a pinch. Perhaps she was unwell, quite apart from Orsini's pretended swoon.

"Are you quite well, miss?" Orsini asked as they reached the foot of the stairs. He rested his hand on the banister, peering into Harriet's large eyes. She was pretty, there was no denying it, but she had a curious mix of her mother's stern countenance and her father's thin-lipped appearance that gave her an almost angry look.

Furious, in fact, Orsini realized as it hit him that he wasn't Orsini at the moment, but her rival if she was a willing participant in the betrothal. *Perhaps we won't be friends after all.*

"You shan't have him," Harriet hissed in a whisper. "You shan't. I won't let you take him from me. He's mine — not yours. He's supposed to be mine."

Her petulant, bratty tone made it sound as if she was talking about a fought-over toy, not a human being. Orsini knew that he had two choices now. The first was to let her know that Cosima was a force to be reckoned with, but no general showed his enemy the full extent of his Army before the battle. Instead he asked with wide-eyed concern, "Miss Tarbottom, is that decision not for the *capitano* to make?"

"Yes, and of course he'll choose me!" Harriet accompanied her arrogant claim with a stamp of her delicate foot. "He won't want a trollop for a wife! And besides, he won't be able to resist Papa's money!"

"You are as charming as you are kind," Orsini told Harriet, giving a firm tug that released his arm from her grip. "I shall go to my room now, Miss Tarbottom, if you will excuse me."

Harriet stepped away from Cosima, her face transformed into a scowling mask of hate. "Pack your trunk, you Haymarket harlot! You're not wanted here!"

"Harlot?" The word stung. Orsini had been called far worse in his day, for what gentleman with his proclivities could escape the occasional barb, but Cosima was no harlot, not by any standard. She had fallen in love with Ambrose Pendleton, just as hopelessly as Amadeo Orsini had.

"You theatricals are all the same — that's what Mama tells me!" Harriet poked her nose into the air. "Enjoy your lie-down — and thank you so much for leaving Captain Pendleton to me."

With a smile of triumph, Harriet curtseyed, then hurried back to the drawing room at frankly unladylike speed. Her speed, however, was nothing next to that of Amadeo Orsini, who dashed upstairs and along the hallways to the pretty room that had been allocated to him by Mrs. Pendleton. He closed the door and turned the key, then pressed his back to it and drew in a deep, shaking breath. Every insult that had been hurled his way in childhood came flooding back, every cry of *culattone* from his youthful peers. How cruel they had been when they'd learned of his mother's operatic past, calling her *baldracca*, and how he had wept more bitterly for that than the beatings they doled out whenever they decided the *piccola* among them needed to be taught what it was to be a man. Harriet Tarbottom might not share their gender, but how well she would have fit in among them, with her sneers and her insults. And how he would enjoy keeping Ambrose Pendleton from her talons.

It was the thought of waving her off at the door that slowed Orsini's breathing and stilled his trembling limbs. He was a boy no longer, curled in a ball on a dusty ground as his playmates kicked him into submission, but La Cosima, the toast of the continental stage, a noblewoman who had turned notoriety into devotion among her audiences and an actress who could play any role. Amadeo Orsini had been a middling sort of thespian, a handsome lead in a few worthless plays, but La Cosima had a grace and charm that he did not. Let Amadeo be the impresario and Cosima be the star and all would be well. Tonight, however, even Amadeo must play his part.

Orsini tugged at the door handle once more, just to be certain of his security, then began preparing the room. Eventually he had made a passable Cosima of pillows to give the impression of a figure sleeping beneath the covers should anyone find a key and think to check that all was well. It was a trick in which he was well-practiced, having used it whenever the traveling players arrived in the village. As little Amadeo had clambered down from his window, his pillow-self had slept on, undiscovered by any in the household. He washed away the makeup that made him Cosima and tied his hair in its familiar queue then dressed once more in his male clothes, resplendent as ever in a suit of rich midnight-blue velvet and silk, the waistcoat embroidered with shimmering, colorful hummingbirds and blossoms.

Then he need only wait for night to fall. Wait for night to fall and pray he didn't snap his neck or the trailing ivy beneath his window on the journey from bedroom to solid ground.

Chapter Nine

On the pretext of looking for a piano score, Ambrose had managed to escape the drawing room and the post-dinner hell of music and tedious conversation. He wandered through the vast house with one aim in mind, but knew very well that aim could not be realized.

Although Orsini was in one of the many guest rooms, only up the stairs, Ambrose could not go to him. Propriety would not allow it. And as he wandered into the hall and sat on one of the chaises that were never used in that drafty chamber, he realized he could not linger long or he would risk being accused of paying court to the swooning Cosima.

But he snatched a few moments more away from the Tarbottoms, away from perfect, sparkling, nauseating Harriet and the specter of a future he most certainly did not want. Yet Cosima had vacated the field of battle and he knew not why. All Ambrose could see was their common enemy advancing, threatening to overwhelm his defenses with every mention of her father's fortune and every sparkle of her diamonds and pearls. Barnaby Pendleton was a man of business and in Harriet Tarbottom and her accursed family, he saw all his ambitions realized.

Ambrose was startled from his reverie by an almighty hammering on the front door, loud enough to wake the dead in their tombs, if the family chapel and its crypt had not been too new to contain any.

Surely a servant would appear at any moment to answer it, but the loud, thunderous knocking grated on Ambrose's nerves and his hand trembled again. He shoved it into his pocket and strode to the huge oak door.

"What is the meaning of this?" he bellowed.

"Release my sister, you fornicating beast!" Amadeo Orsini stepped out of the darkness and seized Ambrose's lapels. Though easily the more slight of the two men, Orsini's momentum carried them both backward into the entrance hall and he howled in fury, "Devil, rogue, *stronzo*!"

Ambrose's eyes widened at the spectacle of this enraged embodiment of Orsini. He had never seen the fellow in such an ill humor before and was taken quite by surprise. He rather liked this firebrand Italian.

But there was a scheme to play out, he reminded himself.

"Release her, you madman?" Ambrose's voice echoed through the corridors, audible, he was sure, to the sitters in the drawing room. "She came here of her own accord! And she has taken to her bed – though heaven knows by now you must have woken her, as you have no doubt woken all the hounds of hell!"

"Shall we settle this in a duel, sir?" Orsini's dark eyes blazed and Ambrose was reminded once again that this was the man who had enjoyed no success on the stage until he donned rouge and gown. What were audiences thinking? "Like men?"

"You stand here in my father's house and challenge me—a former captain of His Majesty's Army—to a duel, sirrah?" Ambrose threw back his head and laughed. "No harm has come to your sister, you blackguard!"

Footsteps were hurrying along the corridors now and Ambrose knew an audience would soon appear. Orsini responded by hurling him back into the wall, finally releasing Ambrose's lapels. He strode to the center of the hall and tipped back his head, calling out, "Where is the father of this base creature? I demand reparations for my sister's lost honor!"

Ambrose was impressed by Orsini's strength and grinned giddily at him. Then he sharply changed his expression to one of dismay as his father's quick, short steps sounded over the marble floors.

"Would you shout such a thing abroad, Amadeo?" Ambrose gasped in shock. "Accuse me of such villainous acts and besmirch your own sister?"

"What on earth is to do?" Mr. Pendleton demanded. The women had, of course, remained in the drawing room, though whether they could resist the temptation to peek out at who was making all the noise, Ambrose couldn't be sure. There was Theodore Tarbottom though, his lips slightly parted, his eyes narrowed as he took in the scene. Mr. Pendleton tutted and asked, "Come now, who's hollering and bawling when we've a sickly lass upstairs?"

"Sickly?" Orsini's head flicked round and his gaze settled on Mr. Pendleton. When he spoke again, his voice was low with menace. "Are you the father of this seducer?"

"I am Mr. Barnaby Pendleton, of Pendleton's Coal." He nodded, gripping his lapels. "And this is my fine son, Captain Ambrose Pendleton, who you may have heard of due to his fine showing at Waterloo. I will not have my boy shouted at by a common caller at the door!"

"A common caller? I am Amadeo, *nobile dei conti d'Orsini*, and I will speak to this false friend however I so choose!"

"I am not false, Amadeo!" Ambrose ran his hand back through his disordered hair. "I cannot help it if your sister and I are in love—such a tender, sweet love as I have never known before. And you, my friend—you would run me through for the crime of adoring the beautiful contessina!"

"Now just one moment!" Mr. Pendleton frowned and hopped from one foot to the other as he considered his next move. "That letter can't have arrived already. It only went off this afternoon?"

"Letter?" Orsini demanded. "There is a letter?"

"I wrote to you—on my father's urging—to ask you here because…" Ambrose bowed his head before Orsini like a penitent. "For I dearly wish to wed your sister, and without a father to approve, and with the contessa out of reach, there was only you whom I could ask."

That seemed to pull Orsini up short and he blinked, then shook his head.

"Alas," Mr. Tarbottom spoke up, as though this house was his to command. "Would that it were so simple as all that. Come, sir, you must be tired from the road. Join us in the drawing room for a refreshment?"

"So you are the father?" Orsini gave a pantomime of confusion, raising his hands as if in surrender. "Who is the master in this house?"

"The bloody parrot," Ambrose distinctly heard his father murmur. Then he said more clearly, "I am the master of this house, sir, but Mr. Tarbottom is merely trying to calm your continental fire. No need to throw any coal on you, eh?"

For a moment, as Orsini's dark gaze landed on his father, Ambrose actually felt himself tense. There was such anger in his friend's face, such barely controlled rage, that he allowed himself to forget that this was Amadeo, the most kind-hearted soul he had ever known. This was Cosima, for heaven's sake, and Cosima would never strike a little fellow like his father.

Then, like the sun breaking through a storm cloud, Orsini laughed. He strode toward Mr. Pendleton, placed his hands on the Yorkshireman's shoulders and kissed him first on one cheek, then the other. Then he said, "To the drawing room, as your Mr. Tarred-Bottom says, and I shall meet your wife. Your son and I though, we have unfinished business."

Ambrose swallowed. "I have long wished to introduce you to my mama, Orsini — would that it were under happier circumstances. Do understand — please — I would move the earth and all the heavens to marry Cosima."

"We shall talk later." Orsini, his arm still around Mr. Pendleton, pointed at the three men. "But for now, women!"

As they headed back to the drawing room, spirited along by Orsini's boundless energy, Ambrose mumbled an awkward introduction. "Father, Mr. Tarbottom, may I introduce my good friend Amadeo d'Orsini. And Orsini—may I introduce my father, and his...erm...business acquaintance, Mr. Tarbottom?"

"Sirs." Orsini dropped into a flamboyant bow, twirling one hand ornately. "I am honored to know you."

A rustle of skirts by the drawing room door signaled that while the women had not ventured from the room, they had ventured from their chairs. Mrs. Pendleton was flushed, her cap askew once again, and sat half on the edge of her armchair as if she had only that second dropped into it. Pagolo sat at her shoulder again, his head inclined very slightly toward hers.

"Another guest? My, we are popular!" Mrs. Pendleton grinned at the apparently new arrival. At the sight of Orsini Pagolo opened his vast wings wide and squawked a merry Italian song of greeting which, Ambrose suspected, might be obscene.

Ambrose made the introductions, and Mrs. Tarbottom and her daughter smiled at Orsini. Again they received the flamboyant bow and again, when Orsini glanced toward Ambrose, his expression grew momentarily fierce.

"What a pleasure to make your acquaintance." Harriet grinned. "I am already a firm friend of your sweet sister."

"Two sweet young ladies together," he told her smoothly, winning another grin for his efforts. Then he addressed Mrs. Tarbottom and Mrs. Pendleton, adding, "And two ladies whose acquaintance it is my pleasure to make, one of you squired by our good Pagolo. *Buonasera*, Pagolo!"

"*Buonasera*," Pagola replied, hopping over to Mrs. Pendleton's shoulder and fluttering his wings again. "*Buonasera!*"

"Madame, I must apologize for my sister's parrot." Just as Cosima had earlier, Orsini moved to correct the cap, but he paused at the last. "Forgive me, madame, I almost handled your person. Pagolo has spoiled your attitude. Might I be permitted to correct it?"

"Oh, how very kind of you!" Mrs. Pendleton blushed a shade redder. "And please don't apologize on the parrot's behalf. Pagolo is a dear little fellow!"

"Mamma," Pagolo pronounced. With an approving smile Orsini straightened Mrs. Pendleton's cap, pinning it in place. Ambrose couldn't help the swell of affection in his breast at the sweet gesture as he watched his friend's gentle movements. He cared not for the jewels and silks of Harriet Tarbottom nor the pious gold cross and subtle diamonds of her mother, his eyes were only on that misbehaving cap.

"Thank you, kind sir! Will you take a drink, or refreshment? Do you wish for something to eat? Do take a seat." Mrs. Pendleton gestured to the various empty chairs dotted about the room. "Your sister took to her bed, should you wish to see her. She came over in a swoon, poor girl. She said she wanted rest and that no one should disturb her, but I'm sure she'd be glad of a visit from her brother."

"I shall see her in the morning, Madame," Orsini decided, descending into a seat in a rustle of silk and a cloud of perfume. "Forgive me my ejaculations on entrance. I am known for my hot-blooded passions."

"Oh? I didn't hear—we didn't hear, did we? Mrs. Tarbottom, Miss? Not a thing. What was that about your entrance, good sir?" Mrs. Pendleton was not a convincing actress and Ambrose briefly turned to face the mantelpiece in order to hide his rising amusement.

"No, we didn't hear a sound," Mrs. Tarbottom remarked. Orsini glanced to her and smiled, inclining his head in thanks. Then he knitted his hands in his lap and looked around the room in clear appreciation

"I trust La Cosima is not proving any trouble?" he asked, looking now at Ambrose. "She has always been impressionable. You can well imagine my late father, God rest him, and my mother when Cosima told them of her wish to perform. She is fortunate indeed not to be residing in a distant convent as we speak."

"Your English is impeccable," Mr. Tarbottom commented. "As is your sister's."

"We are known for our nimble tongue," Orsini told him innocently. "It is an Italian talent."

Mrs. Pendleton giggled and nodded toward her son. "You have the most charming friend, Amby! And as for Cosima—no, Orsini, she is no trouble at all. Save for…well."

Mrs. Pendleton shot her husband a Gorgon stare. Everything she could have said on the subject of potential daughters-in-law was bound up in that one expression. Orsini followed her gaze then turned to Mr. Tarbottom once more and said, "Mr. Tarred-Bottom, from whence do you hale?"

"Philadelphia, sir," he replied proudly. "As does my good lady. We hope to show our good city to Captain Pendleton, for I believe he is considering returning with us. Isn't that right, sir?"

"Indeed it is," Mr. Pendleton said quickly. "But that is part of a conversation we gentlemen shall have elsewhere."

"Oh, is it indeed, Husband?" Mrs. Pendleton sniffed. "I think perhaps that Mr. Orsini might be involved in your discussions, considering that his unhappy sister will meet with great disappointment if you persist in your plan. And as for the gentleman whose hand—and future—is at stake, does he not have a say either?

"To think nothing of me, his poor mother." A wavering note of distress had entered Mrs. Pendleton's voice, as if she were not entertaining in her grand drawing room but alone in a parlor of the middling sort. "Oh, Orsini, I am plagued by nightmares of shipwrecks and robbers! I cannot bear it!"

"Mother…" Ambrose crouched beside her chair and took her hand.

"All of this shall be discussed," Mr. Tarbottom said, his voice clipped. "Miss Tarbottom, would you care to entertain us with a song? Perhaps your mother might accompany you on the piano?"

"I should be delighted, Father. And what should you like me to sing for you, Mr. and Mrs. Pendleton?" Harriet rose with practiced elegance and curtseyed to Ambrose's parents. She was so intent on showcasing her talents that she seemed either not to notice or care that her hostess was exhibiting distress.

Mrs. Tarbottom smiled at Orsini. "And our new visitor, what should he choose?"

"Do you mind, Madame?" Orsini addressed Mrs. Pendleton gently, his attention on her alone. "Are you of a mind for music, dear lady?"

Mrs. Pendleton clenched her jaw, then said, with one eye on her husband, "Music is supposed to heal the spirit. And at least it means we shan't require too much conversation, for heaven knows my opinions are not required here this evening."

Mrs. Tarbottom and her daughter swept by to the piano. "Music is a balm, indeed, Mrs. Pendleton. Let my daughter and I gladden your hearts with song."

A petulant remark rose to Ambrose's mouth, but he decided not to say it. Orsini nodded and decided, "Then let it be Figaro, if you have it. My sister gives a wonderful *Deh vieni, non tardar*. I should dearly love to hear an American's interpretation."

Ambrose was fairly sure he had heard sarcasm in that remark, and he pressed his lips together to prevent himself from laughing. Of course though the girl could sing and of course her mother could play, for both were well-tutored in what it took to secure a husband. Yet there was no passion in each note-perfect syllable, each calculated gesture of hand and eye, and Ambrose was transported back in his mind's eye to Cosima on stage, bewitching all who saw her.

"Prettily done," Mrs. Pendleton acceded and smiled at the performers. "What a lovely voice you have, Miss Tarbottom."

"I do so hope we cheered you, madam." Harriet gave her audience a pert smile.

"Yes, well done," Ambrose said with little feeling. Orsini rose to his feet and gave a polite round of applause that was echoed by the Messers Tarbottom and Pendleton, but Pagolo seemed less impressed. He turned his back on the gathering, preferring to look out into the darkened garden.

"Mr. Pendleton." Tarbottom cleared his throat. "Might we discuss matters this evening, you and I and the younger gentlemen? Then we might all go to our beds with clear head and sure of the way forward."

"A capital idea, if an unorthodox one," Ambrose's father decided. "It is time the ladies retired, I am sure, but if you are amenable, sir, we might conclude our business this evening?"

"Of course," Orsini agreed. "Let us discuss matters of the heart, now that we have had our music."

Chapter Ten

Ambrose poured himself a drink. He needed one. Possibly several. "Anyone else?"

"I would be glad of something warming," Orsini told him curtly, though the other men shook their heads as one. "To ease our negotiations, you understand?"

Ambrose poured out a generous helping of brandy for his friend. As he passed the glass to Orsini, his wretched hand trembled. "Sorry. It does that on and off. The downside of this hero lark."

"And never was there a prouder father," Mr. Pendleton announced, smiling broadly.

Ambrose bowed. "Thank you, Father." In soldiering, at least, his father was proud to call him his own. And now he was a bargaining chip.

"The situation is this, young sir," Mr. Pendleton told Orsini. "Captain Pendleton has an understanding with Mr. Tarbottom. He has been offered a position in America with an immediate start and the hand of young Miss Tarbottom. The couple are devoted to one another, you understand."

"And Mr. Pendleton and I intend to go into business together," Tarbottom added. "He shall be investing in the Tarbottom Mining Company, making us partners as well as family!"

Orsini frowned and looked from one industrialist to the other. "Then let him invest and do whatever he might wish, but why must a marriage be part of the deal? Why can Mr. Pendleton not throw his money at whatever venture he so wishes without throwing his son at it too?"

"Choosing and trusting a partner in business is a leap of faith," was Tarbottom's hasty response. "Why, what if one half is ambitious and greedy? Better that they be family, that bond of honor is stronger than any handshake."

"And what of love?" asked the Italian.

"Harriet adores Captain Pendleton," Tarbottom replied. "She would lay down her life for him. It truly was love from the very first."

"But—Father, how can you?" Ambrose held onto his glass even though his hand was trembling again. "I am not devoted to Miss Tarbottom. I barely know her. I cannot speak for her feelings, of course, because I am not her, and besides—she has not told me whether she cares for me or not."

"Then tell me, sir, what profession do you intend?" his father asked. "You have left the Army behind and can linger no more. Waterloo is two years past and these months since you came home, you have frittered away your time! Your brother is a man of business with half a dozen children to call his own already. You can hardly marry a theatrical lady and live off her!"

"I...could be her manager." Ambrose emphasized this with a nod. He wasn't going to mention his plays again, for his father would only laugh. "Could I not, Orsini?"

"You could not, sir," Tarbottom cut in, "for the lady herself told us that this very gentleman filled that capacity. Besides, the theatrical world is not one for a man of military interests. Mister Orsini, sir, I have had the good fortune to see your charming sister on stage and I saw too the gentlemen who wished an audience with her afterward."

And I'll wager you were among them, Ambrose thought bitterly.

"Go on," Orsini told him, his tone cool.

"What if Captain Pendleton here is simply as enchanted by her as those gentlemen were? There is much that is appealing about a lady on the stage and young men fall in love easily with Titania and her like." He shook his head. "I would not want your sister to pledge herself only to find that it is her characters with whom the young man has become besotted."

"I am insulted, sir." Ambrose put his glass aside and hid his shaking hand in his pocket. "As I said, Cosima and I spent much time together in each other's company during the last season—I very well acquainted with the real woman, I'll thank you to know. And whatever you might think of my fancy for her, did you not hear her declare her love for me? You will break her heart if we are separated!"

"There may be more than one heart at stake," Orsini said, and the room seemed to stand still. Ambrose's eyes widened as his friend went on, pushing their play to the next act. "She may be with child."

Mr. Pendleton nodded. Then he said, "Mr. Orsini, Mr. Tarbottom, would you give me a minute with my son, please?"

Though Ambrose had never lain with a woman, something in Orsini's delivery felt so very real that part of Ambrose almost believed he was about to become a father. A tiny Orsini-Pendleton co-production—imagine that!

Tarbottom and Orsini seemed to sense the change in the air too, for both departed with nothing but a polite goodnight, leaving the father and son alone. Now Mr. Pendleton rose from his seat and crossed to the window, knitting his fingers behind his back. For a long moment he was silent, then he turned back to look at Ambrose.

"I never thought you would shame this family," he said quietly. "Your poor mother, what will she say? Could you not control yourself, lad? And those two poor lasses, what in the blazes do you think we will do now?"

"I have shamed nobody." Ambrose jabbed his finger at his father. "That's your doing—not mine. I only want one woman, my Cosima. You're the one who's dragged Miss Tarbottom into this—I never wanted to marry her. You did not even ask me!"

"I have indulged you from the day of your birth, sir, and no longer, do you hear me? Maybe if you had been made to pick up a shovel and dig for your living like I was, we wouldn't be here now!" Mr. Pendleton shouted, more angry than Ambrose could ever remember seeing him. "The sorry Italian lady will be sent safely back to the care of her mother and brother and an allowance made for your child. You will marry Miss Tarbottom and accompany her to America as a man of respectable business and you will say nothing of this unpleasant matter to your poor mother, do you understand me? Not one word!"

"And we all know how much Mama likes the idea of this marriage, don't we?" Ambrose shook his head. "She's unhappy, you're angry, and I'm stuck in the middle wishing I'd —"

Ambrose raised both hands before his eyes and crushed them into fists. A red film distorted his vision. "I wish I'd been run through with French bayonets! I'd much rather I'd bled out on the field of battle at Waterloo than live to see the day when my own father sold me off! Is this what you want — to see me unhappy because you resent the bloody luxury you insisted on bringing me up in? I never asked to be born in a palace! And that's how you punish me — a loveless marriage with a woman I barely know, flung off across the seas to a land I've never been to."

"No, sir, it is because I have seen too many rich sons fall to drink and ruin thanks to an indulgent father. My own father drank himself into the grave and gave me no direction and I swore that day I'd always steer my own boys right. This is the end to it. I shall tell your mother the happy news tomorrow and make the announcement at the ball." Mr. Pendleton gave a curt nod. "Good evening, Ambrose."

Ambrose's rage had blown itself out as suddenly as it had whipped itself up. Exhausted, he held back the sob in his throat for long enough to say, "Goodnight, Father."

Obedient, dejected and lost.

"I do love you, son," he heard his father say as he turned for the door. "And when you're as old as I am, you'll realize that I steered you right, as my own father never did."

Ambrose did not reply, and threw the remainder of his brandy down his throat in one go.

Chapter Eleven

Muttering imprecations against his father and the Fates and every cruel device that had brought him to this unspeakable juncture, Ambrose headed off to bed. Some captain he was. Though, of course, in the Army he had taken orders often enough, orders which had sometimes seemed suicidal to accept. And he hadn't been knocked off his horse by a cannon ball, had he?

Maybe Philadelphia had theaters. Maybe Orsini could be convinced to perform there. That was something to look forward to, at least. Though how he could go through the wedding and promise to love a woman he wasn't even sure he liked was a problem Ambrose didn't want to address before bed.

He threw open the door of his room and halted. There, sitting on the bed, was Orsini. At the sight of Ambrose he leaped to his feet and asked, "Pen, what happened?"

Ambrose blinked in surprise before closing the door firmly behind him. He urgently needed someone to speak to. Doing his best to sound chipper, Ambrose said, "I don't suppose you're averse to long ocean voyages, eh?"

"You're coming home with us?" He clapped his hands together. "Though we shall stay here on your shores until things are a little more settled in my homeland, I think. All is upheaval at the moment, alas."

"No, I mean—to America." Ambrose's smile faltered as his eyes filled with tears. "The devil take it—I'm far from a hero! My father will have his way. Poor Cosima will be paid off, and I...I am to marry Harriet Tarbottom whether I wish to or not!"

"No!" Orsini crossed the room in a few bounds and took his friend's hand in his own. "I will not allow it, Pen. Did you tell him of your play? Of Harty and the Regent? What did he say?"

Ambrose shook his head and tears began to track down his cheeks. "I said nothing about my plays. He would only have laughed at me. Coal and industry, cogs and wheels, that's all he can see in my future. He believes he is doing this for my own good, Orsini! I cannot convince him otherwise."

"I would bring the Regent here myself but he is loathe to drag himself out of bed, they tell me, unless to torment your friend Wellington." Orsini lifted his free hand and brushed away one of Ambrose's tears with the soft pad of his thumb. "You are the best man I know, *Capitano*, and if I have to marry you myself to keep you from America, I shall."

"If only we could hop off now to see the reverend. A license, and we marry tomorrow before breakfast." Ambrose smiled at the thought of it.

"Married to an Italian actress who has turned down kings and emperors." Orsini laughed gently, his hand still resting on Ambrose's cheek. "A marriage of convenience, to save you from a marriage of convenience. But at least I do not have a silent mother and a smile that never moves."

Ambrose closed his hand over Orsini's where it rested on his cheek. "Do you know — it's ridiculous of me, but when you told my father that Cosima might be big with my child, I…wished it were true."

"There are so many children in need of a loving home, we could — " Orsini flushed and shook his head. "I had almost forgotten we were not betrothed. I was picturing us surrounded by a half-dozen orphans, all spoiled rotten and well-versed in theater!"

Ambrose touched Orsini's soft hair. "Do let's think of it. What a happy daydream that would be."

"Come and sit." Orsini reached his free hand into his coat and produced a silver hip flask. "And share a drink with Orsini. Or Cosima, if you would rather."

"Either. I'm fond of you both." Ambrose nodded toward the bed. "It's not quite up to the standards of your bed in London, but I'm sure you'll agree the bed curtains are more than elaborate enough."

"I know a thing or two about fathers." Orsini drew Ambrose to the bed by his hand and together they settled against the pillows. "My father was not pleased that I wished to pursue a career on stage. Less so still when I first showed him Cosima. I have never seen him so angry, nor so disgusted, Pen. I thought my heart would break."

"How sorry I am for you, my dear friend." Ambrose slipped his arm around Orsini's shoulders and let him get comfortable against him. "And did — before he passed away, were you two reconciled?"

"My mother did what she could but at first, he would not listen. Not only was I a boy dressing as a girl, I was a theatrical using the Orsini name. But our family has never been orthodox. We have painters and adventurers and even a priest in our number, and you have met them all!" He rested his head on Ambrose's shoulder and settled their linked hands on his chest. "On the day before I was to leave to begin my first engagement in Venice, he called me to him. We had not spoken in a month or more, and I ran to answer his summons. I thank heaven that I did, for he told me that he had fallen ill and thought his time short."

Orsini gripped Ambrose's hand tighter. "We reconciled that day and passed the evening in laughter, the room filled with Orsini children and grandchildren. Around that ancient bed we ate a dinner of kings, Papa sitting up against his pillows and leading us in our merriment. As the sun went down that night, Francesco gave the rites. I have never been so proud of that brother of mine, then Papa asked me to entertain him before he slept."

Ambrose felt his friend take a deep breath, hearing the tears in his voice when he spoke again. "There, before every one of my people, I performed Cosima's song from *Fleet Fortune* and my father cheered louder than any other in that room. As dawn came he passed into the next world, and he went in peace and with love."

Ambrose rubbed away a tear with the heel of his hand. "I'm glad. That in the end, he accepted you as you are."

"And he would be the first to tell you, Pen, he loathed light comedy. If it could make the Conte d'Orsini laugh, then it must be a fine piece indeed." Orsini raised his head to gaze at Ambrose. "And that is why I will not allow you to abandon the theater, nor me along with it!"

"I wish I did not have to, but what am I to do?" Ambrose sighed in defeat. "I can never talk to my father man to man. I try but when I speak to him I'm either an obedient boy or an obstreperous lad. But never a man. Because he never treats me like one unless I'm in uniform. And that's been consigned to a trunk."

"You are still Captain Ambrose Pendleton, a man who is so brave that he does not even fear the tremble in his own hand." Orsini brought their linked hands to his lips and pressed a soft kiss to Ambrose's skin. "And there is nothing that Orsini, Cosima and Pen cannot achieve. Those Tarbottoms have met their match."

"I love you, Amadeo Orsini."

Orsini blinked as though he didn't quite understand, his brow furrowing at the words. He opened his mouth and closed it again, then opened it once more and said, "In that way that soldiers do? That way that is the way men love other men without it being... I love you too, Pen, but in the other way to that way."

Only moments before he had been dabbing at his tears, but now a huge smile spread across Ambrose Pendleton's face.

"Oh, thank God!" He wrapped his arms around Orsini and held him close. His lips against Orsini's ear, he whispered, "I love you, as if...gosh, all this talk of wives, when all I want is a husband!"

"Me?" Orsini's voice filled with confusion, but Ambrose felt his arm around his waist. "Not Cosima? Me? The male me?"

"Cosima is a very sweet young lady, but it's the man beneath the gown who makes my heart thud all the faster." Ambrose stroked Orsini's back, a careful, exploratory touch. "Yes, the male you. And I had no idea that you might — all those beauties in the theater, why for a moment should I imagine that you would have any interest in a man built like a clothes press?"

"Because I am a man built like a very slender young lady. Beauties interest me only when we are borrowing one another's gowns and learning little makeup secrets!" Orsini gave a gentle laugh and tentatively stroked his fingers over Ambrose's thigh. "And what does a young lady need if not a strapping, brave soldier to keep her safe from the villains of this world?"

Ambrose brought his other hand up into Orsini's hair and tried one little kiss just below his ear.

"I shall be your champion, Orsini, your defender and your shield. You can have no worry about that."

"When you went to war, I was beside myself." He shifted just a little, pressing his cheek to Ambrose's. "I thought you would be lost to me forever, and I would die that day too. My heart stopped with every piece of news from the field, Pen, for I have loved you since that first day on the beach."

"I thought about you every day, I swear to you I did. Always thinking, what if I die now, and I've never told him? But how could I tell you?" Ambrose drew his lips down to Orsini's throat to kiss his soft skin. "Although, as it happens — I wasn't expecting to tell you tonight. It fell out of my mouth, darling."

"I have been torturing myself with the thought of you, wishing I might be Cosima so you would love me as you pretend to love her." Orsini closed his eyes and gave a long, happy sigh. "I would never have thought you might look at me and see anything more than your silly friend who looks nice in a gown!"

"I see the man I love." Ambrose smiled. "I'm looking at him now, in fact—he's the most beautiful creature you ever did see. Big, dark eyes, and an elegant nose and a gentle face, and—my word—such lips! I dream of kissing them."

"*Amore mio*," Orsini purred. "I wish that you would kiss me."

"You do?" Ambrose was still surprised that his love was returned. How impossible the very idea had seemed.

Smiling, he brushed his lips over Orsini's. Answering what seemed like yearning in their brief kiss, Ambrose brought his mouth closer and claimed Orsini's lips with own. And Orsini, the middling actor turned great impresario, the cool theatrical negotiator who had steered La Cosima through the great houses of Europe on her way to the pinnacle of comedic theater, showed himself to be little changed from the enthusiastic young man with whom Ambrose Pendleton had spent a rather frolicsome summer some years ago. He gave a little gasp of delighted pleasure and returned Ambrose's kiss with an enthusiasm that stole his breath, clutching his fingers tight to Ambrose's shirt.

Ambrose held Orsini tighter still, delighting in the press of their bodies. They were lost in lips and tongues, their kiss growing deeper, each man reassured by each other's touch. Still kissing, they slipped over sideways onto the bed, then they lay facing each other, cushioned by the plush bedding.

"I had thought you would think it very odd that I made my fortune as a girl," Orsini whispered as they broke for breath. "But most of all, I had not thought you would want to know that I prefer gentlemen."

He dotted a kiss to Ambrose's nose. "And I prefer you most all, *tato*. All that summer, trailing around, gazing at you, wishing you might see me as I saw you."

"I did! My God, Orsini, I think back to our naked swim and I tremble at the force of the desire I felt then. Feel now, in fact." Ambrose saw so much love in Orsini's beautiful face that gazing at him was like gorging on honey. And Orsini gazed back at him through his large, dark eyes, framed by long eyelashes that any actress would likely kill for. He was as beautiful now as when he wore Cosima's makeup, more so, and Ambrose could scarcely recall a sight more glorious.

"I had not imagined you would like men," he murmured, carefully dancing one finger down Ambrose's chest to his stomach. "I dreaded the marriage notices too, Pen. What a bundle of silliness I have been."

Ambrose took Orsini's wandering hand and kissed it. "My precious Orsini, I always thought the same of you — dreading to see some remark in the theatrical gossip page, or hearing at third-hand that you had a bride. And always thinking, what a fool I am, how could he want a beefy fellow like me! But you do after all...so..."

Ambrose raised an eyebrow and worked off his neckcloth, throwing it over the side of the bed followed swiftly by his coat and his jacket. "Should you like me to take off my shirt? So you might see if I'm still as strapping as you remember?"

"I know that you are, for I have dreamed of you often enough." Orsini lazily unfastened Ambrose's shirt as he spoke. He smiled very tenderly and gave another one of those delicate sighs. "Would you take it off, *tato*?"

"Anything for you, dear heart!" Ambrose sat up, and grinned as he pulled his shirt over his head and threw it aside. He enjoyed feeling Orsini's gaze on him, then he stroked Orsini's hair, hoping he wouldn't think him horribly vain. Yet Orsini seemed to think nothing of the sort, for he took in the sight of his shirtless friend with one sweep of a gaze that was suddenly blazing with fresh heat. Then he pressed his lips to Ambrose's again, both hands sliding down over his muscular chest, caressing his skin with no effort to conceal his appreciation.

Ambrose rolled onto his back and brought Orsini on top of him, caressing Orsini's back but steadfastly not going farther, despite the temptation of his rounded bottom. It was enough to feel Orsini's hands on his bare chest, to hold him and kiss him.

Bringing his mouth away from Orsini's, Ambrose whispered, "Do you want to take off your coat too? Only if you want to, of course." At the thought of unbuttoning it, Ambrose's hips twitched and he knew that Orsini could not have failed to notice the hardness in his breeches—just as Ambrose was aware of Orsini's.

"How much of it would you have me remove, Pen?" The Italian blinked, all innocence. "For unlike on Pall Mall, I have no marvelously decadent robe at hand to keep me decent tonight."

"You, in that robe—the softness of it, the color..." Ambrose almost drifted off into his memories of that night, but the man he loved was here in his arms and he soon brought himself back. "Take off the coat."

Orsini shrugged his arms out of the coat and flung it aside. Ambrose cuddled Orsini to him, his shirt soft against Ambrose's chest, and for once Orsini was silent—a rare state of affairs for him—seemingly content with simply snuggling with his love. He let his head rest on Ambrose's shoulder, his soft hair ticklish against Ambrose's cheek.

Orsini's hand was moving lazily, drawing gently sinuous patterns with his fingertips on Ambrose's broad chest. His lips followed just as lightly, soft kisses fluttering to his shoulders like butterflies. The strapping soldier trembled—undone, conquered by the love of Amadeo Orsini.

"I adore you," Ambrose murmured, stroking Orsini's hair.

"Ambrose and Amadeo, and sometimes La Cosima," Orsini whispered, kissing his throat. "From now until forever."

Ambrose smiled, tipping back his head, encouraging Orsini in his kisses. "There's nothing more in all the world that I want besides you."

"Kissing an Italian boy… What would your father say?" Orsini trailed his kisses lower once more, lips softly traveling down to Ambrose's chest.

Ambrose wanted to cry out for joy, but only sighed as he arched his torso up toward Orsini's mouth. "He'd say, thank goodness you're not going after the maids!"

"Why would anyone chase a maid," came the answering murmur, "when there are heroes to kiss?"

"Do you think me heroic?" Ambrose stroked the delicate contour of Orsini's cheek. "It's easy to be brave in a uniform, with a sword, but you, Orsini—you're going into battle in a gown!"

"And there is nobody charging down on me with gun loaded nor bayonet sharpened," he reminded Ambrose. "The stakes are rather less high for me!"

Orsini fell silent, attending instead to another flurry of tender kisses against Ambrose's chest. All the time he was murmuring gentle expressions of affection in his native tongue, his tone melodic and gentle. One hand trailed down Ambrose's side, stroking the muscular lines with obvious appreciation, and the fingers of the other linked with Ambrose's hand, holding tight.

Ambrose returned the pressure of Orsini's hand. "Now we're together, no one will separate us—no one." He gasped, arching his back again, desire taking hold of his every fiber. "Will you let me kiss you, Orsini, my love?"

"You need not even ask," he whispered. "For I have longed for it."

Hand trembling, Ambrose brought Orsini toward him, their mouths meeting in a deep kiss. Gently, never breaking their kiss, Ambrose rolled them over together so that Orsini was on his back. He found the hem of Orsini's shirt and slid his hand underneath, his caresses tender against Orsini's delicate skin as their kiss went on.

"I must tell you a very deep, dark secret." Orsini murmured the admission against Ambrose's lips, but something in his tone suggested that this wasn't about to be too troubling a deep, dark secret. "Cosima's bosoms…they aren't real, Pen."

Ambrose's trembling turned into shudders as he heaved with laughter. "How could you deceive me, madam!" he joked. "But I really should make a thorough examination, just to be certain."

With a bawdy wink, Ambrose roamed his hand higher until he found the little hard peaks of Orsini's nipples. He brushed over them and caught Orsini's answering sigh of pleasure in a kiss.

"Wouldn't it be a marvelous twist if I were a lady disguised as a gent?" Orsini gave another, deeper sigh of delight. "Happily that is not the case."

"You would stand up to the accusations?" Ambrose winked again. He would not be so bold as to touch the shape in Orsini's breeches, although he could feel it against him through their clothes. He was more than content to explore Orsini's chest and enjoy his love's reaction to his touch.

"All night long," was the purred response, and Orsini's dark eyes fluttered closed in an absolute picture of contentment.

"You would, too, you darling devil, and I would match you." Ambrose grinned as he stroked Orsini's nipples more firmly, before drawing up Orsini's shirt. He took in the light olive glow of Orsini's skin, recalling once again their swim all those years before. The memory was undimmed—he could hear the waves crash against the shore and feel the distant sun upon his body.

Ambrose pressed his mouth to Orsini's stomach before slowly kissing his way up toward his chest. Orsini shifted a little, just enough to lift his back from the bed so he could throw his shirt off, his nimble fingers dispensing with the cravat with all the skill of an actor used to the quick change.

Ambrose halted his progress, struck by Orsini's beauty. He'd seen it before—he'd seen a lot more as they had run into the sea, as Orsini had stood naked in his London bedchamber only days before. But they hadn't been embracing as lovers.

"You're perfect," Ambrose whispered, and rested his cheek against Orsini's stomach, just to gaze at him.

"I am a long, long way from that," he replied gently. "But I am yours, all the same."

Ambrose laughed softly and took Orsini's hand, lacing their fingers together. He returned to his tribute, pressing his soft kisses against his lover's body until he arrived at those perfect dark pink nipples. Taking one gently in his mouth, Ambrose tightened his grip on Orsini's hand, as if he feared the moment would end too soon and his Orsini would disappear.

"My Pen," he groaned breathlessly, his back arching up from the bed, and beneath Ambrose's lips, he felt Orsini's breath grown faster. "*Amore mio…*"

Ambrose reached his other hand into Orsini's hair, tangling his locks about his fingers as he tweaked and bathed the dark pink peak with his warm mouth. He twined his leg around Orsini's, their erections pressing together, insistent within their clothes. But Ambrose wouldn't unbutton him, not yet. He would hold back and merely enjoy the knowledge of their mutual desire. Still Orsini sighed and gasped, his heart beating an ever-increasing tattoo as Ambrose's attentions went on. He slipped one leg around Ambrose's in turn, tangling them together, two halves of one.

Ambrose lifted his mouth away and propped himself up with his hands either side of Orsini's dear face. Once he had recovered his breath, which was not an easy task with Orsini gazing up at him with such pleasure in his eyes, Ambrose was ready to speak.

"We must behave ourselves, mustn't we?"

"Are you going to court me, Pen?"

"I fully intend to." Ambrose sighed. "Would you like that? We can dance together at the ball—that would be a lovely thing for a courtship, wouldn't it?" He felt so close to Orsini at that moment, legs wrapped around each other's, bare torsos pressed together. And as for their loins—it was a promise, a gift reserved for later.

"I would truly love that," Orsini told him, dotting a kiss to Ambrose's forehead. "And Cosima would adore the chance to be wooed by a gentleman soldier such as yourself, Captain. I usually politely dismiss those who would pay their respects to my protégé but I believe you are worthy of the lady!"

Ambrose lay down beside Orsini, encircling him in his embrace. "Even having romped shirtless with a handsome fellow?"

"I shall not tell Cosima if you don't."

"It'll be our secret. Just as much a secret as Cosima's true identity." Ambrose crossed his heart and pressed his fingers to Orsini's lips. "Won't tell a living soul."

"And you, sir, courting an impresario *and* a leading lady." He kissed Ambrose's fingers. "Your secret is safe with me, *tato*."

"You know what they say about soldiers." Ambrose grinned. "Actually, they—whoever they might be—say rather a lot!"

"Whereas everything they say about actresses is a bawdy lie!" He closed his eyes and laughed, adding, "But everything they say about Italians is entirely true!"

"Based on this evening alone, I would hasten to agree there about Italians." Ambrose trailed his fingertips across Orsini's chest. "But the actresses, well…"

He nuzzled his lips against Orsini's neck. "You're so lovely and warm and soft. I shall curl up around you and never let you go."

"What a fine gentleman I have found." Orsini smiled, running his fingers through Ambrose's hair. "My very own soldier! Oh, Pen, how I longed for you when we traveled together… You were the most terrible temptation!"

"Perhaps I should apologize, but I won't." Ambrose danced his fingertips down to Orsini's soft stomach. "Lying there night after night, knowing you were only on the other side of the wall… Longing to go out onto the balcony and climb across it to get into your room, if only to see you. One night, I actually got out of bed and stood there on my balcony, and I had to clutch onto the rail to stop myself from enacting my silly plan. For I was sure you would only laugh at me. The sight of a ridiculous Englishman in a nightshirt down to his ankles, appearing like a phantom on your balcony!"

"I think I would prefer you without the nightshirt, but I would certainly have welcomed you with very open arms indeed. I always thought you were hoping for a lovely young lady to sweep away into your embrace!"

Ambrose rolled onto his back and stared up at the bed's canopy. He hoped Orsini wouldn't misunderstand what he was about to say. "Do you know—I tried most hard not to feel the way I do. Not because I didn't want to love you, but because I oughtn't to. I tried to picture a bride, but whenever I did, she always had your face." Ambrose laughed softly. "Isn't that a funny thing?"

Orsini propped himself up on one elbow and gazed down at Ambrose, his eyes shining in the candlelight. After a few moments he pressed a very gentle kiss to Ambrose's lips and asked him, "Will you marry me, *tato*?"

Ambrose answered without a moment's hesitation. "Yes! For heaven's sake — yes!" He pulled Orsini down to him and kissed him with fervor, until a thought occurred to him. "And how do we accomplish that, darling — does Captain Pendleton wed Cosima?"

"He does!" Orsini agreed excitedly. "Alas, though, she cannot give you any little Pens, Pen."

Ambrose kissed him tenderly. "We can borrow some little Pens. We shall fill our house with foundlings and the orphans of unfortunate theatricals."

"You are truly a hero, my darling." Orsini settled his head against Ambrose's shoulder. His warm skin pressed to his lover's. "I shall have to write to my mother. Happily, she has thrown up her hands and said, Orsini shall do what Orsini shall do!"

"Orsini shall marry a soldier." Ambrose tangled his arms around him. "A retired one, but I do still have the uniform, of course. The sash has huge tassels on either end of it. Funny, really — whenever I wore it, I always thought, Orsini would love this sash! I pictured you flouncing about in it!"

Ambrose felt rather silly for admitting to that, but he had carried Orsini in his thoughts wherever he had gone, whatever he had done.

"What would you have me wear it with, *amore mio*?" As he spoke, Orsini began to dot those small, sensuous kisses against Ambrose's jaw again. "Something in silk and lace? A manly uniform? Nothing at all?"

As if it were a terrible thing to want, Ambrose held his reply back until he could restrain it no longer. "Not a stitch else! Just you and the golden sash."

"Well, perhaps you might get your wish," murmured the coquettish actor. "And I shall say nothing of cavalry sabres."

"I shall unleash my mighty sword!" Ambrose tickled Orsini, then gasped when he realized what he'd said. "Not at this precise moment, however...courtship and all that."

"And when you are not cozy in the countryside with your Cosima, you might raise hell in town with her brother," Orsini realized, snuggling down against him again. "Pen, we shall have the finest life anyone might imagine!"

Ambrose laughed. "Indeed! Let us go to Vauxhall Gardens again, but with you in the garb of a gentleman — oh, the larks, Orsini, just think!"

"Yes!" He clapped his hands merrily and kissed Ambrose's shoulder. "Yet as the younger son, I can never make you my comtesse, my darling, you must simply remain Captain Pen."

"Perhaps I might sign my plays as Captain Pen — or might people think me rather full of myself?"

"I think they would love it," Orsini assured him. "And when we wed, Cosima might wear a gown fashioned to capture a certain feminine sense of that splendid uniform of yours. What say you, sir?"

"With gold braid and little buttons?" Ambrose tapped his fingertips up Orsini's chest as if suggesting the track of the fastenings. "And frogging. And a sash..." He kissed Orsini's ear, which at that moment, so pink and perfect, he couldn't resist.

"And a feather in my hair, because La Cosima must have her feather!"

"Oh, yes — the tallest we can find in all of England!"

"All the better to tickle you with!"

With their legs still locked together, they tickled each other and rolled across the large bed. On they went until they were quite breathless, and drunk with the silliness and joy of being in each other's embrace.

At the end of the landing the grand clock that Mr. Pendleton had proudly purchased last Michaelmas chimed the hour, yet Ambrose barely heard it, entirely lost in this delightful encounter. Instead the kisses went on and on, his embraces more loving than ever.

Ambrose fidgeted with the corner of the bedclothes. He knew that what he was about to say was fraught with danger, for what would be said if they were found? But not to ask seemed even worse, for he couldn't bring himself—and didn't want—to usher Orsini out into the cold corridor.

"Would it be a naughty thing indeed if you stayed in my bed tonight? To sleep, just as we did in Pall Mall?"

"I must be back in Cosima's room before breakfast, for tomorrow Orsini will spend the day in business, and Cosima shall leave her room," Orsini told him, chewing at his lip as he considered the question. "But I shall take the risk!"

Ambrose's heart beat so violently that he was sure Orsini must have heard it.

"I shall keep on my breeches, as we're courting." Ambrose ran his thumb under the waistband. They wouldn't be the most comfortable clothes to sleep in, but if they both—no, he could not think of that now. Their evening so far had been chaste. At least, as chaste as two shirtless men very much enjoying each other's company could be.

"What do you usually wear for bed, Pen? Just wear that." Orsini stifled a soft yawn. "I wear nothing, as you know, but I shall throw on my shirt for the sake of decency unless you have a silky something I might borrow, as tradition dictates?"

"I have my nightshirt—I sleep in that. Very comfortable it is too. Nice and…erm…loose." Ambrose popped open the top button on his breeches, which certainly were not. "And as a matter of fact, I do have a banyan. I wear it when I'm writing. I drift about in it, like a fool. You should laugh to see me at my endeavors! But you may borrow that, and the next time I wear it, I shall think of that soft silk against your bare skin."

Once again Orsini clapped his agreement, then he pushed himself up against the pillows to watch Ambrose. In fact, even when he leaned forward to slip off his shoes and stockings, his gaze never left his lover, and Ambrose saw in it every proof of the love and devotion they shared.

Ambrose kissed the top of Orsini's head, then left the bed to retrieve his banyan from the clothes press. He draped the silk garment over his arm and trotted back to the bed.

"Well, here we are, my darling Orsini—the silkiest one that I could find, and, so I am told, Mr. Brummell has one just like it! Though I'm convinced you should look a thousand times more appealing."

"My friends tell me that your Mr. Brummell will soon be selling that banyan, along with everything else he possesses, on pain of two broken legs or worse!" Orsini took the banyan and ran his hand appreciatively over the delicate fabric. "Mark me well, Pen, all is not well with our Beau. When you join me in the theater, you shall hear all the gossip!"

"How terribly exciting!" Ambrose took his nightshirt from the chair by the bed and went behind his dressing screen. "I do try, you know, to follow the ton, but as you could see earlier, that cravat knot was entirely ridiculous. I nearly choked myself."

"La Cosima's ladies shall take care of you," Orsini called, and Ambrose heard the sound him discarding what remained of his clothes. "They know how to tie a cravat!"

How tempting to peer around the edge and see what he had once seen, years before, on a sunny beach in Italy. But no. Ambrose Pendleton was a gentleman and he did not peek on naked men as if he were an elder spying on Susanna. Ambrose tugged at his hair and dismissed the temptation, then kicked away his breeches and stockings and pulled his nightshirt over his head. There was no disguising his desire, other than by a discreetly placed hand, and this Ambrose attempted as he made his way back to the bed. Orsini was already there, perched very neatly on the covers against the pillow, resplendent in the banyan that he had somehow transformed into a picture of decadence simply by wearing it. He hopped up onto his feet and greeted Ambrose with a bow.

"I hope you shall find the accommodation comfortable." Unwittingly, Ambrose's careful hand dropped from his loins as he pulled back the bedclothes. "And that looks a lot better on you than it does on me!"

"I think it looks possibly more feminine, but better? I doubt that!" Orsini slipped into the bed beside him. "I should like to see you lounging about in this, Pen, and nothing else. Those gorgeous legs of yours just teasing beneath the silk, a little hint of chest? Say you will when we are married, *tato*?"

His cheeks warm with awkward fire, Ambrose put his arm around Orsini. "Anything you like, darling.

Anything at all. Perhaps we can lounge about together, a banyan each...I can see it now, on a chaise longue before a huge window overlooking...overlooking — well, I can't see what's outside, because the vision of you is so very distracting."

"Mine would be red, yours...blue, perhaps. Or perhaps red also or — " Orsini sighed and snuggled closer. " — or no banyan at all, for you are too perfectly formed to hide, but simply a Grecian sort of diaphanous draping affair to keep us cozy."

Ambrose pulled the bedcovers up to cocoon them, and smiled as the feather pillow sank under his head. "Me, perfect? I'm not sure about that. Although my arms are just the perfect size to embrace you, and my lips are just soft enough to kiss you. So perhaps I am."

"I thank God that He brought you home to me," his lover whispered. "We are blessed, my love."

Ambrose clutched Orsini's graceful hand in his large, square palm. "We are, indeed."

"How does one obtain such a splendid physique, Pen?" Orsini's tone was playful, his free hand gently stroking over Ambrose's nightshirt-clad chest. "One imagines we are made the same, but you? You are perfect!"

"I'm rather solid, I'll grant you." It was only then that Ambrose realized he had accidentally rested his hand against Orsini's thigh, but he made no attempt to move it away. "Out on the horses, bit of bathing...my brother and I used to box, until Mother forbade it as she was scared we'd spoil our noses!"

"Thank heavens she did!" He shuddered theatrically. "You cannot risk that jaw either!"

Ambrose stroked a circle on Orsini's thigh. "Really? You don't like the thought of the two Pendleton boys shirtless, in the stables, hair sticky with sweat as their fists fly?"

"I do not!" And Orsini's tone certainly seemed to confirm his words. "There is nothing to be admired in flying fists, *tato*. And if you are to be shirtless and sweating in the straw, let it be with me, and for a far more entertaining pastime than boxing!"

Now that was certainly more appealing than seeing his brother ready to throw a punch. "Such things you promise, darling Orsini—and shall we romp in the straw before or after our wedding? Shall we make a habit of it, the rest of our lives through?"

"We shall before and after, and forever." He kissed Ambrose's cheek. "Now, tell me, Pen, should I untie my hair or would you prefer your Orsini a little more masculine? What say you, my darling?"

Orsini's hair was so glossy in the dying candlelight, and Ambrose reached for the ribbon that secured it. "Loose, I think, for tonight."

"Loose it shall be. Will you untie the ribbon, Pen?" He lifted his head a little and blinked his dark eyes at Ambrose. "We will be so very happy."

"We will." Ambrose unfastened the ribbon with one gentle tug and combed his fingers through Orsini's hair, humming a half-remembered tune. "Will you let me comb it for you one day?"

"Of course. And will you make me the neatest plait on an autumn evening, my darling?"

Ambrose chuckled at the thought of his large, clumsy hands dressing Orsini's elegant hair. "I might have to practice!"

"We have a lifetime to get it right."

"We do." How quiet it was, the house sleeping around them, not a sound beside their whispers and the slowly failing fire. "If I fall asleep, it's no bad reflection upon you. Only on how content I am, to lie here like this with you, my dearest."

"I love you," Orsini whispered. "*Amore mio.*"

Ambrose murmured something. He was fairly sure it was 'I love you' in reply, but the comfort of lying abed with Orsini was as delightful as reclining on the softest feather down. He rested his lips against Orsini's throat, and he did mean to kiss him, but he began to drift off to sleep, seeing only himself and Orsini before his inward eye.

Chapter Twelve

Orsini opened his eyes slowly, snuggling with a sigh against Ambrose as he did so. They had hardly moved as the long hours of the night had passed, their limbs still entangled, Ambrose's chest still firm beneath Orsini's hair. He lifted his head just enough to look at Ambrose, his eyes still closed, a faint smile on his face, and Orsini pressed a soft kiss to his lover's lips. How far they had come in the space of one night and how far they still had to go to not only save Ambrose's future, but do so without tearing father and son apart, for that would not do at all.

As Orsini watched Ambrose sleep and pondered on their plan he listened to the faint sound of a chiming clock, counting the bells as they rang. It would be seven o'clock, he guessed, for the house was quiet. He could take his time strolling to Cosima's room and changing then be safe in bed, ready to receive any morning visitors who might look in on the sickly young lady.

The seventh chime sounded and Orsini settled down against Ambrose again, just doing so as the eighth chime sounded.

And the ninth.

A theatrical like Orsini was hardly used to early starts and nine o'clock was a time he frequently failed to see but this morning was different. He had a distinct feeling that Mrs. Pendleton might be making an appearance, so concerned had she been at Cosima's faint, and what would she think if she found the door locked and the lady unrousable?

She will have the door broken down!

Or find a spare key.

Nevertheless, the Cosima of pillows and blankets would be revealed by daylight and with that thought in his head, Orsini sprang from the bed. Ambrose slept on as his lover dragged his shirt over his head and tied his long hair back with his discarded cravat then, with a last look back at Ambrose, he fled the room.

Orsini dashed along the corridors toward Cosima's room, expecting at any moment to hear the alarm raised or meet Tarbottom and Pendleton, the padded corsets that made up his female alter-ego clutched in their hands and their demands for an explanation echoing through the halls. He prayed to every saint he could think of as he turned each corner and the Lord, it seemed, was listening, for Orsini unlocked Cosima's door and slipped inside without any interruption. In the darkened room he took a deep breath and turned the key in the lock. Then he crossed himself and whispered, "*Grazie, Dio.*"

All Pen's fault. Orsini smiled and began to undress, his head filled with visions of Ambrose Pendleton, his muscular body accessorized by nothing but a flamboyant tasseled sash and a broad smile.

And maybe something else, but they were courting and he wouldn't be so naughty as to even imagine—

Except now he was, picturing Ambrose naked on their Italian beach, waiting for his Orsini to tumble into his arms with a magnificent, hard—

A knock at the door wrenched Orsini from his reverie.

"Yes?" he called, summoning Cosima's more gentle tones.

"Contessina?" The rich, slightly condescending voice of Mrs. Tarbottom came through the door. "Oh, you are awake now. Are you accepting visitors, only—"

"—only Mama and I felt it our duty to come and sit with you for a time." Harriet chimed in with a sweeter, younger version of her mother's tone. "Would you admit us, dear friend?"

By now naked and far from an innocent, dewy young lady in the thrall of a strapping soldier, Orsini froze. His rather spirited imagining of Ambrose beneath the Italian sun had left very hard proof of his masculinity there for all to see and though Cosima might be able to explain most things away, that certainly wasn't one of them.

Blankets, he decided, quickly snatching up Cosima's stays with their delicate padding in all the right places. And closed curtains.

"A moment, if you would," he called back. "I look a terrible fright to visitors!"

"Very well, we shall wait," Mrs. Tarbottom drawled. She chuckled, arrogant and self-assured.

"God bless you!" Orsini pulled his nightgown over the stays and let his hair tumble over his shoulders. He put his hands on the dressing table and peered into the mirror. He was always feminine but there was no doubt that he was Amadeo. It was a subtle shade here and there, a gentle color and a touch of rouge that brought out Cosima.

And one doesn't become a girl for a living without being able to put on a face in the dark, in two minutes or while the watch is knocking at the door and your partner is scrabbling out the window.

He kept the women waiting longer simply because he could, and because Cosima would look all the better with every extra second he spent on her face. She needed less makeup than Harriet Tarbottom, Orsini noted with a smile of mischief, as he patted powder to his skin and teased a few ringlets into place.

Perfect.

With that thought Orsini pulled his shawl around his shoulders, kicked his suit under the bed and turned the key in the lock.

"Forgive me, you must think me terribly rude," he simpered, turning toward the bed. That troublesome appendage might have softened somewhat with the arrival of the cold water that was the Tarbottoms, but it was still something of a risk to go *au naturel* beneath one's nightgown. He slipped beneath the covers and pulled them up, suitably decent to call, "Come in, please!"

Mrs. Tarbottom and her daughter crossed the room in slow, stately fashion, their faces masks of pious kindness. But they couldn't hide their pride. This was no mercy visit—they were here to gloat. They sat near the bed on a sofa and neatly folded their hands in their laps.

"Have you recovered from your faint, Contessina?" Harriet asked. "Only we were so concerned for you yesterday, but you did want to rest, so we couldn't bear to disturb you."

Does Harriet's mother know what sort of a girl she is? Orsini wondered. *Or does she think her as sweet as she seems?*

"I am recovered," Orsini replied, resting one hand meaningfully atop the richly brocaded bedcover, just against his stomach. "My brother has told me that my *capitano* has made his choice, Miss Tarbottom."

Harriet dipped her head, her eyelashes lowered. "He has, yes. He will marry me."

She lifted her eyes to Orsini, her smile brittle with triumph.

"Once you are well, Contessina, you ought to leave," Mrs. Tarbottom advised. "I really do not feel that your presence would be welcome at the wedding breakfast — neither for your sake nor anyone else's."

Mrs. Tarbottom tipped her head to one side as if she were trying to appear sympathetic, but the import of her words robbed her of any tenderness. She was rejoicing at making a bastard of Cosima's child, of breaking lovers' hearts. Ambition had turned many hearts to stone, and Mrs. Tarbottom's was no exception.

"I cannot travel in my condition," Orsini replied, the hand on his stomach shifting just slightly. "You are a lucky lady indeed, Miss Tarbottom, but I have not yet accepted defeat. My brother would have me leave today, but I will not go. He is furious with me and Captain Pendleton, and believes me cruelly misused. I had not thought he would be your ally."

Orsini sighed deeply and shook his head, turning away just a little. Some instinct, he wasn't sure what, told him that these ladies might like to think of Amadeo Orsini as their friend, angry at his sister and her seducer, not to mention as keen to clear up this sorry matter as they were.

"He believes that I should forget the captain," Orsini went on sadly, dabbing at his eye with a silk handkerchief. "It would seem that he has been my suitor even as he was preparing to be yours, Miss Tarbottom. Perhaps we are both misled. You might well seek another man as your betrothed, or my brother believes that the *capitano* will break your heart one day too."

And I believe that you will think this a scheme of mine, a very poor ploy to try and make you give up Pen for me. Which is precisely what I want you to think, so your mother might see your true colors.

Harriet gasped. "I realize you are saddened by this turn of events, but there is no need to attack the character of the gentleman I happen to love — the man who shall take me for his bride!"

"Harriet, my girl — quieten down. We don't want to upset the *contessina* in her condition." Mrs. Tarbottom's lips curled into a cruel smile. "She cannot even look to her own brother for succour at this tragic time. Oh, poor friendless lady!"

"My brother has always been a fool when presented with a pretty face," Orsini told them, though in truth he had never really cared for pretty gents. Better a man who looked like a man, strong and broad and handsome. "And your daughter certainly possesses one of those. When he came to me last night, his anger aflame, it was all I could do to keep him from striking Captain Pendleton or coming to your room, Miss Tarbottom, and telling you to flee before you marry a false man!"

"Aflame?" Mrs. Tarbottom seemed to be trying to sound shocked at such a carry-on, but there was no disguising a certain light that danced in her eyes. Not victory, no, but a flicker of desire. "I confess we heard his imprecations when he arrived at this house — a very, shall we say, passionate man, is he not?"

Oh.

She couldn't possibly, not the Godfearing, crucifix-clutching Mrs. Tarbottom… Could she?

It wouldn't be the first time, Orsini knew. One only had to visit the right houses in Rome to discover that the priests with the biggest crosses were often the ones with the biggest appetites too.

And their housekeepers can be even worse…one always has to know where the exits are.

And Amadeo Orsini, handsome, flamboyant, charismatic, was no stranger to interest from ladies of rank, bored with their husbands and their respectability and in search of a little continental fire. How amusing it had been to realize that Cosima's noble male suitors offered her love and devotion whereas Amadeo's noble ladies and gentlemen wanted a quick bit of fun in the shrubbery.

But Orsini had never had an interest in ladies.

"He is," Orsini told Mrs. Tarbottom, glancing to Harriet to see if there was anything other than malice in her eyes. "And, Mrs. Tarbottom, he has no right to chastise Captain Pendleton for following his own passions, for Amadeo is certainly no stranger to such heated desires. Why, he lives for passion and romance. How dare he denounce the *capitano* for doing the same? I believe Amadeo taught the captain all he knows about women and I can tell you, I believe he knows a lot."

Mrs. Tarbottom's artfully pale face turned red under its layer of makeup. Her neat hair appeared to be pinging out from its pins, the curls she had created by what must have been an uncomfortable night in curling rags were unraveling as if subjected to a humid afternoon. Which was no doubt what was playing out in her mind at that moment. An afternoon with a passionate Italian who knew a lot about women.

"Really, Contessina, you might move in laid-back circles, but in front of my innocent daughter—pray, keep your counsel." Mrs. Tarbottom's tone did not ring true. She spoke for effect in front of her daughter, because what mother would wish her child to run to Papa with news of Mama's latest fascination?

"Mama, I do not understand what she speaks of, really, I do not." Harriet smiled with pert conceit.

"Oh, to be so innocent," Orsini lamented, stroking his stomach.

Mrs. Tarbottom patted her daughter's hand in distracted fashion. "Yes, yes, she is quite the innocent, my darling Harriet."

"Oh, I thought I could hear voices!" Mrs. Pendleton had introduced her cheery face through the gap in the door. "Good morning, dear Cosima. I do hope you're feeling better—given the…ah…circumstances."

She turned the most wooden smile Orsini had ever seen on the visiting Tarbottoms.

"Signora Pendleton, come in. I trust Pagolo did not keep you awake with his chatter?" Never was a woman more welcome than this one was now. Such a warm lady, one with whom Orsini could happily spend long hours dispensing the very best gossip.

She swept in, her smile genuine now as it fell on Cosima. "I did not sleep well, my dear, but it had naught to do with Pagolo. He slept all night on the back of my chaise longue! Are you recovered from your swoon?"

Mrs. Pendleton perched on the edge of the bed and rested the back of her hand against Orsini's brow. It would come away dusted in powder, he realized, but that could not be helped. Besides, what young lady wouldn't make herself halfway presentable when faced with the women who had bested her?

"I near swooned again when I heard my brother raising hell," Orsini said apologetically. "I am so very sorry. He should not behave so."

"Hush, now, Cosima, there's no need to apologize. He's only doing his duty to you as your brother." Mrs. Pendleton's smile wavered as she glanced across at the Tarbottoms. "You should've seen my brother when — Mrs. Tarbottom, Miss...perhaps you might be good enough to leave Cosima be for now. She shall be perfectly well in my company."

"Contessina?" Mrs. Tarbottom and her daughter rose from the sofa in one synchronized movement, as if they had been practicing. "Do you wish to dismiss us?"

"Dismissed," Pagolo decided as he strutted through the door. "*Addio, addio!*"

It was all Orsini could do not to laugh and he could only follow the parrot's lead and say, "Thank you for looking in on me but please, you have spent enough of this beautiful morning with me. Go and enjoy the day."

"*Addio,*" said Pagolo again as he hopped onto the bed frame, cocking his head to watch the two women.

The two Tarbottoms inclined their heads and left, the door banging loudly behind them.

"Don't worry," Mrs. Pendleton told Cosima. "The walls and doors of this house are tolerably thick. They shan't hear a word unless we're shouting! Now where was I? Oh yes…"

She giggled as if she had been transported back to a young miss again. "My brother did just the same to Barnaby—my husband, that is—when he found out that I was with child! 'You'll marry my sister, you cur, or I'll thrash you!' Imagine that! And Barnaby did right and we were wed. I only wish he would allow his own son to do the same."

"Has your husband told you that—" Orsini shook his head, his sadness suddenly real, for father and son were at daggers drawn now, there was no pretense in that. "Last night, the decision was taken. My captain is to marry Miss Tarbottom, to protect the business agreement."

"My husband came to my bedchamber last night and told me what had been decided, and I told him—never mind that." Mrs. Pendleton took her lace-edged hanky from her sleeve as if she were about to cry. "I told him he was a hypocrite. Though it isn't easy for poor Barnaby…it's not only business that's on his mind, my girl."

Something about Mrs. Pendleton told Orsini that this was an ally, a sister in arms. He could do anything with the love of Ambrose Pendleton but with the support of his mother added to that heady brew, miracles might become possible.

"I saw Pen last night, signora," Orsini admitted. "And we are truly in love, there is no fancy, no silly romance born out of our Italian summer. But we have lied to you already, and I cannot have you think your son…"

Orsini fell silent for a moment, then went on, "We thought that if your father and my brother believed us already intimate, your husband would have no choice but to give us his blessing. In truth, the *capitano* has been a gentleman toward me. We have not…how to say it politely? Just, we have not."

Mrs. Pendleton giggled again, as if she and Cosima were fond, girlish friends. "Then you are better behaved than Barnaby and I! But I do not blame you for your subterfuge. I only wish there was something I could do, but Barnaby is so very set on this course of action. And he is not well disposed toward theatricals, not after… Oh, it is all so long ago, but his grudge lingers yet."

"At least it is not Italians he despises." Orsini managed a smile, but it felt a little weak. He reached out and took the lady's hand softly. "Why does he dislike theatricals so, when even your princes have such a liking for our kind?"

Mrs. Pendleton glanced over her shoulder at the parrot, who nodded as if promising not to repeat what she was about to say. "This goes no further, mind. It was his father. Fond fool that he was. Barnaby was only a little thing, and his father abandoned him and his mother and the Pendleton brood and pursued a theatrical, for he couldn't ignore her pretty ankle."

And the pieces fell into place with a resounding thud. This was not some heartless man of money and ambition—it was yet another who saw Pandora, Eve and Lilith combined in any woman who called herself an actress, no matter what activities that description covered, from boards to bedroom. A little boy, abandoned for a woman of the stage.

It would not end happily, he knew, even as he asked, "Does Pen know, signora?"

"No, Barnaby does not want such a history known far and wide. But maybe the time has come to tell Amby about his grandfather." Mrs. Pendleton sighed. "I took the boys to the theater once, when they were small. Barnaby was off looking at some mines somewhere, and Amby was enchanted! Like his grandfather, I suppose. Must be in the Pendleton blood, though Barnaby won't thank me for saying so."

"I shall not tell him without your permission," Orsini promised, squeezing her hand. "Theater is in the Pendleton blood, Mamma, for your son has written the most marvelous play and one of your finest producers is desperate to put it on in London, but—what can we do? I love Pen, but he cannot be at odds with his own father!"

"Has he really!" Mrs. Pendleton gasped with delight. "He's forever scribbling, and he had a poem printed in the newspaper—I'm sure he told you that. I was so proud of him, but Barnaby was not pleased. I should love to read this play of his—nay, I should love, more than anything, to see it performed! And would you be in it, Cosima? He surely wrote a part for you, did he not?"

Her grin faded and she shook her head. "But what would Barnaby say to all that? It'll sound like naught but dreams and nonsense if I tell him. Who is this producer you speak of?"

"Tonight, after dinner, perhaps I might perform a comic song from the play? A duet, and Pagolo knows the male part!" Orsini exclaimed. "We shall not tell your husband who wrote it, and see how much he will laugh and applaud? The producer is Viscount Hartington. There is no man with more influence in all of London theater!"

"Now that name sounds familiar! And a viscount no less—Barnaby couldn't help but be impressed by that.

You don't suppose—" Mrs. Pendleton had turned rather pink with excitement. "—no, it's silly, but would the viscount come to the ball? Is he an acquaintance of yourself and your brother? If he were to appear in person, Barnaby would be hard put to ignore that Amby's quite capable of making his own way in the world. There's no need for him to be packed off with those Americans."

"Would you like me to write to him?" Orsini asked, wondering if this might not be an opportunity to lift the peer's unhappy mother from her sadness too. What better to cheer a lady than a ball? "His mother was robbed of her wedding jewels this spring and has been left heartbroken by it. She is a sweet and gentle lady, one of Pagolo's favorites. Might we invite the dowager too?"

As if to add his support to the request, Pagolo hopped onto Mrs. Pendleton's shoulder and pressed his face to her hair like a kitten. Orsini knew there and then that the bird had found his retirement home and felt a pang of sadness, and a great swell of happiness too, for he could not have chosen better. Mrs. Pendleton giggled again and stroked the parrot's iridescent feathers.

"Well...I think you should, my dear. Barnaby has given me free rein to invite whomsoever I choose, and I think a viscount and his dowager mother would be wonderful guests for the ball." Mrs. Pendleton shoved her handkerchief back up her sleeve. "Now—have you paper and ink?"

"I do! Do you think your husband will tell Pen of his father?" Because Orsini couldn't, he had made his promise to the woman whom he hoped one day to call Mother. "For he should know, shouldn't he?"

"He should." Mrs. Pendleton kissed Cosima's brow, then rose from the bed with Pagolo still perched on her shoulder. "You write your letter to the viscount, and I shall look in on my Amby. And I'll tell him about his grandfather. All is not lost."

"I believe Amadeo intends to show his best behavior today after his sorry performance last night." Cosima smiled. The day was going to take some planning if brother and sister weren't to be expected in the same place at the same time, but he was sure he could do it if anyone could. "I will rest a while longer but by supper, I will be ready to perform for your husband."

For now, I'll just be performing for everyone else.

Chapter Thirteen

The morning was half done by the time Amadeo Orsini emerged from his room in a haze of rose scent, clad in his favorite summer suit of emerald green. Today the embroidery was floral, vivid reds and yellow blossoms that clustered on his waistcoat, and the colors were picked out again in the rubies he wore on his fingers and in his stock pin. Yet it all felt so very restrictive after Cosima's muslin dresses and loose hair, and on a day as warm as this, he longed to be dressed in her airy gowns and soft shoes.

How delightful to have the choice!

The heat in Mrs. Tarbottom's eyes was hotter than any summer sun though and he was sure now that there might be something in that of use. More than saintliness lurked behind her pious smile, Orsini knew.

He knocked at Ambrose's door, only to be informed by the young maid within, her arms filled with linens, that the gentleman was already off about his day. Of course he was, Orsini thought warmly, for he was a man of action.

Only now, as he trotted through the halls and past the portraits of horses and landscapes, the shelves heaving with rich leather-bound books, did he think of the future they had planned. Could they really dare to wed, this hero and his pretend contessina? Would their future truly be as they had planned, Ambrose and Cosima, happy together through the long years?

"*Si,*" Orsini told a painting of a fine white steed that stood resplendent before the portico of Pendleton Hall. An English horse, he reminded himself, as he added, "Wait and see, Signore Cavallo!"

He descended the stairs and skipped through the entrance hall, past closed doors and even the occasional maid, each one of whom he greeted with a low bow in return for an amused giggle. One of the girls pointed their flamboyant visitor toward the morning room and he paused outside, hearing the hum of voices within. Then, with a deep breath, he pushed open the door and stepped inside.

"Good morning, Orsini!" Mrs. Pendleton nodded as he entered. She was sitting beside Ambrose, who was somewhat pale in the face, but he smiled at Orsini nonetheless. She had told him about his profligate grandfather, Orsini was sure of it.

"Good morning, my friend." Ambrose rose to his feet and bowed neatly. "I hope we might be on better terms this morning than we were yesterday. My mother tells me that your sister improves."

"*Buongiorno.*" Orsini bowed to Ambrose and his mother. For good measure, he offered a nod to Pagolo too, who was watching the garden beyond the window. "Madame, sir, I must apologize for how I comported myself last night. It was unforgivable."

He put his hand on Ambrose's arm, the gesture one of friendship, but as Ambrose would know, something far deeper than that too.

"For the sake of appearances, let our American adversaries believe us still at odds." Orsini offered Mrs. Pendleton and her son a smile. "For the sake of love and Cosima, let us be friends and allies."

"I forgive you, Orsini. It is quite understandable, really." Mrs. Pendleton returned his smile.

Ambrose blinked at him, then stiffened his posture and smiled too. For a second he touched Orsini's hand. "We none of us asked to be swept into this situation, but we are here and we are resolved to fight."

"And have a picnic!" Mrs. Pendleton grinned. Ambrose hid his mouth behind his hand, clearly trying not to laugh.

"A picnic?" A lance of panic shot through Orsini. Would Cosima's presence be required in addition to his own? A hundred scenarios charged through his imagination, each worse than the last and each resulting in discovery. Surely a picnic wouldn't be their undoing.

"Mrs. Tarbottom wished that we should all go on a picnic," Mrs. Pendleton explained. "To enjoy our beautiful English weather! I for one can think of nothing nicer than sitting out on the damp grass while swarms of wasps attack us, but if it keeps Mrs. Tarbottom happy, then we may as well."

"And she wishes for you to attend, Orsini, you lucky fellow!" Ambrose clapped his hand against Orsini's shoulder.

"Me?" He grimaced. Oh for a return to last summer, with its deluges and chills, when no thin-lipped American could force one off to a picnic. Last year

Ambrose had still been in the service of his country though, still risking his life and limbs, and Orsini remembered those days too clearly. He had no wish to feel such weight of worry ever again. "Nothing is better than a day beneath the summer sun, but can I not decline on this occasion?"

"I should very much appreciate it if you would attend." Mrs. Pendleton glanced from Orsini to her son. "I realize you must be worried about Cosima, but…she will be with us in spirit, if not in person."

Ambrose glanced at Orsini, his brow furrowed. "Erm…of course, Mother. Orsini—think not of the Tarbottoms, but of you and I and our picnics in Italy! Though, alas, that we cannot finish it with a spirited swim."

"Whyever can we not?" The thought of it sent a thrill of excitement through his blood, though, of course, he knew Ambrose was right. "I shall endure the picnic, for the sake of my good captain and his mother."

Chapter Fourteen

The sun was bright as the little party of five strolled through the gardens toward the shaded hills beyond. At the head of the group, Orsini and Ambrose carried a generous hamper each, the air between them crackling with manufactured tension as the supposed seducer and his supposed enemy did their best to remain civil. Behind them strolled the ladies, one with a parrot on her shoulder, one with her face unreadable and the youngest dressed as though she were about to enjoy an audience with the queen herself. Harriet was relishing her triumph and her diamonds were almost as fine as Orsini's rubies. She knew it too — he'd seen it in the way her eyes had widened when the group met to begin their promenade.

Harriet Tarbottom had an eye for jewels, just as her mother had one for Italians.

"And in your country, Orsini, do you take picnics?" Mrs. Tarbottom's voice rang across the gardens.

"Indeed yes!" He slowed to allow the ladies to draw level. "Have you visited my homeland, Madame? It is a paradise. All gentlemen with Italy in their blood are raised to appreciate only the finest beauty."

Mrs. Tarbottom laughed, her head tipped to one side as she toyed with the cross around her neck. "I have never visited Italy, but I long to. And so does my daughter."

"Oh, yes, Mama!" Harriet smiled at both men. "Papa says I should take my honeymoon there before we head back to America."

"Things are politically interesting at the moment," Orsini informed her with a laugh. "But it is the finest land, is it not, Captain?"

"I cannot think of a finer place. Besides England, of course, but I am biased!" Ambrose nudged Orsini, as if indicating to the ladies that they were being polite, yet still combative.

"Yet I think America might prove to have attractions of its own," Orsini purred.

"You have never visited?" Mrs. Tarbottom turned toward Orsini and managed to brush against him. "You might enjoy it."

"I shouldn't like to visit America myself," Mrs. Pendleton remarked, apparently unaware of the adulterous flirtation occurring under her watch. "I've never been one for sea journeys. We traveled down the English coast once and—oh, heavens, I have never in all my days been so unwell!"

"I believe my mother would agree with you. She is of a mind to make her life here in England." Orsini sighed. "The country has stolen her heart."

Ambrose glanced at Orsini, heat in his eyes but nothing else in his demeanor to hint at what battled within his breast. He dropped his gaze.

"Will you take my arm, Orsini?" Harriet beamed at him. "It is not every day I can claim to be on the arm of the son of a real Italian count!"

"The brother of a count now," he pointed out. The hamper made it somewhat difficult but he lifted his elbow to accommodate her. "My eldest brother is the head of our family today."

Harriet nodded with enthusiasm, her ringlets springing about her face, for all the world giving her the appearance of an excited spaniel. She surely wouldn't transfer her affections—or her attentions, at least—from Ambrose?

"Somewhat more exciting than being the brother of a colliery magnate!" Ambrose laughed as he took his mother's arm.

"I can tell you, being a colliery magnate's wife has its compensations," Mrs. Pendleton remarked, her eye on Mrs. Tarbottom. "Though it's not quite the same as having a title, I'm sure."

"My brother is married and father to a brace of fine children, his title is shared already," Orsini informed them. He lifted his other elbow slightly and met Mrs. Tarbottom's gaze. "Madame, might I escort you too?"

"I should be delighted." A soft timbre had crept into her voice, the tones of a seductress hiding in plain sight. She took Orsini's arm with delicacy, but ensured that every few steps her bosom would collide with some part of Orsini's person. The thought of this creature daring to pass judgment on Cosima left Orsini's blood boiling in his veins, for no woman so accomplished in the art of deception was new to the practice. From the grip of Harriet's hand on his arm he knew that the mother had tutored the daughter just as well, though as Harriet's gaze slid over his ruby stock pin, he wondered again if it wasn't the jewels that she found attractive, not the fellow wearing them.

"Do all the men in Italy dress as you do?" Harriet asked him.

"We are a colorful people," he replied. "But few are as colorful as Orsini!"

"Very true!" Ambrose laughed, and his mother laughed along with him.

Not to be outdone, Harriet and Mrs. Tarbottom joined in, laughing with droll amusement as if Orsini had made the most hilarious comment ever heard. Orsini joined in, though he couldn't help but think that this heavy hamper could be doing La Cosima's slender arms little good, let alone that he would have to compensate for the sun with even more powder tonight, when she sang before the guests. It was that thought which caused him to slow as they reached the shade of a spreading tree and glance back at the house and its beautiful gardens beneath them.

"Shall we make our camp here, ladies, where we might look out over our world like those on Olympus?"

"What a charming spot—you have such an eye, Orsini!" Mrs. Tarbottom finally relinquished his arm, but it was clear that she expected to sit beside him.

"Oh, he does, Mrs. Tarbottom!" Mrs. Pendleton sank down onto the grass, her silk dress billowing up around her. Ambrose assisted her, and the two laughed as her parasol got caught in her shawl. How Orsini wished he could join in with their chuckles but instead he was stuck with the Tarbottom women, one staring at his jewels, the other letting her gaze roam where no married woman should. Even Pagolo squawked with mirth, before he straightened Mrs. Tarbottom's lace cap with a tug of his beak.

"As much as I like a picnic, you can't beat a chair!" Mrs. Pendleton laughed. "Now, if you two gentlemen would unfasten the hampers, we can enjoy our p—"

Mrs. Pendleton swatted at a wasp that was dancing between her and the food. "Picnic. That is, if the wasps behave themselves."

"Your house is beautiful." Orsini opened the hamper he had carried and waited for Ambrose to open his too. "And built from coal, after a fashion? Mr. Pendleton built his own fortune, I believe, but I'll wager it took a special sort of lady at his side to do it."

"You are too kind, Mr. Orsini!" Mrs. Pendleton blushed under his gaze, and nudged Ambrose to unfasten his hamper. "But I am sure Mrs. Tarbottom has had a similar experience. What was it like, in the early days, Mrs. Tarbottom? Tough work, I imagine, like it was for me?"

"No, not at all." Mrs. Tarbottom poked her supercilious nose into the air. "My family were already wealthy."

"We Orsinis were wealthy a few hundred years back, then we were not, but we were still happy." Orsini shrugged. His family history was filled with the sort of drama that would keep Ambrose in drama for a long time, after all. "We had palazzos and jewels and the ear of the pope and the doge but money? Not so much. Presently we are back in the financial sun, thanks to a few generations of sensible Orsinis to put us straight. Let us hope the sun never sets."

"Indeed, let it not!" Mrs. Tarbottom nodded. She was trying very hard to look elegant and seductive with a checked cloth on her knee bearing a slice of game pie.

"Bread?" Ambrose offered round a plate with sliced and buttered bread. "There's cheese too if anyone should want it."

"Would you please pass me a slice?" Harriet had asked Orsini rather than her intended. Orsini was sitting nearer, it was true, but it left an unpleasant tang in his mouth. Orsini made great play of taking a piece of bread and offering it on his palm as though it were a fine jewel, his head slightly bowed.

Then he asked her mother, "Madame, might I oblige you?"

"Indeed you may." She leaned toward him, the soft mound of her bosom heading his way at nightmarish speed. Mrs. Tarbottom delicately sniffed the air. "And what is that scent?"

"That'd be the cows, Mrs. Tarbottom," Mrs. Pendleton helpfully informed her. "Home Farm's only on the other side of the rise."

"No—" Mrs. Tarbottom sat back, adjusting her sleeve. "No, I mean to say, Orsini, that cologne you wear, it has such a marvelous aroma."

"Me, Madame?" He pressed his hand to his embroidered brocade. "It is a simple fragrance from the east, delicate as a spring dew."

Mrs. Tarbottom danced her fingertips against her neck. Orsini was taken aback that she dare be so forward as that, for it was bold indeed, there in front of Mrs. Pendleton. "It really is a beautiful scent. I adore it."

"Yes, I noticed it too." Harriet beamed at Orsini. "It is very pleasant."

He lifted his hand to brush away the compliment, watching Harriet's gaze follow the ruby. What a magpie this girl was. What an expensive bride she would make some poor fellow.

From Ambrose's side of the picnic, Orsini heard a distinct cough. Was he trying not to laugh?

"My sister tells me she intends to entertain you with a little post-supper music this evening," Orsini observed, seeing the American girl's face harden. "Alas I cannot be present for I have a mountain of correspondence to attend to. Our mother must know that all is well, and a good many others besides."

"I shall look forward to her performance, as shall Harriet." Mrs. Tarbottom finished her sentence with a stern tone which told her daughter in no uncertain terms that she would look forward to Cosima's performance whether she wished to or not. "What a shame you are to be busy, Orsini! Can you really not put your correspondence aside for the sake of an evening's entertainment?"

"My mother worries so," he said by way of an explanation, sensing an opportunity for a little more mischief. "I believe that a little distance would do my sister and I no harm either, for a good many angry words were exchanged this morning. All is happy now, but I know she will enjoy performing without my scrutiny."

As he fell silent, Orsini shot Ambrose a dark look as though all was certainly not well with him.

Ambrose did a passable impression of his mother's haughty sniff. "Mother, you are looking forward to the contessina's performance as well, are you not?"

"I most certainly am! We are lucky to have such a well-known personage of the stage perform at Pendleton Hall." She smiled down into the valley where her many-windowed house nestled. "Of course, I should love one day to see Cosima on stage."

"And one day, I hope, you will all be my guests at a performance." Orsini opened a bottle of homemade lemonade. "When all of this is behind us and the delightful Signorina T. is instead a delightful Signora P.!"

Mrs. Tarbottom laughed politely. "You are most magnanimous, Mr. Orsini."

"I am known for my tender nature as well as my passions," he replied, meeting her gaze. Those eyes, so avaricious and cold when turned on his sister, flashed with heat now and an understanding passed between them, an unspoken promise. What a horrible thought that was. "Both beat in the heart of Orsini."

And both beat only for Ambrose Pendleton.

And that damn sash.

"Is that so?" Mrs. Tarbottom replied, her voice but a wisp escaping her pouted lips.

"It is why he and I were friends," Ambrose said through a mouthful of cake. He swallowed and went on. "And why I lament the wedge that has come between us — my dear, tender Orsini."

"Time shall mend it," Orsini told him, barely glancing away from his admirer. "If I do not have at you with my weapon first."

Ambrose pursed his lips. To the Tarbottoms, it must have seemed as if Ambrose was reining in an imprecation, but Orsini knew that his lover was reining in something else entirely.

Weapon, indeed.

"There are many stones strewn along life's highway." Mrs. Pendleton nodded sagely. "One steps around them or over them and continues on the way. But the journey is easier if we have our friends beside us."

"Hear, hear!" Orsini filled their glasses then lay back on the grass, his hands pillowed beneath his head and his eyes closed against the sun. Oh to be here alone with Ambrose, the grass beneath them, the clouds above and only kisses in between. That would be perfection.

Chapter Fifteen

After returning from the picnic, Ambrose spent most of the afternoon with his mother and the Tarbottoms, with Orsini tantalizingly within reach but lavishing all his attention on the ladies. Pagolo provided most of the entertainment so Ambrose was free to sit at a discreet distance and write.

"Letters, Mother," he said. But it wasn't letters at all, but a new play—*Avarice and Ambition; or, the Magnate's Misfortune*. The main character was a put-upon young man with a stubborn father, who was about to be hoodwinked by a liar. However, a charming young lady from the continent was about to rescue them all.

Really, where did Ambrose get his ideas from? He just couldn't say—they appeared in his mind as easily as daydreams.

Eventually, as the shadows lengthened and even the gentlemen must be setting their business aside in the study, Orsini was the first to rise. He bowed low to the women and told them all, "Forgive me, ladies, I should look in on my sister before I retire to my correspondence. I am still tired from my journey. I believe I will be abed before you leave the table! Forgive me my absence at dinner, please, it is not my usual way."

With another bow of gratitude at the assorted gentle good wishes from the ladies, Orsini was gone. It seemed to signal that the day was over and the night was to begin. Time to dress for dinner which, far from being its usual chore, was suddenly the start of something even more exciting, for Cosima was to appear once more.

Ambrose bundled up his papers and hurried upstairs to dress. If only he could see Orsini for even a moment or two, to relate what his mother had told him about the grandfather he had never met—the man whose name was never mentioned, as if Barnaby Pendleton had risen from the dust like Adam himself. But Orsini would be in Cosima's chamber by now and by no means could Ambrose enter, or be seen anywhere near the door. He paced back and forth in his own room until it was time to go back downstairs again.

Harriet was on Ambrose's arm as they went in to dinner, but she seemed almost as reluctant as he was. He tried his best not to stare too much at Cosima, but it was very difficult not to. Though Harriet was wearing one of those perfectly chosen gowns, understated and expensive, the height of fashion, Cosima had let fashion be damned. Just as Amadeo Orsini had once told Ambrose proudly that he didn't follow fashion, but led it, so too did Cosima, it seemed.

And for dinner with her rival, Cosima and Pagolo matched. Her dress was bright blue, a shimmering silk that clung to her slender form while the dainty, embroidered yellow and red feathers that formed a pattern at the skirt's hem and along the edges of the sleeves and neckline must have taken somebody — Orsini, probably — long hours and immeasurable patience to stitch. She wore a pendant of a single sapphire set into a teardrop of gold and it nestled against her olive skin, though Ambrose reminded himself that he mustn't look too long at that embroidery nor that jewel, let alone imagine what lay beneath the delicate blue silk. Not for her the fussy hair of Harriet Tarbottom, pinned and primped into place, instead she wore her locks scandalously loose over her shoulders, her only ornament a dainty silver comb into which she had pressed one of Pagolo's fallen feathers. There must be makeup, Ambrose knew, for there was no Cosima without it, but what there was subtle and soft, like the woman his friend had created.

Mrs. Tarbottom's displeasure was clear from her smile, which was curling into a snarl. Whether this was because Cosima had outshone both Mrs. Tarbottom and her daughter, or because Mr. Tarbottom was obviously enchanted by Cosima's outfit, it was impossible to say. If Ambrose had to place a wager, he would have said it was both.

"Now is that an Italian gown, my dear?" And with that question, Mrs. Pendleton was off, initiating a conversation between the women about silks and satins and fashionable cuts. In Ambrose's other ear, all he could hear was his father and Mr. Tarbottom trying to out-compete each other with tales of their industrial exploits.

From the corner of his eye, Ambrose saw Cosima lean forward and gently touch her fingers to Harriet's neck. Then she said, "Those pearls are the most perfect I have ever seen, Miss Tarbottom, they are exquisite! I have an eye for jewelry and I have never seen pearls like these!"

Harriet beamed. "Oh, Cosima, really? What can I say, other than that I am very lucky to have an indulgent papa!"

"Wherever did you find them?" Cosima asked Mr. Tarbottom, who lifted his gaze from the sapphire at her breast and blinked. "The pearls, Mr. Tarbottom?"

"A family heirloom," he said with a wave of his hand, then turned back to Mr. Pendleton to continue their discussion, but Cosima was far from finished.

"No heirloom like this exists without marvelous stories attached to it," she told him sweetly. "Do tell!"

He took a sip from his glass and said, "I confess I hardly recall, Contessina, I'm sorry to disappoint."

And that seemed to be that, as the ladies went back to their chatter and the gentlemen to their talk of money. Eventually cutlery was laid down and the bustle at the table grew less and less until dinner, it seemed, had reached its natural conclusion. Pagolo, who had been contentedly dining from his own silver dish of nuts at Mrs. Pendleton's elbow, now hopped onto her shoulder again and told her in a cryptic, low squawk, "Painting, Mamma!"

Mrs. Pendleton smiled and rose from her chair. "Gentlemen, I'm sure you'll happily delay your port for ten minutes? Only Pagolo and I have something rather exciting to show you. Come, everyone!"

Without waiting to be escorted from dinner—though, arguably, that was Pagolo's role—Mrs. Pendleton swept from the room and beckoned her dinner guests to follow. Through the corridors they went until they were in the entrance hall.

"There! It's been off to have a new frame fitted. Is it not glorious?"

Mrs. Pendleton gestured toward a huge painting that now adorned the hallway. The vast canvas showed the Pendleton family, nearly thirty years ago. They were posed before a backdrop of dark foliage, with Pendleton Hall peeping through the branches, minus its two most recent wings. Barnaby Pendleton was grand in profile, neatly bewigged, his chest proudly puffed. His expression was almost stern, but softened perhaps by the angle of his gaze, which took in his lady and their boys. A younger version of Mrs. Pendleton held out one hand to a lively boy on a hobby horse, a drum around his neck—this was Ambrose's older brother. And on Mrs. Pendleton's lap, nestled in the shiny blue silk of her gown, was a baby in a lace cap and frilly frock. None other than the infant Ambrose Pendleton, his little pink lip stuck out as he held a silver rattle aloft to his mother.

"He's grown a bit since then!" Mrs. Pendleton grinned. "I was young once, truly—and back when Mr. Pendleton took me for his bride, I had no idea what my life would become. Posing for a grand painting—I ask you." She nodded, as if imparting the wisdom of the sages. "But the wheelwright who I nearly married...he's still making wheels."

Cosima gazed up at the painting, her eyes roaming over the magnificent canvas, taking in every inch of it, every individual piece of pigment that went to make up this chronicle of the family's early days. Ambrose watched her as she did, seeing wonder in her eyes and such love that it almost stole his breath. How he adored his friend, the man who would risk everything to keep them together.

"This is magnificent," Cosima eventually breathed. "And, Pen, you are so very, very tiny!"

"So very, very fat! Look at those big round cheeks! And why was it so important that I showed my mother the rattle? I'm sure she'd seen it a hundred times!"

"A christening present from a viscount," Mrs. Pendleton told them, in hushed, reverential tones. Mr. Tarbottom nodded approvingly and his daughter cooed but now Ambrose was looking to his father, who was regarding his wife with a look of affection and —

Sadness, he realized, and he rarely saw Barnaby Pendleton sad. The couple had argued, Ambrose knew it without a doubt, and it sent a pang of regret through him, for theirs was not a union built on conflict. What had his father endured in childhood, pushing down the memory of his own errant parent as though he was never there in the first place, making Cosima the target for his ire against that earlier actress as though all women of the stage must now carry the cross she had forged for Barnaby Pendleton's sorry father.

Not for the first time, Barnaby Pendleton was wrong.

"Now then," Mr. Pendleton said suddenly, turning around to address the group. "Let us process into the drawing room. This has put me in the mood for a little entertainment. Captain Pendleton, will you play for us awhile before the ladies sing?"

"Tradition can hang," Mr. Tarbottom agreed. "We would love to hear you play, Captain!"

Ambrose rarely played now, and never in company as the tremble might come into his hand and make a clown of him. But he cared not if it did tonight. "I would be happy to, Mr. Tarbottom."

Ambrose went ahead of the party into the drawing room. He pushed back the lid of the piano, uttering a silent prayer. *Please, God, let the thing be in tune.*

His parents and their guests—and the parrot—processed in, while Ambrose played a sonata. He tried to find something in the notes, as each plaintively rolled from his fingertips, that might carry him out of this world of determined industrialists and their daughters, of fathers who measured everything in gold.

Ambrose moved into a waltz, playing at sarcastic speed. The notes hurtled from his steady hands as the music moved by faster and faster, losing control like a desperate horse escaping its reins.

"Who would have thought the little plump lad from the painting outside would grow into such a man as this!" He heard his father's voice, filled with pride despite their conflict, and knew he was addressing the portrait of his son in uniform.

"The brave Captain Pendleton!" Harriet declared to the room. At which remark, Ambrose played faster still, his fingers almost stumbling on the keys as the tremble returned and took over his hand.

"Our very own British hero!" Tarbottom declared. "At the vanguard of Philadelphia's industrial might, with me as his guide and mentor!"

Ambrose thundered to a crescendo and the piano was suddenly silent. He turned on the stool to face the party and briskly brushed his hands.

"My dear Cosima," Mrs. Pendleton declared. "Will you sing for us?"

"Miss Tarbottom sings marvelously," her father told them quickly. "Perhaps our young ladies might join forces. Mrs. Pendleton, what say you?"

"I should love to hear the two of them sing!" Mrs. Pendleton replied.

"Figaro's Letter would be perfect," Cosima told him, rising to her feet and crossing to sift through the music available. Ambrose was sure it would, not only for the voices it needed but perhaps the rather germane subject matter. Cosima certainly shared Orsini's mischief, it seemed!

Harriet glided across the room on tiny steps that barely disturbed her gown, hands neatly folded. She leaned in at Orsini's elbow.

"You must sing the soprano," Cosima told her, holding out the music for Harriet to inspect. "I freely confess that I cannot always do justice to the highest notes."

"Now, ladies, are we ready?" Ambrose placed the score on the music stand and rested his fingers on the piano's keys, looking from one woman to the other. His hand had stopped shaking now, and he softly counted the singers in.

Only as they began and Cosima came to sit beside him on the stool did Ambrose realize her ruse. She had surrendered the larger role and taken the more comic, for what was Orsini if not famed for his comedy? Here she was transformed into Susanna, her brow furrowed and her character emerging as she mimed taking down the dictation of the cunning young countess, played rather aptly by the cunning daughter of a cunning industrialist. The rolling of her eyes was just so, the warning looks of bewildered surprise perfectly timed and though Harriet might possess a sweet voice, she seemed unwilling or unable to interpret the song as her adversary was doing, rigid and poised while at her side Cosima pantomimed and playacted and stole the scene from under her nose. On a few occasions Ambrose saw Cosima look to Harriet in an effort to involve her in the comical scene but the other woman was too focused on wringing what emotion she could throttle out of the piece. It was left for the Italian to walk off with the plaudits, Cosima's mimes and attitudes growing sillier with each passing note.

Mrs. Pendleton clapped and laughed, clearly loving every moment. Ambrose glanced up from the piano to see her, and smiled. His gaze moved to the Tarbottoms, who were unimpressed, which made Ambrose smile all the more.

When the song came to an end, Tarbottom told his daughter, "Give us your Ruhe Sanft."

He said this with a sly smile that suggested this was something of a specialty. No doubt this was Harriet's crowning glory, and it would now be employed to devastating effect. "She will break your heart."

Cosima, of course, retained her place beside Ambrose and whispered to him devilishly, "Or shatter your windows."

Ambrose nudged Orsini, biting his lip to avoid laughing once again.

"Very well. I have the music here. Do bear with." Ambrose shuffled through the scores until he found the one he needed. If only it were Orsini who was singing instead.

Harriet did a very good job of her sweet rendition — one could almost suppose that she was capable of loving someone, even someone who didn't have a vast fortune. But the way she took her breaths at the beginning of each line told Ambrose that this was a young lady who had been subjected to music lessons, drilled relentlessly like a private learning to charge with a bayonet. Her voice quavered slightly on her highest notes, in a way designed by music tutors to tug at the heart, which all seemed a little too obvious to Ambrose's ears.

Gentleman that he was, however, Ambrose played on, and when Harriet ended her song, he turned to her and clapped.

"Bravo, Harriet, a wonder!" Mr. Tarbottom decided. "Accomplishments and beauty, her mother's daughter to her toes, is she not."

Her stern faced, thin-lipped mother's daughter. Indeed she was.

"Very pleasant," Mrs. Pendleton replied, as if she had been asked her opinion on the soup they had had for dinner. Still perched beside him, Cosima now rose to her feet.

"I have a little piece to perform, a duet. I need no partner, just..." She turned to the music scores atop the piano and took one from the bottom of the pile. "This is a pretty and funny little song from a piece that Viscount Hartington hopes to produce in London. It has never been heard in public before. An amusing duet for a star-crossed girl and her barrel-chested, pompous but lovable papa. If you would, *Capitano*."

She put the handwritten score before him — the song from *Fleet Fortune*.

Ambrose's hand shook so much when he realized what song Orsini had chosen that he had to sit on his fingers to make the trembling stop. "Ahhh...it is familiar, Cosima. It uses, I believe, a simple melody, so I should be able to play without too much trouble. I shouldn't wish to ruin the song's debut!"

His hand now still, Ambrose placed the music on the stand in front of him.

"One can hardly sing two roles." Cosima beckoned to Pagolo and he fluttered carefully from Mrs. Pendleton's shoulder to the mantel, where he took up his place on the edge. Then Cosima inclined her head to the parrot, whom Ambrose now realized was intended to be her partner in the duet. A pompous little fellow indeed.

"Captain Pendleton." She beamed and placed one delicate hand on Ambrose's shoulder. "Would you be so kind, sir?"

"Absolutely." Ambrose decided to show off a little himself, and embellished the introduction with his own stylistic quirks, until he began the song.

And Cosima, who had already almost stolen the show, now claimed it as her own. The words that he had written, the little melody they had composed together in Italy, now sprang into life as though they were on the stage at Covent Garden. It was as funny as it was beautifully sung—by Cosima at least —and it was so absurd that it was impossible not be charmed. Unless you were Harriet and Mrs. Tarbottom, of course, though they were doing a passable impression of amusement even though their faces looked like they might crack, forced to smile too widely for too long.

Cosima and Pagolo performed their duet and, to Ambrose's delight, he heard his father's chuckles turn into belly laughs. He gave little spontaneous applause now and then, too, his foot tapping along in time with the music each time Cosima flicked her fan toward him. It was a showstopping performance, and by the time it was concluded, with Pagolo finishing up perched atop Cosima's head, it had turned Harriet Tarbottom quite, quite green.

"Oh, Cosima, love—you are right to be on the stage!" Mrs. Pendleton smiled fondly. Mr. Pendleton was nodding his enthusiastic agreement, his cheeks ruddy with humor and alcohol.

"A pretty comical piece," Tarbottom agreed with no trace of the annoyance that he must surely have felt. He looked to his daughter and said, "Harriet's comedy is sublime but her soprano is angelic—it would be a travesty indeed to employ it in anything less than the finest arias. Yet I think comical pieces can be so well chosen for those of us who lack the clarity of Harriet's own soprano."

Ambrose nearly snapped down the lid of the piano. "Would anyone else care to play?"

"You play so beautifully," Cosima told him as she took a seat beside her mother. "Will you not give us a little more to accompany our conversation?"

"I'd be delighted." Ambrose gave a formal bow and returned to the piano. He flipped the piano lid open again. Lazy afternoons spent doodling at the piano while he pondered his plays had not been ill-spent, and he nimbly darted his fingers along the keyboard, chasing after each note. The tremble had gone. For now, at least.

"I am not a man with a love of the theater," Mr. Pendleton admitted, "but when that play appears, I might be convinced to venture along to see it. I confess I have not laughed so hard in a long time. The parrot put me in mind of someone, though I cannot think who!"

Ambrose was about to suggest they go to the theater as a family, but the specter of a square rigger with him on it, heading out across the Atlantic, robbed him of that thought. He shook the vision away. If Barnaby Pendleton had found much in the song to laugh at, then surely—surely there was a chance that his future might be saved? Perhaps his play was good enough after all, not just scribbled whimsy.

"What a shame that Amby won't be able to join us," Mrs. Pendleton remarked. She sipped at her drink with pursed lips.

Presently, as the conversation ebbed and flowed, Mr. Pendleton excused himself as his son knew he was wont to do after one glass of claret too many. The gathering seemed barely to notice his absence, even though even by his standards it seemed drawn out. Eventually, however, as Ambrose played on and the ladies discussed the finer points of Harriet's immense talent for needlepoint, the door opened again and his father returned.

He crossed to the window to peer out at his kingdom and, as the ladies chatted and the parrot dozed, Tarbottom joined his fellow captain of industry to survey the grounds. The two men were speaking, Ambrose could see, but their voices were hushed, their topic of conversation a mystery. Tarbottom was all confidence, he surmised, and had won Pendleton over wholeheartedly.

Ambrose's fingertips froze above the piano keys. Was this really a man he could take on and win? He glanced at his own portrait. The artist had followed his mother's demand and added a brave glitter to her son's eye, but that bravery was not pretend. It had carried Captain Pendleton onto the field of battle at Waterloo. He had helped to defeat Napoleon, and whatever Theodore Tarbottom might think about his wedding plans, Ambrose would defeat him.

Or, at the very least, put up a fight that no fellow could be ashamed of.

Chapter Sixteen

It was torture to wish Cosima goodnight and retire to bed without knowing whether he would see Orsini again that night, but Ambrose had no choice. He couldn't even hope to steal a moment with his father, for Mr. Tarbottom had monopolized him until the very last, talking of the vast returns Barnaby Pendleton's investment promised and the future that awaited in Philadelphia. Yet Ambrose was a man who was used to the nuance of conversation — he was a playwright, after all — and he could hardly help but note that only one man seemed to be parting with any money and it wasn't Theodore Tarbottom.

"*Capitano*, are you abed?" Orsini's voice was a singsong melody as he stepped into the room, clad in the bright suit he had worn for their picnic. "Today has been most eventful, has it not?"

"I can't think where to begin." Ambrose embraced him and softly kissed Orsini's cheek. "Although perhaps — let me apologize on behalf of my father. My mother told me a most tragic story today, which has

been hidden from me all these years. My grandfather —
Orsini, you do not look surprised?"

"Your mother came to see Cosima this morning." He
slipped his arms around Ambrose's waist. "I told her
that you had not compromised the good, Catholic girl
who so loves you and she told me in turn of your
grandfather's ruin. It has simply made me more
determined, Pen. We will save you and see your father
singing the praises of theatrical ladies, for we are not all
ladies of dubious repute. Why, Mrs. Tarbottom is far
more dubious than Cosima has ever been, and her
daughter is more dubious than even that!"

"She was — I did not imagine it, did I? — Mrs.
Tarbottom is somewhat taken by Orsini?" Ambrose
chuckled as he caressed Orsini's beautiful face. "Mr.
Tarbottom was certainly fascinated by Cosima's
bosom, or was that just your sapphire?"

"Miss Harriet Tarbottom, of Philadelphia, was
wearing the pearls stolen from Dowager Viscountess
Hartington, I am sure of it." He lifted his head to look
at Ambrose. "Nobody knows jewels as I, Pen, and those
pearls are the pearls of Lady H."

"I wonder if perhaps Tarbottom bought them,
without realizing they were stolen?" Something, a
notion he had not previously entertained, was nudging
at the edge of Ambrose's mind. "But there is also the
very real chance that the Tarbottoms somehow
contrived to steal the pearls. Though I cannot think
why they should have bothered when they could easily
buy whatever they wish."

"Tomorrow, Pen, I want you to do all you can to keep
the ladies busy so that I might examine the jewels of
Miss Tarbottom and send word back to the city, to ask
those who know such things whether any of them

might be purloined!" Orsini frowned. "Just this morning your mother agreed to invite the dowager to the ball. Let us see what she says when she sees those pearls, and what if Harriet is the creature who has liberated half a dozen other jewels during the season's balls?"

"Will we be in time, I wonder? But my goodness…I'm not sure I'm much good at entertaining ladies, though I shall do my best so that you can examine the jewels undisturbed." Ambrose unfastened the ribbon from Orsini's queue and ran his fingers through the loosened hair. "Unless that lady happens to be called Cosima, that is."

"How I love you, and I long for the day when we walk arm in arm together as Captain and Mrs. Captain, the envy of all." Orsini's elegant fingers began to work at the knot of Ambrose's cravat as the two men kissed again. "Oh, Pen, can we? Would it be a deception too far?"

Ambrose stroked Orsini's delicate face. "You are a woman when you are Cosima. So when you stand beside me at the altar in a gown, what objection can there be?"

"You have yet to ask my mother for my hand in marriage." The cravat whispered free and Orsini cast it aside. "She shall say yes. She is long since resigned to Cosima occupying five days out of every seven!" Then he moved his hands to Ambrose's shoulders, holding him there. "I believe Mamma believes that there is a Cosima, that we have somehow conjured her from the rouge and powder!"

"Perhaps Cosima was your twin, lodged at a palazzo in a different city?" Ambrose brought his hand between them and stroked it over the front of Orsini's breeches. "But tonight, I am most certainly with the brother."

He smiled in reply, dark eyes glittering, and began to lazily unfasten Ambrose's shirt. Once again Orsini's hand caressed his lover's chest through the fabric as, beneath Ambrose's palm, his arousal was all too evident.

Ambrose began to unbutton Orsini's jacket. There were no words then, only kisses and their hands, shedding layers of silk and velvet until Orsini was easing Ambrose's shirt over his head. He threw it aside and dipped his mouth to feather gossamer kisses over his lover's strong shoulders.

Ambrose stroked across Orsini's chest, then down under the waistband of his breeches. "May I?" he whispered into Orsini's hair.

"You may," came the breathless reply. "Please…"

"Thank you, dear heart." Ambrose popped open the buttons, slowly, teasing, and gasped as he reached inside to caress his lover's erection. Orsini gave a sound that was somewhere between a gasp and a whimper, one hand flying up to seize Ambrose's shoulder again. The warmth and the heft of Orsini in his hand made Ambrose sigh. He carefully edged down Orsini's breeches and took him more tightly, stroking with firm rhythm. "Oh, yes, definitely the brother."

"Would it be dreadfully forward of me if I suggested a move to the bed?" His voice was caught in gasps of pleasure, his hips pushing forward.

"To bed!" Ambrose grasped Orsini about the waist and put him over his shoulder. He playfully tapped his bottom as they crossed the room, then lay Orsini down upon the bed. Ambrose grinned at him, embarrassed. "Sorry—I'm enthusiastic."

Orsini, however, was gazing up at him with wide, wondrous eyes, his chest rising and falling quickly. He opened his mouth and closed it, then opened it again and gasped, "Heavens!"

Ambrose felt awkward and silly, but he lay down beside Orsini and kissed him as he took his erection again. His hips stirred against Orsini's as he stroked him, moaning softly against his lips. He felt his lover's hands at the fastening of his own breeches, felt cool air as his erection was freed from the fabric then only warmth, the firm touch of Orsini's fingers encircling him.

He had wanted to ask Orsini if he had been too rough or too fast. Had he failed him as a gentleman by lugging him about like a shepherd running to a haystack with a hoyden? But as he felt Orsini's hand on him, any doubts or fears flew away. For Orsini wanted him—Orsini loved him.

"I had always thought myself too short and too skinny," Orsini murmured, his hand matching Ambrose's pace and rhythm. "But not anymore, not if I can be carried over the threshold!"

"You are neither too short, nor too skinny. You are perfect, and you are beautiful, and you are also—" Ambrose watched his hand move upon Orsini, and whispered, "very hard and very long."

"And very, very enthusiastic."

"I've—I've..." Ambrose's hips rose up off the bed and he struggled to bring them back down again. "I've waited so long for this moment, my love."

"Since that day on the beach when I first saw you," Orsini whispered, tightening his fingers and looking down to watch their hands moving together, "I have dreamed of you like this."

"Let's go back to the beach and swim there together again." Although it wasn't swimming that was on Ambrose's mind, only their intimate, shared pleasure. He had put his hand to himself in this very bed many times before, dreaming of Orsini's touch. Now it was real, and his heart swelled.

"Beneath the moonlight," Orsini whispered, his fingers growing tighter as his hand moved faster. "Will you make love to me on the sand?"

"Yes—just as we should have done back then." Ambrose gasped as his hips rose from the bed again, from the force of the joy that coursed through him. "I'll make you so happy, just as you do me."

"I love you," Orsini whispered as he entwined his leg with Ambrose's and kissed him again and again, his tongue teasing and exploring as they brought each other to the edge of that wonderfully overwhelming, helpless pleasure.

Ambrose forgot how to speak, existing only in the place where their bodies and their pleasure met. He stroked Orsini all the faster, sensing that his lover was nearing his bliss just as Ambrose was. It was the Italian who surrendered first, shuddering through his pleasure with a soft, almost singsong cry of delight, his large eyes fluttering closed in the moments of his deepest ecstasy. Yet his hand didn't pause or slow and his kisses didn't falter. The sight of Orsini reaching his peak overwhelmed Ambrose with a sense of such tender beauty that his own bliss soon followed. This time, when his hips rose from the bed, he made no attempt to still them, and all the love he had for Orsini blossomed into his lover's hand. He brought Orsini into his trembling arms, half-undressed and glorious both.

"*Amore mio*," Orsini whispered, snuggling his soft, slight body against Ambrose's muscular form. "My soldier."

A rather shaky soldier at that moment, but Ambrose smiled. "You are quite the loveliest person on earth. I cannot tell you how happy I am to lie here, like this, with you."

"And at the ball, will you wear your uniform?"

"Oh, but of course! A proper captain, with shiny leather boots and well-fitted breeches, an elegant tunic and —" Ambrose punctuated each word with a kiss. "Lots. Of. Gold. Braid."

Orsini settled back onto the mattress and blinked up at his beloved, his eyes so bewitching and dark that Ambrose felt as though he might fall into them. "Will you wear it for our wedding?"

Ambrose smiled gently. A wedding, between himself and Orsini, between Ambrose Pendleton and the man he had loved so long and had never thought he would hold. "If my darling wishes it."

"You in your uniform, and me in my military-inspired gown, with hair cascading down over my back," Orsini murmured. "Perfect."

"And just think, when we first met you said I was a stuffy English gent." Ambrose grinned at their debauched appearance. "I am not such a stuffy English gent now!"

"You never were really, *tato*." Orsini lazily entwined his fingers with Ambrose's. "You have always been my *capitano*."

Ambrose lay down on the bed beside Orsini, feeling the heat of his body against him. He brushed his lips against his Orsini's, tangling a delicate kiss before it grew deeper. He felt Orsini's arm slip around his waist and draw them together, holding him there. Ambrose sighed into their kiss at the touch of Orsini's skin as he fluttered his fingertips over his lover's body. Reverentially they eased each other from what remained of their clothes, what remained of the world.

"Make love to me, Captain." Orsini sighed. "Make me yours."

Ambrose gazed into Orsini's dark, gold-flecked eyes. All he had ever wanted was here in his arms. All he could see in Orsini's face was desire and love. He kissed Orsini again, caressing him, stroking his way down his back. As they continued to kiss, more heated now with each breath, Ambrose danced his fingers at the base of Orsini's spine, then tenderly circled his way farther down, catching Orsini's every melodious sigh with his lips.

One of those graceful hands, elegant and assured, moved to rest on Ambrose's buttock, stroking the firm skin appreciatively. The other slid in sinuous patterns over Ambrose's muscular back, as toned and contoured as Orsini was slender and soft.

Ambrose gently rolled their entwined bodies over until Orsini was lying beneath him. He broke from their fevered kisses, and smiled gently. Ambrose was not without experience, but he loathed the very idea that he could spoil their first encounter with enthusiastic yet ill-timed passion.

"I want you so much, my Orsini, my Cosima—will you guide me?"

"Have you never—" He blinked then smiled rather serenely. "A man so handsome as you?"

"I'm not entirely vestal." Ambrose blushed. "But...you're too precious to be treated with roughness. Do you — do you mind me being above you? Am I heavy?"

"I would not like roughness," Orsini agreed, reaching up to stroke his fingertips down Ambrose's face. "But I am rather partial to a strong sort of fellow. A man who is a man."

Ambrose pushed himself up, his hands on either side of Orsini's face. He glanced down at their bodies. "I am fairly strong."

"I am fairly delicate." Orsini blinked. It was a coquette's blink. "And you are very big. But I will not break, Captain."

"Erm…big. Yes." Ambrose blushed even more. His erection had returned with impressive yet unsurprising speed. He moved a little so that he might stroke his way down Orsini's chest, teasing Orsini's nipples as he dropped his hand farther still until he closed his fingers around Orsini's revived erection. He nibbled Orsini's ear as he began to pleasure his lover again with firm strokes. Gently holding his other hand before Orsini's lips, Ambrose asked, his voice low and catching with desire, "Will you prepare me?"

"You have a most delightful bloom to your cheeks," Orsini told him sweetly. Then he lifted his head just a little and drew his tongue over Ambrose's palm, holding his gaze all the time.

Ambrose kissed Orsini a thank you, and, lying between Orsini's legs, applied his hand to his erection. He touched the tip of his nose against Orsini's, gazing at those glittering, loving eyes as he gently brought their bodies together. They could not be any closer, and Ambrose had no wish to let Orsini go.

"*Amore mio*," his lover sighed, lifting his hips. His legs encircled Ambrose's waist, holding him there as the two men began to move together. Orsini's lips parted slightly and he let out a sigh of unrestrained pleasure, his hands clutching at Ambrose's back.

Ambrose kissed his way around Orsini's face, pressing his mouth to his lover's neck as Orsini arched back against the pillow in delight. The closeness of Orsini's body, and the pleasure Ambrose felt, and which he was bringing to his lover, drove him on. To think that he had never imagined his love for Orsini was returned—but it was—twofold, threefold. Ambrose didn't pause in his lovemaking, for he was intoxicated by adoration for his theatrical.

Orsini's mouth slipped over Ambrose's jaw until his teeth were nibbling at his lover's ear, his voice a whisper as he purred soft words of affection. His hands slid down to grip Ambrose's bottom tight, encouraging him to thrust harder.

Ambrose sighed. Still clutching Orsini's erection, he stroked him as best he could as their bodies were pressed close, for he did not want to deny Orsini any pleasure that he could possibly bestow.

"How do you want me, darling? Gentle, like this?" Ambrose delicately moved his hips, almost as if in a dance. "Or do you like to be taken by an energetic sort of fellow—like this?" He moved a hand to Orsini's waist, holding him steady as Ambrose thrust with increasing vigor.

Orsini's reaction gave him his answer, as he gave a cry of delighted pleasure and arched his back from the mattress. His kisses were hungrier than ever and, in reply to Ambrose's heated thrusts, he slipped his hand lower on his lover's bottom, clutching tight until, in one smooth movement, he pressed one finger between Ambrose's buttocks.

At Orsini's touch, Ambrose thrust inside him as far as he could, throwing back his head as he moaned with joy. The delicious sensation of Orsini's touch had brought Ambrose to the verge of bliss again, and he struggled to keep his pleasure in reserve as he thrust harder still.

Yet Orsini seemed intent on pushing him further along to his climax, adding a second finger as he moved his hand in time with Ambrose's hips. His kisses were deep and fierce, his own hips rising from the bed with each thrust.

Ambrose groaned deeply, trembling once more on the edge of bliss. Though his pleasure had increased, he went on stroking Orsini. This was without doubt the most perfect bedchamber encounter of his life. There was so much joyful debauching to be had with his darling lover.

"Pen," Orsini cooed, arching his back from the bed as, in one perfect thrust of his hips, his orgasm claimed him. He clutched one hand against Ambrose's bottom, the fingers of the other still working at him.

"Amadeo Orsin—" But Ambrose couldn't frame the words as the sensuous movement of Orsini below him, around him, was too irresistible. His orgasm finally took him as his hips bucked firmly against Orsini one last time. He sagged down onto his lover, still holding him, their bodies slick with perspiration as they exchanged slow, sloppy kisses.

"I shall be the finest bride you could wish for," Orsini whispered. "I will love you until the end of days."

"And I the most true, most faithful, most adoring of husbands." Ambrose combed his fingers through Orsini's hair and gazed at him, utterly dazzled by his lover. Orsini blinked up at him, his eyes dreamy and joyous. Then he lifted his head a little and kissed Ambrose tenderly.

The lovers kissed, adoring and soft with bliss, and Ambrose began to slide into sleep, his arms around his Orsini. The last he knew were his lover's embrace and the gentle, harmonious sound of their mingled, dreaming sighs.

Chapter Seventeen

What a day it had been for Amadeo Orsini. Exhausting, frustrating and ultimately, when it came to his scheme to unmask Harriet Tarbottom as a thief, pointless. To make matters worse, he had barely glimpsed his lover since breakfast thanks to the necessary comings and goings of the day and their plan.

The morning had begun in fine style in the arms of the captain, making love as the dawn bathed them in its gentle light. To leave that embrace, those kisses, had not been easy, but leave them he must and long before the household awakened, Amadeo Orsini was supposedly bound for business. Clad in orange silk, he bade farewell to the maids and footmen, merrily dismissing their offers of horse or phaeton in favor of a bracing walk. No doubt they thought their Italian visitor quite mad, since his bracing walk would be long indeed were it to take him into town, but they were too well-versed in the ways of service to inquire further. Of course none inquired of the valise that swung from his arm either, concealed within it his stays, as well a sensible walking dress and spencer for Cosima while a reticule that had been a gift from a Russian duchess of some renown contained the actor's makeup and a mirror. Thank heavens his bohemian creation preferred her hair loose, for at least there was no call to squash a bonnet in there too!

Mere minutes after Orsini left the house he could be found only by the most observant, concealed in the shade of a thicket of trees. There he became La Cosima again, slipping into her gown and sensible boots and painting on her dainty face. Into the valise went the trappings of Amadeo Orsini and he concealed it beneath the trees, satisfied it would remain undiscovered until nightfall.

Nobody questioned Cosima when she strolled back to Pendleton Hall, for it was her concern whether she woke early and strolled as the sun rose. Indeed, in doing so she had happily coincided with her brother on his own constitutional, or so she told the household who bustled about their duties as their employers slept on. Returning from her morning walk and a fond meeting with her brother, Cosima was full of the joys of summer at breakfast. No one could steal the smile from her face, least of all the captain when he joined the party around the table, and it was all Orsini could do not to gaze at Ambrose quite openly, filled with memories of the night they had spent together and those strong hands on his body. What kisses they had shared, and what strength they had given him for the day ahead.

Orsini had glided on his happiness upstairs to examine the jewels of Harriet Tarbottom, leaving his companions with tales of a letter that must be written to his mother in Scotland. Poor Ambrose was to escort the ladies around the grounds as Orsini went about his subterfuge but of course, nothing could be as simple as all that.

Harriet Tarbottom was a rather security conscious sort of girl, it seemed, for the walnut box of jewels was locked, its brass lock and bands holding firm against every hairpin and blade Orsini could find. Worse still, that failure was compounded by an afternoon spent sitting with the blasted Tarbottom women, listening to the droning catalogue of Harriet's accomplishments, when they should have been listing the charges against her for robbery, he was sure. Yet at least Pen was there too, sitting quietly at the writing desk, scribbling away at his work. It was a privilege to watch, and none but Orsini knew what an artist was in their midst.

And a thief too.

Those pearls…

He would see her accused though, and the pearls would be returned to the elderly lady who mourned them even now.

Orsini was missed at dinner, of course, by none more than Mrs. Tarbottom, though she did her best to keep her interest subtle. In her eyes that lust burned again and Orsini was sure her husband must know — how could he not? Perhaps he blessed it, for it meant he was spared her attentions. One could hardly blame him for that.

What a frightful family they were.

Seducers and braggarts and thieves, one and all.

And he had met such charming Americans. They were letting down their whole people.

After her early start, bedtime for Cosima came a little earlier than it did for her friends and, her face washed clean and concealed beneath a heavy cloak, she stole from the house one last time. The moonlight was her lantern as she hurried back to the thicket where she became Orsini once more, wearing the very clothes in which he had left the house that morning.

How exhausting this would be as a life!

One would never get anything done.

It was with a sigh of relief that Orsini greeted the porter at the door, the valise swinging from his hand as he did. A long day of walking and business, he reminded himself as he heard the key turn in the lock to admit him, nothing more than that.

"What a day of it!" Orsini told the porter with a suitably elaborate stifled yawn. "I spied a light in the drawing room. Is there still time to wish the family a fond goodnight?'

"Indeed there is, sir. Shall I take your bag?" The porter reached one immaculate, white-gloved hand toward the valise.

"A gift for my sister," Orsini told him, seized with a sudden naughty plan. Let Cosima steal along to Ambrose's room tonight. Or better yet, Orsini and Cosima as one, silk gent's suit, bosoms and full female face! "Put it in my room, please. I shall unpack it tomorrow."

A quick goodnight then upstairs, makeup, stays and a couple of feathers then off to see Pen. He smiled to think of it. *If only I'd thought of the idea before I washed the powder off!*

But Orsini must show his face, or questions would be asked.

"Thank you, sir." The porter bowed as though the most mundane of tasks was something to be grateful for. He went off into the house with the valise, leaving

Orsini to go to the drawing room. His hand was on the door when he glanced down and saw, on his finger, Cosima's most dazzling diamond ring, that had so attracted the attention of Harriet at dinner.

Almost.

Orsini slipped the ring into his pocket and stepped into the room, calling, "*Ciao*, all, *ciao*, Cos —"

He tutted upon seeing that his sister was not present, but bowed to the rest of the party. "What a day I have had, I declare myself quite exhausted yet I could not be so rude as to fail to wish you goodnight!"

"How charming of you, Mr. Orsini!" Mrs. Pendleton smiled. "I do hope you were able to complete all your business. Perhaps we shall see more of you tomorrow?"

Ambrose had risen from his chair as Orsini had come in. "I must retire myself. Goodnight, all. And Mother, I'm sure we shall see Orsini tomorrow if he has attended to all his affairs today."

Mrs. Tarbottom yawned delicately. "I must retire myself."

"I might tell all of you one very important thing." Orsini laughed, draping his hand theatrically over his brow. "Never attempt to walk to town. It is a long, long, long way."

At the third long he looked toward Ambrose, sure that his lover would appreciate the rather saucy double meaning he intended. It seemed to work, as Ambrose fiddled with his neckcloth as if it was suddenly too tight.

"Walk from here?" Mr. Pendleton laughed and shook his head. "Good heavens, sir, I'm surprised to see you back before tomorrow! Was the mail coach glad of your custom?"

"Delighted." Orsini laughed. "Or I might not have found Pendleton Hall again! I confess I failed to reach town at all, but had a delightful day exploring your county instead, especially one or two rather well-stocked inns. I shall sleep soundly tonight!"

"I'm sure you will, Mr. Orsini!" Mrs. Pendleton laughed.

Mrs. Tarbottom ushered Harriet from her seat. The younger woman wrinkled up her nose in obvious disdain at being packed off to bed, but Mrs. Tarbottom appeared not to brook any refusal.

"We shall see you all in the morning," Mrs. Tarbottom announced to the room. She let Harriet go ahead of her into the corridor. Apparently unseen by everyone else, Mrs. Tarbottom ran her fingertip across the back of Orsini's hand as she passed him in the doorway. He smiled in response, hoping it didn't come out as a grimace.

With a low bow to those still remaining, Orsini followed the party from the room. What delightful torture to say goodnight, but what fun awaited once he had donned his costume of Cosima and Amadeo combined. He would not think of the touch of the American's cold fingertip, though it sent a shiver through him despite the warmth of the night.

At the top of the stairs the group went their separate ways, with Pagolo singing Mrs. Pendleton a gentle song as they receded along the corridor. Orsini slipped into his own room and began to undress again, for what felt like the hundredth time that day. From the valise he took Cosima's stays, which he fastened himself into. Then he sat at the dressing table once more. He took his time now because he could afford to, safe in the knowledge that there was no point in going anywhere until the household was sleeping. This was the greatest risk he had dared to take since he arrived here, but once the hallways were dark and the only sound that of slumber, it was a risk that he was willing to take. After all, were he to be disturbed the worst that would be suspected was the revelation that Cosima had taken to trysting while disguised as a boy, and he suspected that nobody would be at all surprised. Only when Cosima blinked back from the mirror did Orsini pick up his shirt, satisfied that the time had come to finish dressing.

Someone knocked at Orsini's door, and a swish of fabric suggested it was Ambrose in his banyan.

With the tasseled belt?

A loud whisper followed that told Orsini it was most certainly not Ambrose, but the insinuating voice of Mrs. Tarbottom.

"Orsini...you dropped something while you were downstairs. A button. You dropped a button."

Oh God.

The door handle was already turning and Orsini, his face painted as Cosima, his padded stays there for all to see, was caught in the middle of the room. He looked left and right then, in a scene he would reject from his own plays as too ridiculous to be believed, darted behind the heavy curtains that hung down to the floor. A cool breeze blew through the open window and Orsini shivered, peering through a sliver in the fabric at the candlelit room beyond.

Don't come in, he prayed, drawing the curtains firmly together. *Please, madame, stay on the other side of that door.*

The heavy wooden door creaked as it slowly opened. Footsteps on the polished wooden floorboards made it clear that Mrs. Tarbottom had crossed the threshold.

She closed the door behind her with a soft click, then pattered over the floor.

"You naughty Italian gentleman—you're here somewhere, I know it!" Her husky voice was rich with lust, a tone Orsini had of course never heard her use. It wasn't a timbre that any married woman should use to address a man who was not her husband, but Mrs. Tarbottom's boldness told Orsini that this wasn't her first attempt at making a cuckold of the American industrialist.

He heard her feet moving around the room then the sound of the pillows being arranged and, horror of horrors, rustling sheets. She was on or—heaven forbid—*in* his bed and he was trapped, half-Cosima, half-Orsini, behind the curtain.

She won't stay.

Yet stay she did, and long minutes ticked by as each waited, one for an arrival, one for a departure, both in vain. There was nothing for it, Orsini decided from his helpless perch on the window seat. He would have to risk his neck again.

Moving painfully slowly lest he disturb the curtain, Orsini tugged his shirt into the waistband of his breeches and scrambled out through the open window and onto the ivy. Then, as though the devil himself were at Orsini's heels, he clambered down onto solid ground.

Orsini stood and peered up at the house, breathing deeply. The night was warm but a cool breeze touched his skin, so he pulled his shirt on over the stays, glad at least that he hadn't taken off any more of his suit before he was disturbed. Yet where could he go now, with the house locked up and his own room occupied by the enemy? Other windows on the first floor were open but he could hardly risk climbing into Theodore Tarbottom's bedroom, let alone Mr. Pendleton's. In fact, the only window he could risk was Ambrose's, and open it might be, but the ivy had yet to climb far enough around Pendleton Hall to make it accessible from the ground.

For a while Orsini made a circuit of the building, yet it was shut up tight against invasion. At the ornamental fountain in the garden he paused and considered washing away Cosima's face but what was worse than Cosima in her brother's clothes than her brother with bosoms? Instead he scooped up a handful of stones and returned to Ambrose's window. Then, with the accompanying chirrups of the nightbirds as the only sound in the almost still night, Orsini began to throw pebbles up at the panes of his lover's window, missing three times for every one that tapped against the glass.

A gap appeared in the closed curtains and a sliver of Ambrose's face appeared. He was blinking, dazed, as if he'd only just fallen asleep and was now awake. Then his gaze roamed down to the terrace below his window, and he began to smile. He opened the window and leaned out.

"Ors—? Cos—Evening!" Ambrose leaned out a little farther. "What are you up to down there?"

"Help!" Orsini whispered, laughing despite himself. He made a gesture that was intended to indicate a door being unlocked, but somehow it managed to look utterly obscene. Then he shrugged glanced around, seized by the spirit of mischief. "Fancy a wander?"

Ambrose grinned. "Why not? I'll be down in a moment!" He disappeared from the window and drew the curtains. Long minutes passed and a door somewhere along the terrace opened to reveal

Ambrose wearing boots, breeches and his banyan. His toned chest showed between the folds of loose fabric.

"It's a warm night," Ambrose told him by way of explanation. Orsini trotted over to his friend and slipped his arms around Ambrose's waist. Instead of replying he simply greeted him with a kiss, any concerns melting away now they were together once more.

"This day has not been a good one." Orsini pouted. "But it has already improved."

"It most certainly has." Ambrose gave him a cautious kiss in return. "Come, let us walk—there is a delightful corner of these gardens where we might dip our toes and speak without eavesdroppers."

"Then lead on, *Capitano*, for a dip sounds perfect to me!"

They headed down from the terrace onto the lawn, taking a walk that was shaded with thick hedges. Ambrose looked over his shoulder until, presumably satisfied that they would be unseen from the house, he held Orsini's hand and they walked on with their fingers entwined.

"It is not far, but it is secluded. A spot where I go when I need peace for reflection." Ambrose spoke fondly of the place and once more Orsini was reminded of the unconscionable wrench his lover would face if he was forced to leave England forever. "Now pray tell me why the day has been a bad one."

"The jewel box was locked," Orsini told him, hearing frustration in his own voice. "Understandable, one imagines, but I can only hope that it will not always be so. Then to spend all day with those dreadful women as you worked! Is it a new play, Pen? Your father so adored Cosima's song last night, did he not?"

"I wonder where Harriet keeps the key?" Ambrose pondered this a moment, then grimaced. "Somewhere I should not like to venture, I expect! But yes, I wrote much today—a play about an ambitious industrialist who overreaches himself and—oh, but I cannot give it away. Wait until it is finished and you shall be the first to read it, I promise! As for Cosima's song, my father did indeed enjoy it. What he would say if he discovered that I had written it, I daren't imagine."

"I hope that Lord Hartington accepts the invitation to the ball, for I know that his mother's pearls are in that box," Orsini told him. Then he opened his eyes wide and gasped, "You will never guess who is in my bed as we speak, Pen!"

Ambrose stared at him, wide-eyed. "I think I can! Of all the—so this is how you happen to be outside, half-Cosima'd? To escape the unwanted attentions of Mrs. Tarbottom? Good lord."

"I had an idea that I would creep along to see you, *tato*, as Cosima herself, clad saucily in the clothes of a boy. It is like something from one of your plays, after all!" He grinned, then winced. "But Signora Tarbottom stole into my room and I had no choice but to flee the field before she discovered me!"

"Or did anything else!" Disgust rang in Ambrose's voice. "I wonder what my father would say if I were to tell him? Though I doubt he would believe me—he would think it a mere lie to discredit the Tarbottoms and end this dreadful engagement. But…look before you, Orsini. Under starlight, do you see how beautiful this corner is?"

Sheltered from the gaze of the innumerable darkened windows by a bower of pale pink roses that joined a hedge that had been trimmed to resemble a peacock to another that looked like a vast acorn, Orsini smiled. He felt as though they were the only men on earth who were awake at this moment, the soft breeze singing through the trees on the horizon just as he had sung Cosima's song, a voice of longing and love.

In America Ambrose would have a home grander than even this, grander than any Prince Regent even, and a wife who was beautiful and accomplished and everything society thought a young lady should be, and he would be the most unhappy man alive. Sitting in his office, moving men and money around, counting his gold, raising a glass to his own accomplishments in clubs full of Theodore Tarbottoms and Barnaby Pendletons, wasting sadly away amid the splendor.

Ambrose wasn't made for a life like that, and Orsini would not let it claim him.

Orsini clutched at his arm as though he was a blushing young lady, then whispered, "To Gretna, Captain?"

"In a heartbeat!" Ambrose whispered in reply. He brought Orsini into his arms. "Might I kiss you again, my darling Orsini?"

"Of course you should." Orsini wrapped his arms around Ambrose's waist, his full lips already brushing against Ambrose's, the scent of powder and perfume filling the air around them. "As often and as keenly as you wish."

"Then I shall—whatever my darling wishes." Ambrose tightened his embrace and sighed as his lips met Orsini's in a delicate kiss.

But it didn't remain delicate for long. Orsini was utterly intoxicated by his lover, by the man he had longed for all those years. And he had thought it hopeless. Now, he knew, it was not. He felt affection in every touch, not lust, even though their kiss deepened and became ever more passionate. Ambrose was positively bewitching, as much now as he was years ago when they toured the continent as carefree youths. He slid his hands over Ambrose's back, tracing the contours until one palm came to rest very firmly on his buttock.

And squeezed.

Taken by surprise, Ambrose groaned into their kiss. Orsini slipped his hand between their bodies and stroked it over his lover's breeches, seeking out the erection that strained at the fabric. He began to softly caress it, all the time kissing him with that same heated intensity.

And where might this lead?

Hopefully to two men, splashing naked in the lake, just as they once had swum together naked in the sea.

Gasping with pleasure, Ambrose brought his hand between them and stroked his way to Orsini's erection and began to unbutton him.

Ambrose broke from the kiss to whisper, close to Orsini's ear, "May I? Can I touch you without the hindrance of clothes, my love?"

"Oh yes," came the answering whisper, full of longing and heat. "Please, Pen."

Ambrose grinned as he nimbly unfastened Orsini's buttons and brought down the flap on his breeches. It was a work of moments to slip inside, and both men sighed as Ambrose's strong hand closed around Orsini's erection. Ambrose paused to enjoy the firmness and heft of it before he began to stroke with determined movements.

There was the slightest change in Orsini's manner, a lessening of tension in his muscles, a softening of his kisses into something deeper than before. He seemed to sink into Ambrose's arms, his own hand still stroking over his breeches, his breath mingling with the softest sounds of pleasure.

"I've wanted you for so long, Pen, dreamed of you all these years." Orsini abandoned words and returned to kisses. He felt Ambrose move into his touch, and Orsini matched his rhythm to his lover's, wanting more than anything to bring pleasure to this man, yet Ambrose's hand on him stole his breath as well as his heart and he felt Ambrose's fingers move over his back until they clutched his long hair. The night was theirs alone, full of secrets and sighs.

Orsini's soft gasps were more frequent in reply, the fingers that clutched at his hair growing tighter as his release approached. His hips moved with a little more force, pushing into Ambrose's hand until, with a stifled cry of pleasure, Orsini finally reached his climax.

"A year from now we will come back here," Orsini told Ambrose, bringing his hand up to caress his lover's face, "as husband and — Husband and Cosima, wife and husband in one. I love you, *mio capitano*."

"And I love you, dear Orsini." Ambrose guided them to a bench in the hollow of the roses and they sat down together.

"Will you allow your Orsini to take your mind from your worries?" Orsini whispered softly, his hand stroking Ambrose still, already reaching down to unfasten Ambrose's breeches. He slid one hand inside, gently caressing the erection that he found there and purred, "As only Orsini can?"

A soft groan escaped Ambrose's lips as Orsini touched him. He leaned back against the bench and half-closed his eyes.

"My darling Orsini, how I've longed for this moment."

One more kiss found Ambrose's lips, then Orsini slipped from the bench to kneel on the grass at his lover's feet. He gazed up at Ambrose even as he dipped his head to stroke the tip of his tongue along the shaft of his erection.

Ambrose sank his fingers into Orsini's hair, gasping in response to Orsini's tongue.

Those full lips that Ambrose had kissed so fervently now formed into a perfect, sensuous O. Orsini slowly took Ambrose's erection into his mouth, teasing the very tip with soft, delicate strokes from his tongue. All the time he was gazing up at Ambrose with eyes that were lit with love, his hands settling softly against his thighs.

There was only here, only now, only the bench and the garden and Orsini and Ambrose. Orsini could feel Ambrose battling to keep his hips on the bench, to stop them rising up to Orsini's questing mouth with most ungentlemanly haste.

"I love you, Orsini!" Ambrose moaned. In reply, Orsini lowered his head farther, taking Ambrose fully into his mouth even as his hands tightened, holding Ambrose's legs against the bench. Now he moved with more purpose, his tongue sweeping and tasting, the tightness of his lips as he rose and fell, driving his lover on.

A gentleman wasn't supposed to creep about gardens in the dark, he wasn't supposed to cavort with theatricals. He was supposed to be a good son and do as his parents wished and find a bride who would please him or risk them finding him one who did not.

But Orsini knew that Captain Ambrose Pendleton no longer cared. He had spent years doing what he was supposed to do, and it had not brought him happiness. The joy they had found together was all that they wanted. On and on it went, Orsini's hands keeping him down, his mouth drawing him on to the pinnacle of pleasure and all the time those eyes, that loving gaze, was fixed on him. Orsini heard soft murmurs of pleasure in Ambrose's throat, mingling with the sounds of the night.

Despite Orsini's efforts to hold him down, Ambrose's hips bucked up off the bench and his bliss claimed him.

All was quiet until Ambrose murmured, "Thank you, darling Orsini — thank you!" He sagged back against the bench, a soft smile on his lips.

Orsini, ever the theatrical, dabbed demurely at his lips with a lace-edged handkerchief then sprang nimbly to his feet and dropped down onto the bench. He rested his head on Ambrose's shoulder and gave a happy sigh.

"I'll definitely have to marry you now!" Ambrose joked.

"You will!" Orsini agreed. "And I shall be a most fetching bride."

The warm night was still and very quiet as Ambrose led Orsini to the edge of the lake. There, they threw aside their clothes and swam together in the cool water, as happy and as free as Orsini remembered they had been in their days under the hot Italian sun. Until, from the stableyard, came the shimmering chime of the clock striking one.

Chapter Eighteen

As the day of the ball approached and guests began to arrive in the house, life settled down for Amadeo Orsini somewhat. Two days had passed since Mrs. Tarbottom had crept into his room and for those two days, thanks to the arrival of various men far more titled and impressive than he, the social climbing Americans were suitably occupied with filling up their already bulging address books. To be Cosima and Orsini was easier too, for with the new arrivals came opportunities for Orsini to supposedly play cards or drink port or go out riding with the gents, while Cosima was strolling with the ladies or entertaining with gentle songs and readings.

Nobody watched the men as they did the ladies, and when the women retired to bed, Orsini could indulge himself with real games or cards and real glasses of port but better than that, with the company of Captain Ambrose Pendleton. After all, two men, once old friends now torn asunder, might stroll together by moonlight as they renewed that friendship, and nobody would suspect that anything was out of the ordinary whatsoever. And if, as they strolled, they kissed or found a hidden spot in the trees and did more than that, then it was nobody's concern but their own.

The ladies had broken into parties this particular afternoon, some to walk, some to ride, some to read and Cosima, sensitive soul that she was, had taken the opportunity to retire for an hour or so. That freed Orsini to receive an item of particular note, packaged with care amid much ribbon and paper. He excitedly unwrapped the costumes that he would wear to the masked ball, a matching set for brother and sister that were intended to take away the breath of all who saw them. Audacious, he knew, but one way or another, both would have to be seen, for there could be no room for doubt. Both Orsinis must attend. How he longed for something more simple though, yet still the reply from the viscount did not come.

Say you will be at the ball, he begged the Fates. *Say yes.*

He wrapped up the costumes again and carried them with great care across the room. There he opened the door to the small anteroom that had served as an admirable closet for Orsini's many garments and jewels and laid them out side by side, ready for the ball. Then he returned to the bedroom, sure that a little trip to Ambrose might be in order, simply because twelve hours had passed since they had shared an embrace.

What a glorious thing it is to be loved by Ambrose Pendleton.

And God help whoever now commanded Mrs. Tarbottom's amorous attention!

He hadn't got very far before a figure stepped out from a doorway and blocked his path. The proud bosom and pouting lips of Mrs. Tarbottom.

"Orsini, why, there you are! I've been searching high and low for you." Her honeyed, insinuating voice made Orsini's skin itch. He was an actor, though, and swallowed his distaste into a smile.

"Madame," Orsini purred, dropping into a bow. "I have been unforgivably preoccupied. My sister, you understand."

"Such a pity for the girl—and you so devoted to her." Mrs. Tarbottom touched the cuff of Orsini's sleeve. "I wager you'd do anything to make her unhappy situation better if you could."

She can't be suggesting—

"It matters not what I would do." He sighed. "The decision has been taken by the fathers, has it not? Your daughter's engagement is to be announced at the ball, I believe."

"I can be a very persuasive woman if I must." Mrs. Tarbottom smiled proudly. "My husband needs my family's money and connections to maintain his business interests—he must keep me happy. So if I were to tell him I'm very unhappy at the impending nuptials between my Harriet and Captain Pendleton, he would call it off."

Where this was going, Orsini wasn't sure, but he was certain of one thing and that was the simple fact that, if she was about to propose some dreadful quid pro quo, then she wouldn't do it in a corridor.

For that fact alone, Orsini told himself, *be grateful.*

"Come, Orsini, let us converse in private." Mrs. Pendleton returned her hand to his sleeve. "I promise you won't be disappointed."

Orsini's confidence evaporated not only at her words and touch, but at the glimmer in her pale eyes. It was like a vulture spying carrion and preparing to strip the unfortunate carcass to its bones. Yet Orsini could only nod, and allow her to lead the way to the scaffold.

Mrs. Tarbottom led him along the corridor to her sitting room. Her bed, looming like a sacrificial altar, was just visible through the connecting door. "Do sit, Mr. Orsini. It's so kind of you to help me with my Italian lessons." She spoke loudly, as if hoping that anyone overhearing would think their meeting entirely innocent. Orsini settled on the sofa, a fly in the spider's web. Yet perhaps he would be proved wrong. Perhaps she was as kind as she seemed brittle. Perhaps the gold cross she always wore was not simply for clutching, but meant something to the lady after all.

Prove me wrong about you.

Mrs. Tarbottom sat down on the sofa and half-draped herself over its arm. She twirled one of her abundant ringlets around her finger and smiled. "Well, Orsini, here we are... I wonder, how you would like to go on a little trip?"

"Alas, Madame, I can go nowhere today," he replied, not quite following. "I have an appointment on horseback in ten minutes with a gent who I believe owns most of Devon. So many interesting people are gathering for the ball, do you not think?"

"Indeed they are." Mrs. Tarbottom arched her eyebrow. "I shall be quick and to the point. I think it will be best for everyone if I do. Before we Tarbottoms return to America, we intend to make a trip around England, and I would very much like it if you should accompany us. If you agree, then, simply put—I will intervene in my husband's plans and the captain won't be marrying my daughter. He will be able to stay here in England, rigid and uncomfortable in his neckcloth, and perhaps marrying your sister. I can guess that a marriage would be expedient—I know what can cause a woman to faint, Orsini. I am not a fool."

For a moment, he was speechless. A tour of England in return for a future with Ambrose? That was far too easy though, as well he knew.

Act pretty but dim, Orsini decided.

"You would truly do my sister such a kindness?" he asked. "I warn you, I would be a dreadful tour guide. I hardly know England at all!"

Mrs. Tarbottom laughed, shaking her head. "Tour guide? Oh, no, Orsini, it is not as a guide that I need you. I rather need instead your company."

She shifted toward him a little along the sofa, one elbow resting on its back as she played with her hair. "Traveling with Theodore gets so very dull. I would do anything to have some entertainment—of my own. Private entertainment, Orsini. Do you understand? For your *particular* company while my husband goes to visit collieries and cotton mills and shipyards, I would free Captain Pendleton to marry your compromised sister."

His heart lurched at the very thought of it, yet what if the plan failed? What if he was somehow wrong about the pearls or the dowager didn't identify them? What if the unthinkable happened and Mr. Pendleton resisted their efforts?

He could hardly bring himself to imagine it.

"What of the investment Mr. Pendleton is making, though?" Orsini kept his voice steady. "What will your husband say?"

"It is an investment, Orsini. A business arrangement." Mrs. Tarbottom ran the tip of her tongue over her lower lip, her voice still husky as if she weren't talking about cold finance. "Even without the marriage,

Mr. Pendleton is keen to expand his interests into North America."

"A man's pride might be wounded if his son is rejected though," Orsini reasoned. "And wounded pride might see an investment withdrawn. Then there is your daughter. Will she not be heartbroken?"

"Investments might come from other quarters if it came to that." Mrs. Tarbottom nodded. Yes, Orsini had noticed the charming smiles and amused laughter she had turned to the new guests. "Besides, Harriet is young and passably pretty. There are plenty of gentlemen who would happily accept her hand. She will not cry for long over the captain."

Indeed, she will not.

"The proposition is certainly a tempting one," he lied. "But at present I have engagements from now until Advent. However, if you will give me just a week or so in which to see if they might be rearranged, I will give you your answer."

And a week carries us safely past the ball and all will be well.

"Until then," he added, "do you think we might refrain from announcing any engagements?"

"If you wish." Mrs. Tarbottom moved closer still and ran the tip of her finger down Orsini's cheek, pouting. "For your sister, remember."

"For my sister," Orsini agreed. "And for us, of course."

He took her hand lifted it to his lips, placing a soft kiss on her cold skin. It took all of Orsini's mastery of himself to suppress the shudder that passed through him at everything that had just transpired.

Such people in the world.

Then he stood and bowed. "You will excuse me, dear lady. Believe me when I say that I will be thinking of you."

Chapter Nineteen

For the next hour or so, Orsini felt like a man awaiting his death sentence. Ambrose was nowhere to be found, escorting some of the house party's visiting dignitaries on a tour of the gardens, and Orsini knew that it wouldn't do to interrupt, nor could anything be achieved by doing so. Instead he haunted the porters, hoping for a letter from Viscount Hartington that did not arrive. So desperate did he become to escape the clutches of Mrs. Tarbottom that he found his way to the kitchen and, as the panic of the domestics turned to indulgence, allowed them to ply him with cups of tea and the sweetest jam tarts.

It went little way to mending his troubled heart, but at least no American vulture could sink her clutches into him here. Here in the kitchen, his silken figure surrounded by bustle and business, Orsini was safe. Safe and trusted it seemed, for he was even allowed to stir the gravy for dinner under the cook's indulgent smile.

I shall stir gravy more often, Orsini decided as he departed the kitchen for the grounds and, he hoped, the company of Ambrose. *Stirring gravy is a balm for the soul.*

Standing on the terrace, Orsini watched the man he loved entertain the little gaggle of industrialists and peers, showing off his father's greatest achievement. At his side Mr. Pendleton puffed out his chest and beamed across his broad face, a proud little parrot admiring his own nest. Yet as the group fell into discussion, Orsini saw that Ambrose's attention had wandered. He approached and chanced a gentle wave, hoping that the tour might finally be reaching its conclusion.

"Orsini…" Ambrose gave him one of his shallow, stiff bows. No one seeing such a bow would suspect the passion that Ambrose was capable of, although the smile Ambrose shone on Orsini hinted at it. "I trust you have enjoyed your afternoon? We are going in for tea now — would you join us?"

"Might I inconvenience you for a minute or so? I have been strolling and would like to ask a little about the sinking of the lake." Orsini smiled. "Can you spare me a moment?"

"I'd be more than happy to, Orsini." Ambrose's smile increased in brightness. "Do come this way."

Ambrose strolled along the terrace, gesturing for Orsini to follow him toward the secluded path that had become a favorite haunt of theirs. He hurried to do so, his spirits heavy despite the presence of the captain who had stolen his heart. Only when they were safely out of earshot did Orsini admit, "There has been no word from Viscount Hartington, Pen, and still the jewels are locked away, still the fathers are conspiring, still Harriet Tarbottom struts and preens!"

Ambrose slammed his fist against his palm, his jaw clenched. "Damn it all, Orsini, but there must be a way out of this accursed shambles."

"Mrs. Tarbottom has offered me one." He looked at his feet, unable to meet Ambrose's gaze and see the disgust there. Perhaps what they said about theatricals was true, for he would sacrifice anything to save his love from a lifetime lost to Harriet. "She has offered to have the wedding quietly set aside if I will agree to — They are touring the industrial lands of England, you know and Mrs. Tarbottom seeks — "

Yet Orsini found he could hardly force out the words, though he must.

"If I will be her concubine during her stay, you will be freed from the betrothal," Orsini told Ambrose plainly, then pressed his hand to his mouth as though it might silence the words. "And if we cannot find those pearls or the viscount does not come or God forbid I was wrong about their origin — I cannot see you married to her, Pen, nor estranged from your own father! If we have no other choice, forgive me, my love, but I must say yes."

They were at the top of the path, the dark, shiny leaves of the hedges sapping the daylight of all its brightness. Ambrose stared at Orsini, slowly shaking his head, a coldness in his demeanor that hadn't been there before.

"What can you mean, Orsini? Mrs. Tarbottom has asked you to lie with her? How — how can you even countenance such a plan? How dare she suggest it, the dreadful wretch!"

"And if I do not and the pearls are not stolen, what then?" Orsini asked desperately. "Do you marry her?

Do you stand against your father and lose his love? What, Pen, can we do?"

"I cannot ask you to do that! To be a plaything to satisfy a strumpet's lusts! I will not have you do such an odious, dishonorable thing, Orsini!" Ambrose dragged his hand across his face. All the color had run out from it, as if he was staring down the barrel of a pistol. "Better I am banished across the seas than force you to lower yourself in such a debased and vile manner. No—no, I would never ask that of you."

"I could not stand to live knowing that you had been sold to her." Orsini swallowed hard, his eyes filling with tears. "I would give anything for you, *tato*, anything."

"No, no! I won't hear of it!" Desperation was writ in every feature of Ambrose's grayed face. "You must not do this, for I will not make a harlot of you!"

"You would not want me then," Orsini said quietly, the word ringing in his ears. He'd lived enough hours as an actress to have had that word flung at him before, but never had it felt like a stinging slap until now. What a thing it was to be loved, and to see the very moment that love died, for surely it had. "Would you?"

"But of course I do!" Ambrose took a step toward Orsini, then froze, not coming any closer. His arms, which had perhaps been raised to embrace him, fell to his side. "I have wanted you for so long, and to think of you in the arms of that—that—harpy! I cannot bear it!"

"But if the pearls— If all else fails—" He held out his hand but Ambrose remained as still as marble, the distance suddenly unbreachable. "I love you, *tato*, with everything I am, but I am an actor and if that is my next role then—"

Orsini raked his hand through his hair, his next words desperate. "You are a writer, Pen! For God's sake, if this was a play, what would the next scene be? Help me fight, please!"

"If it was my play, it would most certainly not feature a romp between my lover and my future mother-in-law!" Ambrose's voice was steel. Hiding his face in his hands, he turned his back on Orsini.

"You should not call me a harlot," Orsini whispered, his heart breaking. "You should call me a martyr."

As he turned and began to walk away Orsini heard footsteps, and Ambrose placed his hand on Orsini's shoulder.

"Stop, please. I am not angry with you, Orsini. I love you, and I am furious—disgusted—with Mrs. Tarbottom for forcing you into such a bind. She has no respect for either of us—to use you to slake her lusts, to be so determined to drag me to the other side of the world then casually throw the arrangement aside. None for her daughter, whom she would tie to a man who does not love her, none for her husband whom she cuckolds. We are mere pawns as she heads about the chessboard collecting wealth and pleasures. And yet, if this was a play… An idea is forming in my mind. Will you but hear it?"

"I will hear anything but the thought of saving you by succumbing to her," he admitted, relief and love flooding through his blood. Then he turned back to his lover, seeking proof of his words with the softest of kisses.

Ambrose embraced him and claimed his mouth in a kiss that seemed as if it would never end.

Until Ambrose stopped and said, "Ah, yes…the plan. It will require you to play a role, but only for an hour at the most. She must be caught—not in the act, for my plays would not contain such a scene, but as close to it as the Lord Chamberlain could bear. Imagine if she were to be discovered in your bedchamber by her husband! His saintly wife would seem anything but, for what married woman goes alone to another gentleman's rooms?"

"It is genius." Orsini's eyes grew wide as he envisioned it on the Haymarket stage, already hearing the gasps and laughter from the delighted audience. He could see it, the harpy in her silks, the hero in her arms, saved by his love. Yet might there be something he could add, if the playwright allowed? He knew from experience that these creative sorts didn't always take too well to an actor's input. "Might I make a suggestion, my love?"

"Oh—does it not please you?" Ambrose pouted in dismay. "But—go on."

"It pleases me immensely!" Orsini rewarded him with another lingering, gentle kiss. "But would it not be more pleasing still to carry out our scheme at the very ball where the engagement was once to have been announced? It shall not spoil the party for your darling mamma, for she need not know, but we will know that the night of their triumph has become the night of their banishment."

"Ah, now that would draw the threads together nicely—even Aristotle might be impressed by that!" Ambrose laughed as he covered Orsini's face in kisses. "My beautiful, clever, adoring Orsini!"

"As smart as I am beautiful," Orsini teased. "And but still only half as clever and handsome as you, *amore mio!*"

Ambrose caressed Orsini's face, his expression one of gentle concern. "I am so sorry that you thought I was angry with you, my darling. I was taken aback at what you would have sacrificed for me, that anyone could have such love for me, and I—we shall be so happy, Orsini, I know we shall be."

"I thought—" Orsini shook his head. "I was a fool to think it, Pen, but I have loved you for so long, I could not bear to lose you now. I would do anything for you."

Orsini was caught then in the loving gaze of Captain Pendleton. Ambrose's caresses brought them closer until they were embracing tightly, their sweet kisses heated now and deepening. Clinging to Ambrose, Orsini sank against him, losing himself in their embraces as he pressed his body against that of his lover. Ambrose slipped his hand between their bodies and Orsini felt him stroke over the front of his breeches.

A gentle whisper against his ear asked, "Would you like me to take you here?" Then Ambrose brought his mouth back to Orsini's, kissing him with a searing heat. "Anything you want, darling…"

Orsini replied with a sighed "Yes! Take me here, Pen."

A tremor passed through their kiss, Ambrose rubbing more firmly against Orsini's breeches. There was such excitement in being so close to the house and yet so distant. Here in the sunlight they kissed, arms tight about each other, utterly hidden from the world.

Orsini reached his hand between them, massaging it over the hardness that Ambrose's breeches were struggling to contain. They had made so many memories during that heady summer and now there would be more, happiness and love stretching off into the far distant, delightful future. "How I love you, Pen."

"I love you, too, Orsini. Never forget that, never doubt my constancy for a moment." With one hand, Ambrose unfastened Orsini's breeches with admirable speed and slipped his hand inside. How could he ever doubt this man, so strong, so loving? To think that just minutes earlier he had believed himself forsaken. The fancies of a theatrical, as ludicrous as they were mistaken.

He unfastened Ambrose's breeches with a confident elegance and took his erection in his hand, holding it with obvious appreciation. He could feel the heat of Ambrose's passion pulsing through his body, promising pleasure to them both and gently stepped back a little, until he felt the broad trunk of a sheltering tree at his back. Then, still lost in that kiss, Orsini began to stroke his lover, breathless at the thought of what was to come.

Ambrose seemed to mirror Orsini's strokes, and with his other hand, he pushed down Orsini's breeches. He murmured urgently, "I want you. Here...in the garden. Turn, darling, and brace your hands on the tree."

"A capital idea from a talented playwright!" Orsini kissed Ambrose once more, and relinquished his cock. Then he turned and he braced his hands against the rough bark. He gave a wiggle of his bottom and whispered, "How do I look?"

"Marvelous!" Ambrose laughed and gently stroked Orsini's buttocks. "Give me a moment to prepare myself...now..."

As Ambrose kissed the nape of Orsini's neck, he encircled Orsini's cock with his strong hand and gently eased into him. Orsini pushed his body back to meet

Ambrose and, with a low groan, closed his eyes. He was entirely possessed by his *capitano* now, and he wanted for nothing more than this.

Ambrose ran one hand over Orsini's chest, unbuttoning his coat and at last finding the stiffened peak of Orsini's nipple. Orsini murmured in delight at Ambrose's touch, inside him, against him, and turned his head as far as he comfortably could to watch Ambrose's face. He was so beautiful in his transport of joy, but Orsini turned back to look down at the large hand upon him. Sighing, he closed his hand over Ambrose's on his erection.

Together the two men moved their hips and hands, perfectly in time in their dance. Together they moaned, together they sighed, together they left the world behind.

Just two men who adored the very air that each other breathed.

"I love you," Ambrose gasped, his hand running over Orsini's chest once more. "My beautiful, beautiful lover."

"*Amore mio,*" Orsini cooed, the words soft as gossamer. He couldn't say anything more, for every bit of him was swept up in the tide of pleasure. Every sensation was alive with Ambrose, from the feeling of his kisses and hot breath against Orsini's nape to their shared moans and gasps, the scent of Ambrose's cologne heady here in the fragrant woods.

Ambrose gasped, his thrusts growing deeper, harder, with each passing moment. "Amadeo…Cosima…my heart's darling."

"My only love," Orsini moaned in reply. Then he shifted to balance himself against the tree with one arm. With the other he reached behind his head and caught

Ambrose gently around his neck, twining his fingers in his hair. "My captain."

Ambrose held his strong arm securely around Orsini's waist, and Orsini felt a change in him, knew that the peak of Ambrose's pleasure could not be far away. They would reach the pinnacle together, he decided, and only when Ambrose was ready.

"I want to feel you." Orsini sighed. "Together, *tato*, you and I."

"Now?" Ambrose asked through his ragged breaths. "My darling, I cannot —"

Whatever words he was about to say were lost in a sigh of bliss, and Ambrose buried his lips against Orsini's neck, moaning his pleasure. Orsini drove his body against Ambrose's and together they soared, caught up in an excess of joy. The sun suddenly seemed brighter and Orsini closed his eyes, his spirit flying free.

The strength of Ambrose's embrace supported Orsini as they sagged against the tree, worn out by their trysting but utterly together. Ambrose murmured to Orsini soft words of love that were as heady as any perfume. Turning his face, Orsini sought out a kiss that was as sweet as their coupling had been fiery. Their bodies were still joined, still pressed tight together, his nerves still tingling with that rush of delight.

I probably shouldn't put this in a play though.
London isn't quite ready.

C h a p t e r   T w e n t y

Bella donna,
Come to my rooms at midnight as the household dances and
we shall shed our masks together. Let us make the night of
the ball one that we shall always remember.
O

Orsini read the note over, satisfied that it was just the
right mix of anonymous and alluring. Should anyone
discover it the lady need not fear for her reputation, for
she was not named, and nobody would be surprised
that an Italian gentleman of the theatrical persuasion
was intriguing with someone. It was what they did,
after all. Once the letter was sealed he took it in his
gloved hand and, on Cosima's silk-slippered feet,
skipped along the landing of Pendleton Hall. By now
the quiet palace was witnessing a house party of some
renown and tomorrow, at the ball that the Pendletons
had planned for so long, all would be concluded.

Tomorrow, Ambrose would be free.

Orsini glanced this way and that outside Mrs. Tarbottom's door. Then he stooped and pushed the note beneath it before skipping away again, all innocence once more.

All that would improve it was word from Viscount Hartington, but still it did not arrive. Perhaps the curtain had fallen on that particular hope. For now though Orsini pushed that doubt aside, for Cosima had a day of needlepoint with the ladies ahead of her.

Be still my beating heart.

A door opened ahead and a familiar lace cap appeared, askew upon the head of Mrs. Pendleton. She glanced up at Orsini, offering him a distracted smile, but her attention was elsewhere as she anxiously scanned the floor.

"Good morning, my dear Cosima!" She closed her finger and thumb around her wrist then looked up and down the corridor again. Speaking to herself, it seemed, Mrs. Pendleton muttered, "Oh, where can the dratted thing be?"

"Where is it?" Pagolo hopped out of the room behind her, looking left and right like the busy gentleman he was. "For shame, *Mamma*!"

"Have you misplaced something?" Orsini asked, smiling as he watched the parrot follow each move the lady made. "Can I help?"

"My bracelet!" Mrs. Pendleton wailed as she clasped Orsini's hand. "I wore it last night at dinner. Such a pretty thing, a string of sapphires with a diamond clasp! I put it in its case before I retired to bed, I'm certain of it. I had some household matters to attend to this morning, then came back to my bedchamber and found the case open and my bracelet gone!"

"For shame." Pagolo hopped up onto her shoulder. "Gone!"

And Orsini knew then, if he had not been sure before, that he was right about the pearls and that here in this house, the pickings were rich indeed for Harriet Tarbottom. Each of the ladies who were guests of the Pendletons would be as good as a shopfront for Harriet, he realized, but the distress he now saw on this finest of all women was almost too much to bear.

"Might we speak privately, *signora*?" Orsini asked in a whisper, the empty corridor no guarantee that they were alone. "You and I and Pagolo?"

Mrs. Pendleton blinked, as if she was uncertain of what might follow. "Of course—come into my bedchamber, do, and perhaps you might even find it! My husband gave it to me for a present when he'd made his first five thousand pounds, you see—all the days of want were over at last and...and I would hate to think my trinket lost to me."

She ushered Orsini inside, and as soon as the door closed and the unhappy woman was seated before the fireplace, Orsini told her, "I believe Harriet Tarbottom has taken your bracelet, Signora Pendleton, and I believe she has carried out such crimes in London too, and probably elsewhere if truth be known!"

Mrs. Pendleton's cap slipped farther as she gaped at Orsini in surprise. Her mouth formed a perfect circle.

"A thief? That girl is a common thief?" She fanned herself with her handkerchief and took a shuddering breath. "Such does not surprise me, Cosima, I am sad to say. She has quizzed me about my jewels and would you believe it but my husband has inquired, at the behest of the Tarbottoms, which pieces of my jewelry I would bestow on the girl as a wedding gift! I said she'd be lucky if I gave her so much as a home-knitted stocking! My jewels to become part of their dirty *negotiations!*" Mrs. Pendleton spat the word as though it were an expletive.

Yet Orsini was not immune to shame himself and even as he nodded his agreement, he wondered at the lies he had told the lady, the lie he told each time Cosima appeared before her. If only he dared to tell her the truth about Orsini and Cosima, yet how could he? She might put him out here and now, for the number of parents who would smile on a union such as theirs must be small indeed. A lie for sake of love it might be, but it was still an untruth.

Pagolo woke Orsini from his reverie, tugging the lace cap back into place with a sharp pull of his beak and as Orsini blinked, he realized that Mrs. Pendleton was looking at him closely.

Did she know?

Of course not, what an absurd thought.

"Dowager Viscountess Hartington's pearls were stolen during a ball at her home and I am sure that Harriet wore those same pearls to dinner just last night," Orsini explained. "I had hoped that we might have Lord H. and his mother here to identify the necklace but he has not replied to our invitation. One thing I ask though, madame, if he does reply or even better if he attends, please say nothing to the Tarbottoms. I intend to exploit Harriet's naturally rotten character and have her wear the pearls to the ball for if she knows Cosima—I adore them just as I adore Pen—she will certainly flaunt them."

"I shan't say a word, Cosima—until you wish me to speak." Mrs. Pendleton sighed. "I dearly wish I could tell my husband what you suspect, but all he cares for nowadays is money. I fear he would not believe me, and think you and I were intriguing together against his intentions."

Mrs. Pendleton clasped Orsini's hand and smiled. "For I could want no one else in all the world but you at my son's side, whatever obstacles there might be."

Her gaze wandered to a painting on the wall of a round-cheeked child with curls falling to his silk-clad shoulders. It could only have been Pen as a boy.

"Every subterfuge I have practiced here in your home," Orsini told her quietly, "has been for love. Know that I have done nothing that is wicked, *signora*, and I will love your son with all of my heart for as long as we live."

Mrs. Pendleton smiled at Orsini again. "I know you love him, and I know he loves you, and that is all that matters."

"I still have a hope that the viscount will attend," Orsini admitted. "And for that, I believe I have just thought of the perfect way to make sure our madam wears the questionable pearls! Will you excuse me, Mamma P.?"

"Yes, of course, my dear!"

"And worry not for your bracelet." Orsini stooped to hug Mrs. Pendleton. "For it shall soon be with you again, I am sure of it!"

With that, he left lady and parrot alone and went in search of Harriet Tarbottom. She would not be hard to find, Orsini knew, for Harriet always changed after lunch. Even now, as he knocked at Harriet's door, he was certain that both mother and daughter would be here, strapping the younger Tarbottom into stays and silk.

"Who is there?" Mrs. Tarbottom called, with the self-important volume of a dowager duchess.

"Only Cosima!"

"The little contessina!" Harriet said, as if she was addressing her favorite friend. "I'm dressing for the afternoon, but do come in!"

Orsini opened the door and entered the room where the mother and daughter sat together before the mirror, surrounded by a flurry of attendants. Ranged on the dressing table in front of them were a dozen or more jars and palettes, and it was with a note of satisfaction that Orsini observed the preparations and potions. So it took all of this to make ladies of the Tarbottom women when all it took to make a lady of Amadeo Orsini was a few pads and a quick application of makeup.

"I wonder, Miss Harriet, if I might ask a very generous favor of you?" Orsini asked, his tone sweetly deferential.

"Of course, my dear friend! What might it be?" Without turning to Orsini, Harriet met his reflected gaze in the mirror.

"I know it is a great favor to ask, but I wondered if you might be willing to let me wear your exquisite pearls for the masked ball?" She saw Harriet's face harden, knowing that her plan was going just as she had hoped.

"My pearls?" Harriet shook her head and this time turned to face Orsini. "My pearls? Why, Cosima, I simply cannot! For no other necklace I own will go so well with my gown. Besides" — a nasty little smirk came to Harriet's face — "pearls for the bride! And as you well know, my betrothal to the captain will be announced at the ball."

An even nastier smirk twisted her mother's lips at this remark, but Harriet didn't seem to notice. Orsini, however, was nothing but understanding. He inclined his head with grace and told her, "Of course, I should not have asked. Congratulations, miss, you must be very happy."

Harriet grinned. "Oh, I am the happiest girl in all the land!"

Her mother continued to smirk. Orsini gave a neat curtsey, just deferential enough, and said, "I look forward to seeing your costume."

Then he glided from the room, whispering a prayer to Viscount Hartington's guardian angel to bring him quickly to Derbyshire.

Chapter Twenty-One

Mrs. Pendleton spent breakfast describing the various preparations in hand for that night's ball — the arrival of the orchestra, the delicacies for the refreshments, the extra servants drafted in, the excellent and distinguished guests and the unveiling of her new gown. Ambrose was entirely at sea, unable to contribute anything to the proceedings beside polishing the buttons on his uniform or rubbing his boots to a shine.

And a servant had already done that.

There were guests to entertain, however, but the Tarbottoms had monopolized them, falsely charming as they nodded and conversed. The very idea that Harriet had crept into Mrs. Pendleton's room and stolen her bracelet filled Ambrose with impotent rage. Nothing could be said or done.

Yet.

Events had carried him along, and Ambrose wandered the corridors, overcome by sadness. He could be leaving this place forever if the Hartingtons didn't arrive, if Orsini's deceiving intrigue with Mrs. Tarbottom did not come off. Either he would be sent off to America with the Tarbottoms, or be rejected by his father forever and never again see the house where he had been born.

The ground floor of Pendleton Hall was busy with arrangements for the evening ahead. Ambrose could hear his mother excitedly giving directions, her feet tapping back and forth across the marble floors. She was chirping away like the parrot, and Ambrose knew that the moment she laid her eyes on him, she would see his sadness. But he couldn't spoil the happiness of the ball for her.

Alone, he wandered from room to room in the oldest wing of the house. He had played hide-and-seek behind that sofa, he had enacted a play for his grandparents before that fireplace and his father had not been pleased, he had stolen off and hidden behind that curtain to write. Those had been glad days, happy times. He would cling to those memories of the joy he had known here as a boy.

Finally Ambrose came to the nursery, where the Pendleton boys had slept as children. Their two beds still stood side by side, and Ambrose sank down onto the one that had been his. Here he had lain, long after his brother had fallen asleep, conjuring worlds to roam through. He lay back across the mattress and, through a glassy veneer of unshed tears, he magicked a new world—a place for himself and Orsini. A place where they were safe and where their love went unremarked.

And he'd be sent to America as Harriet Tarbottom's husband.

"No!"

Ambrose hurried through the corridors, searching for his father. He wasn't going to marry Harriet or be sent across an ocean. He couldn't. Let his father make him penniless if he would, let him throw him out of the family, but Ambrose couldn't go through with it. He'd go to London with Orsini and he'd shift for himself by painting sets at the theater for pennies if he had to, but he would not marry Harriet Tarbottom.

His father was on the terrace, strolling with his guests. Ambrose approached. He didn't pause, he didn't wait.

"Father, I should like to speak with you."

Mr. Pendleton turned to look at his son and Ambrose was surprised at his father's countenance, a pale tinge now on his usually ruddy cheeks. He greeted the request with a simple nod. After offering an apology to his guests, he drew Ambrose aside.

"How might I help you, young sir?"

Ambrose lowered his voice and turned away from the guests, aware of the Tarbottoms watching him. "Might we speak privately, Father?"

"Walk with me." Mr. Pendleton made his way onto the lawn and began to stroll, knitting his fingers behind his back as he went. "I own that this bother with Mrs. Pendleton's bracelet has caused me some worry. I cannot see her so upset. It upsets me in kind."

Ambrose swallowed, pausing as he chose his words. "Because you married her for love, Father, did you not? You care for her."

"I do, sir, and she has always been constant, as have I."

As he thought a theatrical could not be. As his own father had not been.

"Father, I have always been a dutiful son, have I not?" Ambrose briefly touched his father's shoulder. "I have always done as you wished. I have respected you, even if I have not agreed with you. Because I am your son and I...I love you."

Ambrose had not said as much since he was a boy in silk breeches. The words felt strange in his mouth.

"I love you, son." Mr. Pendleton drew in a deep breath, his eyes clouding. "If only the lady were not a theatrical, perhaps—"

"Pray do not be angry with Mother, but she told me about my grandfather." It hurt Ambrose to say it, and he knew it would hurt his father even more, to be reminded of the cruel hand that fate had dealt him as a boy.

His nod was brisk, his voice likewise. "Did she now?"

"I am sorry, Father, to mention it, but I understand— a little, perhaps—why you are against my union with Cosima. And I know that you will think I am abdicating my duty to you, just as your father did to you—but really—" Ambrose stopped walking, forcing his father to halt his progress. "—I love her. And she and I shall be as constant to each other as you and Mother have been."

"Your mother has spoken to the parrot more than I. She believes the disappearance of her bracelet is an omen of ill fortune." Mr. Pendleton shook his head. He looked back at the gaggle of guests, then returned his attention to Ambrose. "Is she so precious to you, son, that it would cost me the society of my youngest lad and my wife if I stick to this path?"

Ambrose looked into his father's earnest gray eyes. "I would never turn away from you, Father, but if I were to wed Cosima and you hardened your heart to me…that would be your decision. If you decide to close your purse to me, then I shall work to keep a roof over my head, and my darling Cosima's. I never meant for this wedge to divide you and Mother — it pains me to think that it is my doing."

"My heart could never be cold to you, Ambrose." His father reached up to slip his arm around his son's shoulders. "You're my youngest lad. I confess I never slept a night through when you were at war and I'll not see the end of you over something so daft as a lass. I'll make you no promise today but… The young lady's mother is north of the border, is that right?"

Hope began to flow in Ambrose's veins once more.

"She is, Father, yes." Intriguing with an earl, no less, but Ambrose thought it prudent not to mention that.

"Have her son summon her to the Hall, at my expense, and we will see," Mr. Pendleton decided. "I shall tell Mr. Tarbottom that there is a necessary delay, as I'm sure he wouldn't want his own lass married if it's not to a man who loves her. She's a sweet and innocent one, we need to do the right thing by her and cause her no embarrassment."

Ambrose tried to nod, agreeing with his father, when all he could see in his mind was Harriet, smiling while wearing the stolen pearls. "Oh, indeed, sir, she is but an innocent."

Which wasn't something he could say about her mother, either.

"One thing, Ambrose. Is our contessina really compromised as her brother suspects?" He looked Ambrose in the eye, seeking out the truth. "Speak honestly. Is there a child?"

Ambrose shook his head. "She is not with child, Father. I am sorry to have deceived you, but it was the only way, it seemed, to force your hand. I am not proud of what I have done. Cosima is an innocent, I swear to you. But we do love each other, Father, and the thought of being torn from her is too dreadful to bear."

"Summon her mother." He patted Ambrose's shoulder and smiled. "And we shall see."

"Thank you, Father!" As if he were still a lad, Ambrose gleefully hugged his father, forgetting for a moment how much taller than him he had grown.

"Now get along with you." Mr. Pendleton slapped his son's back. "I've a ball to dress for!"

Ambrose laughed as he gave his father a bow, then scarpered across the lawn. The weight was shifting from his shoulders at last. He ran at a trot toward the stables and the coach house, just in time to see a carriage arrive with distinguished guests on board. Ambrose skidded to a halt and at once assumed the demeanor of a grown man. He went up to the door of the coach, ready to welcome—

"Viscount and the Dowager Viscountess Hartington, I do believe?" Ambrose realized his mouth was hanging open like a fish's. He closed it, and grinned broadly. "You are most welcome—sir, madam."

"And the wife!" The viscount climbed down and held out his hand. First emerged his viscountess, smiling graciously at the sight of Ambrose. In her hand she held a rolled sheaf of papers that Ambrose recognized as his own play, the copy that Orsini must have passed to the peer to win his favor. She nodded a greeting and stepped aside to allow the elderly lady Ambrose had seen in the pleasure gardens to descend, her face as sad as it had been then, though she mustered a smile for their host.

"Forgive our coming around the back," Hartington chirruped, placing his hat upon his graying head. "Mama wishes to sneak in and rest without all that fuss they make at these sorts of things. Truth be told, it was all we could do to convince her out of the house at all, so—"

"Teddy," the old lady cautioned, pointing a finger at her son by way of warning, as though he were still in the nursery. A second carriage arrived now and a third, the retinue of the theatrical viscount descending to join their employer in this unorthodox meeting place. Ambrose watched as Hartington dispensed instructions this way and that, while his wife took the dowager's arm and stood aside from the group, the attention of both women taken by the script that she had now unrolled.

"The Ladies Hartington shall need to rest from the road and finish reading their play while I plead with Orsini on theatrical matters," he explained to Ambrose. "One sent late word of our acceptance, but one suspects we passed it on the road!"

Ambrose spirits soared, but he kept a lid on them as best he could. Although he had the advantage now over the Tarbottoms, he would have to play his hand with care. "My mother set aside our best rooms for you and your party, on the off chance that you would attend. She will be overjoyed that you were able to come. Do follow me—I will show you where they are. I know not where Orsini is—his sister is in residence too, however. He might have gone to speak with her, but I shall find one of them at least, I promise you that."

The party seemed happy to simply be off the road and soon the ladies were settled and the business of unpacking the trunks began. With tea summoned, all was soon right with the world, but one thing played at Ambrose's mind. If she learned of the family's presence, Harriet Tarbottom would not wear those pearls and would be sure to hide them away from any chance of discovery.

"They tell me in London that the Tarbottoms are here," the viscount commented. "Such a charming little family. Would that our eldest were not only twelve years old, I might have spied a pretty bride for him in that miss. As it is, he has some years yet before he thinks of such matters!"

"Ah…might we speak, Lord Hartington? It is, I fear, a subject of some delicacy." Ambrose nodded toward the large bay window, which could be screened from the room by heavy curtains. With a comical expression of intrigue, the peer followed him to the window with all the enthusiasm of a child at Christmas.

Lowering his voice, Ambrose told him, "Cosima and Orsini believe they have discovered your mother's pearls…and the thief."

"They have what?"

"The miscreant and the loot are in this very house. I realize you are friendly with the —" Ambrose bunched his hands into fists. He knew Hartington had no reason to believe him, and might not take kindly to him impugning a young lady of his acquaintance. But Ambrose had to speak the truth. "I am a man of honor — pray understand that I do not make accusations lightly."

"No, no, I can well imagine that you do not," the peer replied, his face darkening. "But perhaps you might make your accusations a little clearer, for I fear that I have not quite grasped your meaning! I must speak with Orsini, of course, for I have another pressing matter to discuss with him too. Happily, of a rather more pleasing nature!"

His play. Could it be his play that Hartington was so keen to discuss with Orsini? No, it was a silly hope. The matter of the pearls, however, had to be addressed.

Ambrose shook his head. "I have not, for my father and Mr. Tarbottom have been arranging a marriage between myself and — It is Harriet. She is the thief. Not only has she proudly worn your mother's stolen pearls to dinner, but she has also stolen a bracelet from my mother. Cosima tells me that Harriet intends to wear the pearls to the ball tonight. If she discovers that your mother is in attendance, then, unless she is an utter fool, she will not — so, Lord Hartington, would you mind your presence here remaining secret until Harriet has appeared in the pearls? Meanwhile, I shall hunt out Orsini for you."

The theatrical gentleman regarded Ambrose with a rather narrow gaze and for a moment Ambrose thought he might be about to receive something of a dressing down. Then he nodded and pressed his hand to Ambrose's shoulder.

"I shall do it, for my mother will know the pearls at first glance. I hope for her sake that Orsini is correct, yet I cannot deny that I wish it were not so, for the thought of a young lady indulging in such —" He shook his head. "You shall know me at the ball, for I will be dressed as the Bard of Avon himself. I say, all of this pearl business might be a play in itself, what? I have no talent for it. Alas, I am but a producer."

Ambrose glanced toward Hartington's wife, who was grinning to herself as she leafed through her quire of papers. He cleared his throat, and said, "I happen to dabble in playwrighting myself, you know. I believe you have read one of my works?"

The frown settled again as Hartington no doubt mentally sorted through the plays he had read, eventually deciding, "Alas no, I recall no Pendleton play. I would be happy to, of course, if you wish me to give your work a once-over!"

"Orsini passed it to you, Lord Hartington. It is called…" Ambrose puffed out his chest, as proudly as his father when he spoke of his mines, "…*Of Fleet Fortune; or, The Duke's Disgrace*. I am working on another — *Avarice and Ambition; or, the Magnate's Misfortune*. There's a trunk in my dressing room stuffed with the things."

"You?" He blinked, then glanced to his wife and mother. "Why, the ladies are reading it even now! I have begged Orsini for your name!"

"I have had to keep my plays a secret — my father has never been one for the theater, although…Cosima performed the song from *Fleet Fortune* the other evening and Father did find it amusing." Ambrose could feel his face heat. "But yes, it is me. The Pen behind the pen, if you will."

"Ah, Lady Hartington almost boxed my ears for proposing to La Cosima as a result of her performance of that song. Happily she knows us theatrical sorts well enough." He laughed. "We shall speak of business later, sir, for I must produce it!"

Ambrose grasped the viscount's hands and cheered as if he was swilling pints at a tavern with his troopers. A most ungentlemanly response, but he could not contain his joy.

"Hartington—you are a king among men! My play— oh! And I will forgive you proposing to Cosima because…well, she's lovely, isn't she? My play!"

"Ladies Harty, elder and younger, here is our playwright!" The ladies looked as though they had little clue what the viscount was talking about, but both smiled politely and made suitably appreciative comments. "Our genius!"

"Well, I wouldn't say genius…" Ambrose wrung his hands as he grinned from one woman to the other. "More a scribbler, really."

"That little pompous fellow, parading here and there." The dowager viscountess smiled as she spoke, her unhappy demeanor lifting. "Such a creation, Captain Pendleton. He reminded me of my own late father in so many ways."

"Ah, Mr. Mallett? His inspiration is strutting about in this very house!" Ambrose shone her a conspiratorial grin. "Say nothing, but I based him upon my father!"

"Then let us hope he has a well-developed sense of humor." Lady Hartington laughed, earning an even wider smile from her mother-in-law. "For Harty has every intention of making your play the most sought- after seat in town, sir. We have been reading all the way here, sharing the roles between us, but surely this Cosima can only be played by *the* Cosima?"

"I cannot picture anyone else in the role, it is true!" Ambrose nodded with enthusiasm. "Her rendition of the song is perfect—even better than I had it in my mind as I wrote."

"Sir, we shall see it staged, I swear it." Hartington patted Ambrose's shoulder then withdrew his hand. "If you will excuse me, sir, I shall tell the ladies of your suspicions and our scheme. It is a shock, I confess, but we shall soon have it resolved one way or the other."

"Indeed, sir." Ambrose bowed. "I shall see you all later at the ball!"

Chapter Twenty-Two

Orsini, Amadeo, La Cosima — call him what you would — was the happiest he could ever imagine being. He was in love, he was loved, and he would be the most fabulously dressed person at the ball not once but twice.

There was nothing in life that could not be made even better by a fine suit and frock, Orsini decided as he turned this way and that before his mirror, satisfied that this was the most wonderful collection of silks and laces on the face of the earth. Toiled over day after day, week after week by the finest seamstresses in Italy, it was a creation from the mind of Orsini made into a dazzling reality. For tonight, the Orsini siblings were to be peacocks at last.

His gown was a wonderful vision of peacock feathers, a train draped over one of his slender arms, shimmering black gloves caressing his olive skin to the elbow and a feathered fan dangling from one perfectly-formed wrist. That celebrated hair, auburn and tumbling, hung loose over his shoulders and a spray of peacock feathers rose from it, just as they fluttered at the edges of his bejewelled blue fan. At his throat and wrist emeralds glittered like the brightest stars in a moonlit sky but more priceless than any emerald, more perfect than any gown, he would soon be forever in the arms of Captain Pendleton.

First, though, there was dancing. Dancing and plotting and the marvelous Viscount H., who had arrived just in time for the final act. Before any drama, Cosima would dance with her *capitano* and excuse herself to take the air. Then a quick change would allow Orsini to make his appearance, clad in a suit embroidered with a pattern of those same peacock feathers, capturing attention just as Cosima would before him.

And Harriet will hate it.

When the clocks struck eleven Orsini would be back here in his room, waiting for Mrs. Tarbottom, and ten minutes after that, Ambrose would be at the door with Mr. Tarbottom. What an unsuspecting dupe the American was and how starkly he would learn of his wife's betrayal, but Orsini felt not a jot of sympathy. All the Tarbottoms would receive precisely what they deserved.

Orsini's heart beat fast with excitement as he made his way through the house toward the ballroom, following the sound of happy conversation and sprightly strings. He longed for the moment when he would see Ambrose, his *capitano*, clad in his uniform, and they would dance before the crowd just as they had danced on an Italian beach beneath the noonday sun long ago. At the doorway he paused, a shake of his head informing the bewigged flunkies there that he wished no introduction, not even a witty one to conceal the identity of the lady beneath the peacock mask. Unseen by the dancers, he watched Britannia dance with Caesar, Henry VIII take a turn with a feathered devil who boasted a considerable décolletage, and all around them were the characters of myth, legend and storybook brought vividly to life. He could hear slippers and boots keeping time in the dance, the rustle of silk and the swish of lace their accompaniment while a dozen sweet perfumes and spicy colognes mingled in the summer night, the fragrances suggesting intrigue and, perhaps, a little touch of scandal.

Although he was wearing a mask, it was obvious who the dashing officer waiting by the fireplace was. Captain Pendleton, a breathtaking sight in the shiniest boots Orsini had ever seen, his breeches fitting just so to his muscular legs. The scarlet and gold of his jacket were as bright and alluring as the sun, and the tasseled sash around his waist seemed designed to fall as suggestively as possible over his firm thighs. Captain Pendleton crossed the room in a few steps and bowed before Orsini.

"Madam?" He lifted his mask just a fraction and winked.

"*Capitano.*" Orsini swept his gaze over his lover, glad for the voluminous petticoats and skirts that held up the superstructure of his gown. They hid a multitude of sins, as the saying went, including the response of his own body to those wonderful breeches. "They say it is terribly bad manners to monopolize a gent for every dance, but I may forget my manners tonight. Shall we dance?"

"Throw your manners aside, Contessina. You may monopolize me all you wish." Ambrose took Orsini's arm and led him onto the dance floor, where a set was just beginning. He felt Ambrose's hand slip into the small of his back, wandering over the boning that gave Cosima her shape. Then—because no gentleman's touch should linger—the hand disappeared.

Orsini didn't care to look for the Tarbottoms, for she knew that Harriet's triumphant vanity would see her wrapped in those stolen pearls, and hadn't that been a masked Shakespeare she glanced on the terrace speaking to a Spanish inquisitor? Hartington was here and the thief knew nothing of it, nor her impending and very literal unmasking.

Ambrose and Orsini danced with gleeful abandon and sure steps, their gazes only for each other. Of course there was no mystery as to their identities and Orsini reveled in it, in the freedom to dance with Ambrose in front of all these people and have none of them know the truth of what they witnessed. Two men in love, outdancing their peers and raising such smiles and appreciation from their audience.

They received glances from all, both envious and amorous. Pagolo sailed past on the shoulder of a lady pirate, the blue of her gown matching the parrot's feathers.

Ambrose laughed. "What an outfit Mama has chosen! And who is that she's dancing with?"

"John Bull." Orsini laughed, but surely the stout fellow in his bright red waistcoat and blue coat could only be Mr. Pendleton. The couple looked happy, he realized, for the first time since he had arrived in Derbyshire and begun the subterfuge.

Ambrose had brought his mouth close to Orsini's ear. "I am glad to see them happy again." The weight of feeling in those few words was not lost on Orsini. He inclined his head until his hair gently brushed

Ambrose's cheek, but said nothing in reply until their dance took them a little beyond the set.

Only then did he whisper, "I love you, *Capitano.*"

"And I you, Contessina." Ambrose's hand returned to the small of Orsini's back, a touch that would have to suffice instead of a kiss.

Dance followed dance as the time ticked past and for Orsini, there might be no one else in the room but Ambrose at all. They swirled and stepped on the floor, safe in the knowledge that tonight was the last night that would see the Tarbottoms hold any sway over their love.

Speaking of Tarbottoms, Orsini caught a glimpse of a figure he recognized not by her looks, but by her pearls. Harriet, for surely it was she, chatting with no trace of recognition to Viscount Hartington himself, laughing behind her hand, simpering and giggling, the stolen heirloom around her neck as she did so. She was dressed in Grecian fashion, a Helen of Troy or Penelope in expensive swathes of pale-colored silk. A woman who had been so keen for her engagement to be announced that, rather than make any attempt to dance with her intended, was instead chattering with another man.

Her mother was dancing not far off, dressed as gauzy Titania, her attention divided between her daughter and the door through which the guests arrived.

She awaits Orsini!

Let her wait.

"One more dance, *tato,*" Orsini whispered to his lover. "Then I must seek out my brother. Perhaps you will help me search?"

"Oh yes, one more dance!" Ambrose's lips brushed against Orsini's cheek. It could have been by accident, but Orsini knew better. If anyone were to notice their absence then the scandal would be over soon enough, for Orsini had no doubts that Mr. Pendleton would find much to admire in his mother when she arrived in Derbyshire, and she loved Cosima as much as she loved Amadeo. What a fortunate girl and fellow he was.

There was a lull as the orchestra prepared for the next tune, and the voices around them grew louder to fill the gap. Orsini and his captain took their places, and the music struck up again. On they danced, two men together, seen but unseen.

"Shall we dance ourselves off to seek my brother?" the peacock-clad Italian asked in a whisper. "And whatever else we might find?"

"Yes, let's! To Orsini's bedchamber?" Ambrose's mischief sparkled through his mask as they skipped over the dance floor. The crowd was so thick now that their dance easily became a walk and they slipped through the candlelight and silk and out into the hallway, unseen, or at least unremarked.

Having lived most of his life at Pendleton Hall, Ambrose of course knew unfrequented corridors and staircases. Halfway up a flight of stairs that had been concealed behind a tapestry curtain, Ambrose caught Orsini in his arms.

"No one ever uses these stairs anymore — they're part of the old house. Hear how quiet it is? You'd barely know a ball was carrying on at this moment in this very house!" Ambrose nuzzled against Orsini's cheek, kissing him. "And no one would know a soldier was hiding here with his lady."

"Do you intend to compromise me, sir?" Orsini whispered. "Here in our hideaway?"

Ambrose's breath hitched in his throat as he caressed Orsini's back, sweeping down to rest his hand on Orsini's buttock. "If you would like me to."

"Compromise me." He smiled. "Enthusiastically."

Kisses rained down on Orsini, between murmurs from his lover. "Now what's all this under your gown, you naughty contessina? Might I be permitted to look?"

Orsini put his hand to his mouth in a pantomime of shock, then whispered, "I have a rather sizeable secret, sir."

"A secret, eh?" Ambrose arched his eyebrow. "It wouldn't be the pistol I felt pressing against me earlier, would it?"

"You shall have to discover for yourself, *Capitano*." He pressed his hand to Ambrose's breeches, stroking the hardness that strained within. "What fun we might have with that sash and a sturdy bed!"

"Would you lash your captain to the bedstead and ride him?" Ambrose nibbled at Orsini's ear then kissed his way to his chin before dropping to his knees on the step before him. He unbuttoned the front of his breeches then lifted the hem of Orsini's gown up and over his head. "Now…if only I had my lantern — there is mischief afoot!"

"I shall ride my captain all night long." Orsini laughed. With a sharp gesture he flicked open his fan, batting the peacock feathers before his face. Then he whispered, "I wish you well in your explorations."

"My word…what a construction! And what a — good Lord, there is a pistol under here, and it looks remarkably like a—" No further words came from beneath Orsini's skirts once Ambrose had taken Orsini's erection into his mouth. Murmurs and sighs rose to Orsini's ears, and looking down he saw

Ambrose's polished boots poking out from under the hem of the peacock gown. What a perfect picture it made, bawdy and forbidden and so Pen. Orsini closed his eyes and gave himself over to his lover's touch, sighing his encouragement.

Another sound from beneath the gown told Orsini that Ambrose was pleasuring himself. Unfastening his breeches, indeed. But it did not seem to distract him and he went on teasing Orsini with his warm mouth and his beautiful, soft lips. They could be discovered, he knew, but the thought was a thrilling one and Orsini pressed his hips to match Ambrose's rhythm, gasping his name. He was lost in a world of pleasure, every touch driving him on toward release.

A groan came from underneath Orsini's skirts, then another, and finally a long, drawn-out sigh. But even if Ambrose had reached his pleasure, it appeared that he would not stop until Orsini had found his. Yet the Italian knew that Ambrose wouldn't have long to wait and he bit back a louder cry, his knees buckling as pleasure surged through him. It was all he could do not to stumble and he reached out one gloved hand, steadying himself against the wall.

Slowly, Ambrose emerged from under the gown, his hair disordered and a lazy smile on his lips. He didn't get up at once but stayed kneeling as if he no longer had the ability to stand. "And what a secret that is to hide under your skirts, Cosima!"

"You must tell nobody, *Capitano*," Orsini purred. "Now back to the dancing, sir, and I believe my brother shall soon be with you. Another peacock, you know."

"I shall not say a word of your secret." Ambrose buttoned himself up again and finally rose to his feet. He tucked a handkerchief into his pocket and gave

Orsini a wink before kissing him. Then he bowed. "Good evening, sweet madam."

"Good evening, sir."

They parted with another kiss before Orsini was on his way, ready to play the seducer. It was the matter of minutes to shed Cosima's costume in his chambers and tuck it away in the dressing room. The makeup was washed away, the hair tied up and the second and, he hoped, last outfit of the evening was donned.

The suit that would make a *Cornuto* of Theodore Tarbottom!

He turned before the mirror to examine this costume, rather pleased with how quickly the sister could become the brother. Richly pigmented iridescent colors were blended into smooth, luxuriant fabric to create a jacket, waistcoat and breeches that appear to be made of myriad closely woven peacock feathers, the white shirt that he wore a mass of frills and lace.

Around Orsini's slender neck was a peacock-patterned cravat tied into a bow of ridiculous proportions, fastened with an emerald pin the size of a child's fist, for what was a peacock suit if it could not be accompanied by ridiculously expensive jewels? Emerald buckles adorned his mirror-polished leather boots and around him there was a cloud of delicate perfume, rendering him almost perfect. All that remained was to take a turn around the dance floor and ensure that Mrs. Tarbottom had seen her false suitor.

And pray that Pen does not lose track of the time!

Chapter Twenty-Three

Ambrose returned to the ballroom a little crestfallen to be losing his Cosima, for he could not dance with Orsini in his arms without his lover transformed by a gown and makeup. He registered several lingering glances from various ladies in the room, from the youngest to the oldest, and he smiled at them in return. He wasn't sure he was imagining it but even one or two of the male guests were taking an interest in his uniform. Not for the first time, Ambrose wondered just how many other men were like himself and Orsini, denying who they were and who they loved.

He and Orsini had found a way to be together, as long as this evening went to plan. In fact—

"Amby!" A pirate grabbed his elbow and piloted him toward the window. A pirate who looked remarkably like his mother. "Amby, I don't know what happened—he was here one minute, then the next he'd vanished!"

"Vanished?" Ambrose scanned the room. "Who—Father?"

"No!" Mrs. Pendleton shook her head. The long striped scarf she had tied about her hair into a piratical turban began to come loose, and Ambrose made an attempt to rescue it before it unraveled and slipped off. "Pagolo! He disappeared, and I'm beside myself! He was on my shoulder while I danced with the viscount, then he beat his wings and was gone. And the windows are wide open, Amby! He must've flown outside. Oh, I haven't lost him, have I? Tell me I've not. He's my little companion, and I'll never look myself straight in the mirror again if he ends up—ends up— No, I cannot bear to say it!"

Alarm gnawed at Ambrose. If he had to help his mother look for a parrot in an enormous, dark garden in the middle of the night, then he might not be in time to rescue Orsini from Mrs. Tarbottom's clutches.

"Mama, please—he's a sturdy old beast. He's probably off somewhere romancing a…peacock." He attempted a laugh. "Come, shall we dance? They're about to start another set."

"No. No, I cannot, for I'm that worried I cannot think, Amby! I'll put my feet in all the wrong places." Mrs. Pendleton nudged Ambrose as Harriet wandered into the room. "And where do you think she's been? If they've done anything to my Pagolo, I'll wring their necks like turkeys—all three of the Tarbottoms, the blighters!"

Ambrose placed his hands on his mother's shoulders and steered her to the refreshments table. "A drink will steady your nerves, Mama, then we shall find Pagolo."

Mrs. Pendleton shot away from Ambrose and clasped the sleeve of William Shakespeare, who was taking a drink. "You haven't seen my parrot, have you, Lord Hartington? Oh, please say you have!"

Another grabbed his other sleeve, a woman with white hair whom Ambrose knew immediately was the dowager viscountess. She was clad in an elegant pale blue gown, her face concealed beneath a simple mask, but when she spoke, every word paid witness to her outrage.

"Those are my pearls around that creature's throat," she said urgently, nodding toward Harriet. She was deep in conversation with her father, who pointed a reproachful finger at his daughter before he stalked from the room. "Your father's crest shall be on the clasp, I know it!"

She was silenced by a great shriek of excitement that came from the doorway as, over the heads of the dancers, flew Pagolo. Something glittered in the candlelight, a string of gemstones it seemed, held by the avian in his beak. The crowd parted to allow him to settle in front of Mrs. Pendleton and set down the treasured bracelet she had thought lost.

"Oh, my bracelet!" Mrs. Pendleton gasped as Ambrose crouched to pick it up for her. "Pagolo, you clever fellow!"

"You're a naughty little dipper, Harriet," Pagolo told her in a game approximation of Mrs. Tarbottom's most indulgent voice. "Whatever will your papa say? Lock the box now, keep it safe! Show Papa!"

The orchestra were between tunes and the room had fallen silent. Pagolo's words had rung through the room and as Ambrose and Mrs. Pendleton had turned to stare at Harriet, so had everyone else.

Harriet took off her mask and stamped her foot. "That proves nothing. Only that Pagolo is a thief and should be plucked and stuffed and served for supper!"

Mrs. Pendleton crooked her finger at Harriet. "Come here," she said, in her sternest voice, which Ambrose hadn't heard since he and his brother had skidded down the stairs on a priceless Turkish rug.

Harriet folded her arms in obstinate silence, her nose poked up toward the ceiling.

Mrs. Pendleton beckoned her again. "Come here, Miss Tarbottom, and return those pearls to their rightful owner."

"They're mine!" Harriet screeched.

"Let us not make a show of ourselves," Viscount Hartington said, gesturing to the orchestra to play on, which caused the reluctant audience to disperse. "If the clasp bears our crest, I'll wager the trinkets pilfered through the season will be amongst your haul. If not, then I shall owe you more of an apology than I can rightly give. Perhaps Mrs. Pendleton might remain here with you while the captain and I seek your parents. Then we shall examine the clasp."

Pagolo, however, was having none of that and hopped across to sit on her narrow shoulder, as though appointing himself jailer. The dowager was likewise less than willing to follow her son's chivalrous lead and instead held out her hand.

"My pearls, Miss Tarbottom," she demanded. "Now, if you please."

"I…I was only looking after them. You'd left them lying around. I can't help it if you're careless." As she'd spoken, Harriet had been unfastening the necklace, and she now placed it on the dowager's palm.

"Lying around?" Mrs. Pendleton glared at her. "Just as my bracelet was lying around—inside its case!"

"Let us see what your parents might say about this," the viscount said, fixing Harriet with a dark glare.

Ambrose, however, suspected they knew full well what she had been up to. And her father's money would doubtless see that she escaped any real punishment, though for a woman like Harriet, scandal might be punishment enough. "Captain, will you join me in my search?"

Ambrose nodded. There had to be time—it could only be half past ten, as long as the clock he'd checked outside the ballroom had shown the right hour. "My father and Mr. Tarbottom are doubtless discussing marriage business—let us try his study? Do follow me, your lordship."

Together the men strode from the room, leaving Harriet Tarbottom safe under the watchful eye of the ladies Hartington and Pendleton.

"The parrot is very vocal," the viscount commented as they went. "Do you think— Captain, were the words he repeated truthful? Are we to believe that the girl's mother indulged her stealing?"

"Her mother..." Ambrose's voice trailed off as he tried to find the words without making public slurs against a guest in his parents' home. "I do not wish to speak ill of a lady, and I say this not to escape marriage to her daughter, but it is the truth, sir. Her moral compass is somewhat...you do understand? It might appear that she is a good woman, however..."

Ambrose glanced from the corner of his eye at the viscount.

"They were guests in my home. I confess we all grew somewhat fond of them," Hartington admitted. "There have been three or four thefts to my knowledge during the season, always from houses holding jolly gatherings. This is a bad business indeed if all is as it seems."

"If the Tarbottoms were at all of those gatherings, I believe we can be confident of the thief's identity." And to think Ambrose would have been sent beyond the seas, when Harriet Tarbottom should've been put on the next ship to Botany Bay.

"I doubt that those involved shall pursue this matter in the courts, alas, for what rich man wishes to advertise that he is a dupe who could be robbed by a young lady and suspect nothing?" He gave a bitter laugh. "I rather think that her marital prospects have decreased somewhat, though!"

"Unless she wishes to marry a gentleman of the highway!" Ambrose began to laugh, but it caught in his throat as he heard raised voices from the direction of his father's study. "Excuse me, Lord Hartington, we must hurry, I fear."

Ambrose ran to the door. "Father?"

"Dictated to by a damned peasant like you!" he heard Tarbottom bellow. "Think about the marriage, reconsider the investment, he says! You, sir, have damned me to bankruptcy! I have creditors waiting!"

Ambrose didn't wait to be admitted and shoved his way into the room. There, clad in the ermine robes of a king, Theodore Tarbottom was stood inches away from Mr. Pendleton. The American was a head taller than Ambrose's father but the little Yorkshireman wasn't cowed, his hands balled into fists on his hips and the expression on his face all too familiar from Ambrose's occasional childhood misdemeanors.

"Open the safe, sir!" Tarbottom shouted, apparently so caught in his fury that he wasn't aware of Ambrose's arrival. "You owe me an investment!"

"I owe you nothing—" Mr. Pendleton looked to Ambrose, his expression almost puzzled as he saw his son. "It's all right, lad, you get on and dance."

"No, I'm not leaving, Father. Mr. Tarbottom can address me if he wishes to shout at anyone. Besides, a certain nobleman would like a word." Ambrose folded his arms. "Do you hear me, Mr. Tarbottom? Do not dare shout at my father again."

"Weeks wasted, listening to his boring drone and his idiot wife!" Tarbottom spun on his heel to face Ambrose. "I need that investment and I intend to have it, sir!"

He reached into the folds of his crimson cloak and pulled out a small pistol. "Open the safe, sir, and make your investment."

As the light hit the dull gray metal of the pistol, Ambrose entered a space of calm. He wasn't afraid. His hand trembled, but he ignored it. "I faced down thousands of soldiers on a battlefield, Mr. Tarbottom. What makes you think I'd be afraid of that piddling weapon? Do lower it, sir. There's no need for bullets."

"Your daughter has been unmasked as a thief," Viscount Hartington chimed in. At his revelation, Ambrose saw Tarbottom's face pale still further. "Is that not shame enough on your family, without this outrage? Bankruptcy, sir? Better that than swing for murder!"

"Open the safe, Pendleton," Tarbottom repeated, his voice steady now. "Or I shall shoot your timid sop of a son."

Ambrose closed his trembling hand into a fist. It stilled at once—it was iron. "I am not armed with my sword, Mr. Tarbottom. You should be glad of that. Once more, I tell you to lower your weapon."

"My son is no timid sop," Mr. Pendleton told Tarbottom, his face red with rage, and Ambrose saw a slight movement, the tightening of the American's finger on the trigger. "He's worth more in his little finger than your whole sorry, rotten family!"

Ambrose, who had been so still, now sprang. His fist met Tarbottom's jaw, snapping the man's head backward as he fell. Ambrose grasped Tarbottom's wrist and took the pistol from him. He stood over the man who had come so close to shooting him, and aimed Tarbottom's own pistol at him.

"Anything else to say, Mr. Tarbottom? Timid, am I? Really?"

"I shall summon the watch and some household fellows to act as jailers!" the viscount decided urgently. On the floor, however, Mr. Tarbottom was certainly no threat but lay in a dead faint. "What a family they are!"

As the peer departed, Mr. Pendleton gave a firm nod and smoothed down his costume.

"Well now," he said. "I think, young sir, that I owe you a thanks. No doubt you inherited that right hook from me! I'm afraid that I have bad news, though."

"I'm sure I did, One-Punch Pendleton!" Ambrose joked as he nudged his father. "But bad news? Father, what is it?"

"The wedding to Miss Tarbottom." Mr. Pendleton shrugged. "It's off."

"Reprieved — thank heavens!" Ambrose was about to hug his father when he remembered he was still holding the pistol. He made it safe then dropped it into his pocket. His father's clock ticked away on the desk, and Ambrose made a note of the time. Mrs. Tarbottom would soon be heading to her assignation.

Chapter Twenty-Four

In the candlelit bedroom where Mrs. Tarbottom's inconstancy would soon be revealed to her husband, Amadeo Orsini waited. It was one more role, he reminded himself, to go with the many he had played on stage and that of Cosima, the young lady who was as much the true Orsini as the man he was now. All he need do was spend ten minutes pouring claret and purring sweet words, perhaps reciting a line or two, and his *capitano* would be there at the door, Mr. Tarbottom at his side, to save the day.

There came a soft tap at the door, sly and secretive, and he moved to stand before the mirror, occupying a few more seconds. He brushed down his jacket, straightened his stock pin and called, "Come in!"

The door opened and there stood Mrs. Tarbottom in her Titania costume of gossamer-light fabric. As she came into the room, Orsini realized that she had divested herself of both chemise and stays. None who might have seen her in the corridor on her way to their meeting might have noticed in the dim light, but Mrs.

Tarbottom's abundant charms were all too obvious to Orsini.

"Good evening," she said in her honeyed, sultry tones. She climbed onto the bed and reclined against Orsini's pillows.

"Madam," he said, dropping into a low and flamboyant bow. Her perfume was almost overpowering even from here and he felt his eyes prickling at the strength of it. "I believe that the time has come to set the deal on our agreement, do you not agree?"

"Indeed it has." Her voice was breathy as she gazed at Orsini through her drooping eyelids. "I have been waiting for this moment…"

"And you have spoken to your husband?"

Curling a ringlet around her finger like a coquette, Mrs. Tarbottom grinned at Orsini and shook her head. "Oh, no. Not a word! He shan't know a thing about my Italian lover."

"You are a charming lady indeed and enchanting with it." He conjured a smile from somewhere. "Can I assume that my sister might yet call herself a Pendleton?"

"Oh, yes! Well…by tomorrow morning, I assure you, I will give you your answer." Mrs. Tarbottom caressed herself from her shoulder, over her bosom and down to the soft swell of her stomach. "My dear husband will do whatever I tell him to, and that includes looking elsewhere for a son-in-law of means."

The cunning creature. She must think me as stupid as I am beautiful, Orsini decided. *And twice as easy to mislead.*

"But, madame, I confess I am a sensitive creature." He pouted his full lips. "I had thought you would speak to your husband on this matter already, as it is at this very ball that the announcement is to be made. I could not give my finest performance tonight if I were fretful that even now our dancers might be raising a toast to the happy couple. It would not happen, you understand, were I under such a weight."

"I have delayed the announcement!" Mrs. Tarbottom giggled as if this was the cleverest ruse ever devised. As if she hadn't blatantly misled and manipulated in order to get Orsini into bed. "I explained to Theodore that the negotiations must go on a little longer, so the engagement could not be announced tonight. And it has not been, I promise you. I have told the Pendletons that my Harriet will require a traditional wedding gift—something from the family jewels, of course. But the English have such quaint traditions—I believe Mrs. Pendleton had planned to fashion a homemade stocking instead? And if Harriet hears about that…"

Mrs. Tarbottom raised her eyebrows in mock horror. "But have no fear, Orsini, after tonight, there will be no wedding."

"Shall we drink to it?" He gestured to the decanters available. "Claret? A very agreeable brandy, perhaps?"

Mrs. Tarbottom's eyes shone as she took in the range of expensive crystal decanters. "Yes, *signor*, a drink. To us and our…arrangement."

Orsini poured two glasses of claret, wishing only that there was some way to get it to her without approaching the bed. As timid as a child nearing a spider in its web, he drew closer, holding out one of the glasses to his would-be paramour.

Mrs. Tarbottom reached for the drink, stroking her fingertips across the back of Orsini's hand as she took the glass. "Such soft skin you have," she purred.

"We nobles so often do," he told her, suppressing a shudder. "As an Italian, one is doubly blessed."

"You most certainly are." Mrs. Tarbottom held Orsini's gaze as she drank. She presumably thought it terribly seductive, but it was rather like watching an octopus cling its suckers to an anchor. "Come along, now Orsini...hop onto the bed with Temperance Tarbottom."

"Truffles, madam?"

Anything to avoid the moment of collision, for Mr. Tarbottom need only see his wife on the bed in her state of undress and the plan would be complete. There was no need for Orsini to shed so much as a shoe.

"Won't you pop one into my mouth, dear heart?" Mrs. Tarbottom pouted at him. It was only then that he realized that he didn't actually have any, and she certainly wouldn't allow him to escape on such a spurious errand. As Orsini faltered he saw her mouth set and her face hardening. It occurred to him that he may have run out of delaying tactics.

Temperance Tarbottom took a mouthful of wine before putting her glass aside. Then she sinuously moved onto her hands and knees, crawling across the bed toward Orsini.

"I could just lick you all over!" She giggled, then she flicked her tongue at him like a snake preparing to strike.

"*Oddio*!" Orsini exclaimed. He downed the brandy in one then, as her hand reached out to seize him somewhere, flung himself into the dressing room and turned the key in the lock.

"Signor Orsini?" Mrs. Tarbottom fell silent, then laughed. "Is this one of your little Italian games? You're so naughty! I'm waiting..."

"And a long wait it shall be!"

And that is what it took, it seemed, for Mrs. Tarbottom to realize that there would be no Italian lover for her. Her fists hammered against the door, in the full flight of her rage and humiliation.

"Get out of there now, dissembler! You tried to make a fool of me! But you shan't! And where is your sister, anyway? I have never…my God!—I have never seen the two of you together! Get out of there now and take me to your sister, or I'll tell the Pendletons you've made fools of them too!"

Orsini's heart was beating so fast he thought it would burst out of his chest. There was nothing else for it. This would have to be the performance of a lifetime.

Chapter Twenty-Five

Ambrose hurried as best he could but he had to go slowly enough for his father to keep up with him. Each step was torture as he pictured the lustful matron pawing at his lover. Mr. Tarbottom was even now in the custody of Pendleton Hall's most strapping footmen while Harriet, imperious to the last, was blaming her mother, her father, Pagolo and anyone else she could think of for the presence of the stolen pearls around her neck.

And now the final scene. Ambrose ran ahead the last few steps, panting at Orsini's door. But not for reasons he had panted by that door in recent days, awaiting a meeting with his love.

As his father approached, Ambrose whispered, "I told you I knew where Mrs. Tarbottom was — you must not blame Orsini for this. He is the innocent party in a rotten family's schemes."

"What's all this about, young sir?" Mr. Pendleton asked. "Mrs. Tarbottom isn't — Lord above!"

A pirate, complete with parrot, rounded the corner and appeared before them. "Pagolo insisted I come upstairs to Orsini's room!" Mrs. Pendleton glanced from her husband to Ambrose. "Is he quite all right? He and Cosima have vanished from the ball, and I do hope neither of them has been taken ill."

Ambrose rested his hand on his mother's shoulder. "As far as I know, neither of them is unwell, but…it would be remiss of me as your son if you were to see this."

"See what, Amby?" Mrs. Pendleton glared at the door to the bedchamber. "And who's that banging about and carrying on in there?"

Ambrose shouldered the door and it sprang back on its hinges as he piled into the room, his parents and the parrot close behind. There by the cupboard was Mrs. Tarbottom—rather more of Mrs. Tarbottom than Ambrose wished to see, and he held his hand up over his eyes as if shielding them from bright sunlight.

"Avert your eyes, Husband!" Mrs. Pendleton ran at Mrs. Tarbottom with a blanket from the bed and threw it over Mrs. Tarbottom and her diaphanous outfit.

"Get off me!" Mrs. Tarbottom shouted, her voice muffled underneath the blanket.

"And where is the young gentleman?" demanded Mr. Pendleton. "And his sister, come to that? I think it's time we sat the pair of them down and sorted this marriage business out once and for all."

From within the dressing room there came the sound of a key turning. Then the door opened slowly and from within came Orsini—no, Cosima—

Ambrose wasn't sure who it was, for beneath the elaborate peacock suit was the suggestion of an exquisite female form and peeping out from the mass of loose auburn curls, Cosima's gentle face. Orsini gave a bashful smile and said in melodic tones of Cosima, "We are both standing before you now, and Cosima and Orsini could not be more sorry for the deception."

Ambrose could hardly believe what he was hearing. Was his lover about to confess all, to surrender what they had fought so hard to achieve? In the silence his father began to laugh, booming his mirth into the room.

"My goodness, that's what I call talent! You had me fooled, young lady, I confess!" Pagolo joined in, squawking his own approval as he hopped onto Mr. Pendleton's shoulder. "I thought you a man, Contessina, I really did. A touch effeminate, perhaps, but— You have a rare gift, madam, rare indeed."

"Orsini is a woman?" Mrs. Tarbottom shrieked, before she collapsed to the floor.

"I think she's fainted…" Mrs. Pendleton dropped to her knees and tugged aside just enough of the blanket to reveal the voluptuary's face. As she fanned at the insensible woman, Mrs. Pendleton blinked at Cosima. "A lady? But I thought you were—oh, it matters not!"

Ambrose gawped. Had his mother really just said—? At the suggestion of a disguised wink from his mother, Ambrose stepped across the room to stand beside his intended.

"Mother, Father, with your blessing, Cosima and I should very much like to be wed." He slipped his arm around Cosima's waist and chastely kissed her temple.

"Provided that her mother raises no concern, then I shall happily give my blessing," Mr. Pendleton replied. He took his wife's hand and added with a smile, "So long as I can see mother and daughter in the same room, at the same time!"

"That shall not be a problem," Orsini said sweetly. "And on that, I can give you my word."

Chapter Twenty-Six

The church of St. George's Hanover Square had never before contained such a motley congregation — a melée of industrialists, theatricals, Italians and nobles. And a very well-behaved parrot. A carnival atmosphere reigned among the pews, as if Vauxhall Gardens had temporarily crossed the river.

One month after the Tarbottoms had been vanquished, their reputations in tatters, even the very earth itself seemed to be celebrating. A bright sun shone over the autumn city, burnishing the red and gold trees with warmth and glittering from the stained-glass windows of St. George's.

Ambrose, resplendent in his uniform, stood at the front of the church, his eye on the door from which his bride would appear. He could feel the proud smiles of his mother and he took his gaze from the door for long enough to grin at her. He was about to marry his love, and nothing now stood in their way.

Not even rehearsals for *Fleet Fortune*, the premier of which was fast approaching. He might have imagined that nobody was anticipating the opening night more than the excitable Contessa D'Orsini and Mrs. Pendleton, but in that supposition Ambrose had been proved wrong. Indeed, no one could have been more thrilled about the prospect of the ever-approaching premier of *Fleet Fortune* than Barnaby Pendleton. The obstinate industrialist had not been so stern and immovable after all, it seemed, and Cosima had long since banished his suspicion of theatricals.

A sudden increase in chatter among the congregation, followed by a hushed silence which the organist soon filled, indicated the arrival of the bride. Advancing toward Ambrose was his lover—his Cosima, his Amadeo.

Orsini was on the arm of Mr. Pendleton, resplendent in a gown of ivory silk and lace, gold braid and gemstones glittering in his auburn hair and around his waist, Ambrose's own tasselled sash. His beloved was truly the most magnificent, perfect sight he had ever seen. He had never felt such a rush of love, such an overwhelming dart of adoration, than he did for this man, and Orsini's sparkling dark gaze was fixed on Ambrose, basking in his love.

Ambrose barely registered his father returning to the pew, and he took Orsini's arm as he stood beside him.

I love you, he mouthed to Orsini.

"*Ti adoro*," he whispered in reply.

The moment Ambrose had longed for had finally arrived. He and his Orsini, his love, were united, and for the hero of Waterloo, this was the start of his greatest adventure yet.

Want to see more from these authors? Here's a taster for you to enjoy!

A Late Summer Night's Dream
Catherine Curzon & Eleanor Harkstead

Excerpt

Simeon pulled the ticket out of his pocket as he ran up the steps of the theater. Thanks to the bloody traffic in town, he was almost late for curtain up. He checked his seat number again and hurried through a door from the foyer into the busy auditorium. The house lights went down almost as soon as he found his row.

"Excuse me…sorry." His seat *would* have to be right in the middle of the row, wouldn't it? *Best seat to have, but not if you turn up late.*

With only the green glow of the emergency exit lights to guide him, Simeon found his way to the empty seat. He squinted at the ticket and—*someone is in my seat!*

A tall someone who Simeon could barely see in the dark.

Music began to fill the auditorium, an overture before the play began. Through the strings and brass, Simeon hissed, "You're in my seat!"

Someone tutted, perhaps the lady who was craning to peer around Simeon at the stage. Why was she so keen anyway? The curtain was still down—she was hardly missing the action.

At Simeon's words, the man who occupied his seat peered up at him through the gloom and asked in a cut-glass whisper, "I'm sorry?"

Simeon wafted his ticket at him—not that he'd be able to see it in the darkness. "You're in my seat." Something in the way the man had spoken made Simeon add, without a hint of sarcasm, "…sir."

"Sit down," the lady hissed, patting Simeon's arm with her rolled program. The interloper in his seat reached out one hand and tapped his finger on the empty seat beside him. *His* seat, the seat *he* should be in, not Simeon's central seat.

"Sit down," the man echoed in that same plummy whisper, dismissive and disinterested. "I'm in *my* seat."

Simeon sighed in annoyance. "You're *not*—you're in mine! I chose it on purpose, and you're sat in it!"

"What number seat are you looking for?" He asked it as though Simeon was the most unimportant creature in the universe, with the same throwaway condescension of his worst undergraduate professors. His hand remained on the empty seat and he said, "This is seventeen."

"Yes—seventeen! That's *my* seat. Look—look at my ticket, for heaven's sake!" Simeon held it closer to the man's face.

His nemesis tapped the empty seat again and he told Simeon, "*This* is seventeen, I'm in sixteen and—"

"Fifteen," the woman snapped, patting him a little more forcefully with her program. "Now sit down, you bloody hooligan!"

Simeon popped forward the collar of his denim jacket, a move he had learned long ago from old films. "Hooligan? I merely wish to sit—"

Shit.

Simeon dropped down into the empty seat and looked at his ticket again. His was seventeen, and that was definitely the empty seat.

"Sorry," he whispered. "How embarrassing—but it's so dark, I…"

Yet his neighbor didn't offer him so much as a glance, merely gesturing with one hand, a flick of the wrist that commanded silence. A faint glare of light reflected for a moment from the jeweled cufflink that peeped out from beneath the sleeve of the man's jacket, then Simeon's attention was caught by the curtain which, thank God, was finally beginning to rise.

This isn't going to be an awkward three hours at all, is it? Not at all.

Simeon was soon carried into the play. The scenery was gorgeous, and he overlooked the unimpressive acting because whoever was playing Theseus—if only Simeon had had time to grab a program—was a thoroughly delicious silver fox. As he settled into seat seventeen, Simeon became aware of a scent from somewhere nearby—a very pleasant cologne. The kind that Theseus would wear, in fact. Manly. Distinguished. The cologne of a mature man, who—

Christ, it isn't the grumpy sod sat beside me, is it?

Simeon peered at him from the corner of his eye.

It wouldn't be him. He had the voice and manner of an old-school toff. *Lord knows this city has enough of them, and none of them wear cologne like that.* Oh, for his own Theseus wearing *that* cologne.

Simeon forced himself to concentrate on the play, even though the energetic young actors didn't hold much interest for him. But with any luck, Theseus would turn up again as Oberon, King of the Fairies.

A man can dream.

Before Simeon had time to lament the departure of Theseus too much, the curtain fell and the house lights came up. The interval. He really could do with a drink. Perhaps he should do the decent thing and apologize to the man who hadn't been in his seat?

"Look, sorry—I don't suppose you'd like to—?"

He glanced round at the man who'd sat so quietly beside him in the dark and held his breath as he looked at him.

The woman who had weaponized her program shot Simeon a pointed, disapproving look before bustling from the row. It was only then that he realized the couple weren't together at all. In fact, as the woman departed, the man in seat sixteen was gazing fixedly at his program and clearly trying to pretend that Simeon didn't exist.

Bloody hell, how could I have been so stupid?

The man in seat sixteen was gorgeous.

A head of thick blond hair, stranded with silver, and a strong jaw. Tall. Nicely dressed—far more nicely than Simeon. The man in seat sixteen seemed to have made an effort for going out to the theater, with a shirt and tie and three-piece suit.

And he was wearing that damn cologne.

Simeon turned in his seat and grinned him. "Mate— look, I'm going to grab a drink. Do you—can I get you something by way of apology? Least I can do."

Seat Sixteen lifted his gaze to meet Simeon's and blinked the brightest blue eyes he had ever seen. He looked momentarily bewildered, as though he wasn't entirely sure that Simeon was addressing him, then spoke.

"There's really no need." Seat Sixteen smiled—a friendly, apologetic sort of smile that crinkled his eyes. "These things happen in the dark."

"Yeah, I know, but..." *Straight. He has to be straight.* Not that it mattered—Simeon was only offering a drink to the man because he wanted to apologize. Not because he was even more attractive than Theseus. "Come on—what do you drink? Whiskey? Gin? Maybe a chilled white wine. You've got to be quick though, the interval won't last forever!"

"I couldn't possibly ask you for a rich red, it just wouldn't be the done thing," his neighbor told him, mischief sparking in his blue eyes. "But if you insist, I'm not so impolite as to refuse."

"Good chap!" Simeon raised an eyebrow. "A rich red, eh?" He could well imagine this gent seated by a roaring fire sipping a fine wine. Although he'd now have to sip it in the cramped seats of the auditorium. Simeon gave the man a wink. "I'll be back in a minute— a friend of mine works behind the bar so I won't be long."

Simeon patted Seat Sixteen on his broad shoulder as he went past.

PUBLISHING

Sign up for our newsletter and find out about all our romance book releases, eBook sales and promotions, sneak peeks and FREE romance books!

About the Authors

Catherine Curzon

Catherine Curzon is a royal historian who writes on all matters of 18th century. Her work has been featured on many platforms and Catherine has also spoken at various venues including the Royal Pavilion, Brighton, and Dr Johnson's House.

Catherine holds a Master's degree in Film and when not dodging the furies of the guillotine, writes fiction set deep in the underbelly of Georgian London.

She lives in Yorkshire atop a ludicrously steep hill.

Eleanor Harkstead

Eleanor Harkstead often dashes about in nineteenth-century costume, in bonnet or cravat as the mood takes her. She can occasionally be found wandering old graveyards, and is especially fond of the ones in Edinburgh. Eleanor is very fond of chocolate, wine, tweed waistcoats and nice pens. She has a large collection of vintage hats, and once played guitar in a band. Originally from the south-east, Eleanor now lives somewhere in the Midlands with a large ginger cat who resembles a Viking.

Catherine and Eleanor love to hear from readers. You can find their contact information, website and author biographies at https://www.pride-publishing.com.